I0772896

LOVE FINDS A WAY

By Fran McNabb

ISBN: 978-1-962168-85-4

DEDICATION

To my family at Louisiana Cajun Culture, especially Donna Perkins and Paul and Caroline Hoskey. Thank you for allowing me to write this book while sitting in the little corner of my world.

CHAPTER ONE

INDEPENDENCE, MISSOURI
November 1858

Matthew Jennings slammed the cell door. The clash of metal against metal reverberated throughout the jail as he put his hands on his hips and spoke to man behind bars. "If we catch you staggering down Main Street on a Sunday morning again, you'll never get out of here. Do you hear me, Joe?"

With his three-day beard and two buttons missing on his shirt, Joe grinned and plopped down on the cot. He fell against the pillow, snuggled under the thin blanket, and mumbled something before he started snoring.

Shaking his head, Matthew pushed away from the cell and tossed the key on a hook. With one last look at Joe, he headed to the front door and stepped out on the wooden sidewalk. The empty street gave him a moment of solitude. He breathed in the brisk November air and pulled his coat tighter. He'd been back in Independence, Missouri, for over two weeks but had not ventured out of town. He needed to ride out to Fletcher Ranch to see the family, but nothing would be the same.

He had already spoken to Mr. Fletcher's younger brother, Douglas, and his wife Emma at their medical offices, but the polite thing to do would be to ride out and talk with the rest of the family. That visit never happened. He always let other things interfere when he thought he might ride out.

The ranch had been his home and the Fletchers had been his family since they had taken him in when he was a scared nine-year-old. Lucas Fletcher gave him a place to live and treated him like a son, even wanting him to take the Fletcher name, but Matthew never felt deserving enough to have such a well-respected name.

Living on the ranch had been special. He saw how a well-adjusted family lived, something he'd never had. Everyone accepted him, but it took years before he felt comfortable enough even to sit at the family table.

Now things would be different. No longer was he the young kid without direction. He was a lawman with several years of experience under his belt and a reputation of being someone not to mess with. Not sure how that reputation started, he'd let it grow if it kept him from using his weapon.

Soon he'd have to bite the bullet and ride out to the ranch, but he knew it would be difficult to see Lucas's daughter, Caroline, now that she was engaged to someone else.

A wagon rumbled down the street. He pulled his thoughts to the present and waved to the man. Even on Sunday morning, farmers and ranchers had to keep up their work. Most of them made time during the morning to attend church service, but their duties never ended.

Matthew turned as he heard footsteps at the end of the sidewalk.

Sheriff Victor Sanchez walked toward him with a slight limp. "How're you doing this morning, Matthew?"

"I'm great, Vic, and probably better than you with that limp. It looks as though it's worse today."

"Just my typical morning aches and pains." With a grunt, he sat on the bench and stretched out his legs. "Have you thought any more about taking over for me?"

Matthew laughed and sat down next to him. "You get right to the point, don't you?"

"When I struggle to get out of bed each morning, it's the first thing I think about. Retirement. Blessed retirement." He rubbed his hand down one of his legs.

Matthew wished he could give the man the answer he wanted, but so much stood in the way. "Vic, you know I want to, but there's a lot to think about."

"I know. We've been through this already." Vic sat up straight. "All your reasons are valid, but not strong enough to let me linger in this job. Every part of my body hurts. I need to be home relaxing, not wearing this gun and patrolling the streets."

"What if I take the job then decide to leave Independence? That wouldn't be fair to the people in town"

"If you do, you do. The town would hire someone else. Look. That new jail will be finished soon. I can see you ruling over those cells with an iron hand. You have the experience from your time in Jefferson City. The county needed that jail for so long, and you'll be the perfect man for the job. I've heard the city council gave its approval to hire as many jailers as needed to run the place, and you'd have a place to live right there on the property. It would be a win-win situation for both you and the town."

"Let me think about it a little more. Anyway, it's not as easy as me saying I'll take your job. I hear the new position will be Deputy County Marshal and will be an elected position. How in the world do you think I'd win an election? No one knows me around here. I've been gone for four years."

"You're wrong about that. Everyone I talk to about you is well aware of who you are and what you've done with your life. Those who have lived here long enough remember you from living with the Fletchers. Anyway, I don't know of anyone else wanting to throw his name in the hat for the job."

Matthew laughed again. "So you're saying I could win because no one else wants the job."

"Hey, you know what I mean. You're qualified and can do the job. Period. That's enough to win. I know the council members are behind you all the way."

"I've only been back two weeks. The council can't possibly know me."

"Sure they do. I made sure of it."

"I'm still concerned about your other two deputies. They're the ones who ought to be applying."

"I've talked with both of them. One said he's too old and the other one flat refused it. He doesn't want the responsibility of running a prison. He does want to be one of the jailers though. Both of them said they'd oversee this jail when the facility is needed."

Matthew looked down the street, not wanting to give Vic an answer to a question that should have been easy.

Vic raised eyebrow. "It's Caroline, isn't it?"

"What?"

"My niece is the reason you might not stay, right?"

Matthew looked at him, then back to the street. What could he say?

"Look, Matthew, I know she'll be living in town, but she'll be married and living her own life. You'll be so busy with that new jail you won't have time to watch what she's doing. Anyway, you'll be the most eligible bachelor in town. You'll have a wife and a family in no time."

"Victor, I'm not a school boy drooling over a beautiful girl, nor am I looking for a wife. I'm a grown man. I know Caroline is engaged. She'll have a good life married to. . .whatever his name is. I'm happy for her."

"Sure you are." Vic stretched and blew out a big breath, then stood up and rubbed his elbow.

"That elbow still giving you trouble, too?"

"Always and this cold snap doesn't help. That's why I need to be home with Bettye giving me tender loving care."

Matthew stood up alongside him. He and Victor used to be about the same height, probably over six feet tall, but now he seemed shorter and a little stooped. "Can you give me a little more time to make this decision?"

"Of course, but remember this old man needs his rest."

"You're not an old man."

"Yeah, right. Go get your things and get out of here. Thanks for holding down the fort last night. I'm assuming nothing major went down."

"Nothing. The biggest excitement was trying to get Joe into his cell. He kept falling asleep against me."

"You mean passing out against you. I'm not sure how the man is still living. The human body shouldn't be able to handle as much liquor as he drinks."

Matthew followed Vic inside where he picked up his personal items. "You have a good morning. I'll go to the boarding house and grab a couple hours sleep, then I'll come back before ten so you can join Bettye and the kids at church."

"Thanks, Matthew. She'll appreciate that."

He looked around to make sure he had all of his things, but as he grabbed the door handle, Victor said, "His name is Samuel Brown."

Matthew was about to ask who he was talking about, then remembered Caroline's fiancé. "Thanks, Vic. I'll remember that little piece of information."

Victor laughed. "Go get some sleep."

Main Street in Independence was starting to get a few more wagons and carriages as people came to town to attend church services. After leaving Independence, he attended a few services in Jefferson City, but being in church didn't feel right. He felt like a hypocrite. Tending to Charlie Wright, his step-father, took everything out of him. He wanted to forgive the man for killing the only mother he remembered, but forgiving was harder than he assumed it would be. He thought understanding the man would help, but it never happened. Every time he looked at him, he saw his stepmother's blood splattered all over his clothes.

The church bell rang in the distance. One day he'd surprise Pastor Smith and himself by showing up in church, but not today. He headed in the direction of Molly's restaurant, then realized it was closed on Sundays.

If he had the nerve, he'd ride out to Fletcher Ranch and let Carmella and Bonita fix him a big breakfast as they did when he lived there. As tempting as it was, the visit would have to wait. Instead, he headed to the boarding house and hoped Mrs. Haverty had something left from the breakfast she fixed for her guests.

~

Caroline sat in the back of the new Fletcher carriage with her hat off and her blonde hair flying in the breeze. Her Uncle Douglas drove the carriage with Emma and their new baby in the front seat. Oliver, their three-year-old, slept on the seat next to Caroline. Lucas and Abigail and their family rode behind them in the older family carriage.

Douglas looked over his shoulder. "Are you going to be able to get all that hair tucked into your hat so you can look presentable when we get to church?"

"It's a big hat. It'll hide a lot." She ran her hand through her hair. "You know I'd rather be on my horse than in this carriage."

"That might be, but Samuel Brown wouldn't appreciate you meeting him at the church on horseback wearing your trousers."

"I know." She held her hat in her hand and let out a huge sigh.

Douglas glanced back at her. "I thought you'd come back to Independence a prim and proper lady, but I guess living in the big city and going to that finishing school didn't change you at all."

"Sure it did. While I was there I was *the* most prim and proper lady in town. You wouldn't have recognized me."

"What happened?" He laughed then flicked the reins.

"I got back to the ranch and the old Caroline came out." She laughed out loud as well, remembering the joy she felt when she rode through the gates of Fletcher Ranch. She loved the ranch with all the memories of her earlier life, its expansive lands, and all the animals—

especially the animals.

"And what does Mr. Brown think of the old Caroline?"

"I'd rather not say."

"Oh oh, do I sense trouble in paradise?"

"No, not trouble. He'll let me have fun on the ranch until we get married, then I guess I'll have to be a fitting wife of a banker."

"That ought to be something to see." Douglas laughed.

His wife shoved him. "Be nice to your niece."

"I am being nice. I just can't imagine seeing her all prim and proper twenty-four hours a day and being a fitting hostess to all the teas and socials that a banker's wife has to organize."

"I can certainly try to be a proper Mrs. Brown, banker's wife, but I have to admit I'd rather be working with our animals. I know the old Caroline will squirm to get out."

Douglas glanced back. "You might be beautiful. . ."

"Oh, so you think I'm beautiful?"

"As I was saying, you might be beautiful, but you can ride better, shoot straighter, and rope cows better than any of the ranch hands. How's that going to help with those socials?"

"Maybe I can use my ranch skills as entertainment for the ladies when they come for teas."

Douglas laughed. "Would you send me an invitation so I can watch?"

"Sure. Do you have a flowered hat and white gloves?"

He laughed again.

Emma looked over her shoulder. "You'll figure out married life, Caroline. Being married requires each partner to be selfless. Sometimes it's not easy, but if both partners work at it, the marriage will work out."

Douglas spoke up again. "She speaks from experience. I'd love for Emma to be home with our babies all the time, but she's a fine doctor and the town needs her. Mother and Carmella help with the children and the situation works for us. You and Samuel will have to do the same thing. You might be able to work with the animals on the ranch and be the proper banker's wife as well, but it will take a lot on your part as well as his."

"I know. I've thought about it quite a lot."

"Have you talked to Samuel about the way you feel?" Emma asked.

Caroline squirmed. "We have, but he thinks his family would die if he married a woman who spends her time with animals in the barn."

Douglas relaxed against the seat. "You might have a problem on your hands."

Caroline didn't want to think about that at the moment. She closed her eyes, leaned her head back and enjoyed the cool breeze whipping around her head. She'd missed all this while she studied in Connecticut. Until then, she'd enjoy being on the ranch and helping with the animals.

Thankfully, Emma, Abigail, and her grandmother were excited about planning a wedding on the ranch. She welcomed their help so she could do other things she enjoyed more. The best part of the wedding would be walking through the yard on her father's arm and seeing Samuel standing near the rose garden her mother loved. Even though Samuel wanted a wedding in one of the newer churches in town, she stood her ground and won. Everyone in her family had married on the ranch. She wouldn't be any different, and she'd wear her great grandmother's dress as all the other Fletcher brides had done.

Emma looked over her shoulder once more. "It still amazes me that you ran into Samuel in Connecticut when Independence is so small and you were both here before."

"We both thought our meeting was amazing. I knew him here, but I guess since he was a little older, I never really paid much attention to him. When I saw him on the street in Farmington I was shocked. He was so handsome and debonair and so charming and businesslike. I guess that's what made me fall in love with him."

"What in the world was he doing in Connecticut?" asked Douglas.

"He said he was on banking business. He had never been there before that trip, but after meeting me, he made a journey there several times a year." She smiled remembering how he worked hard at courting her.

"And now, what's it like to be with him in Independence?"

Caroline thought for a moment. "It's different. He's still handsome and charming, but here things are different. I'm different."

Emma smiled at her. "If you love him, the union will work, no matter how different you and he are."

"I do love him and can't wait to get married." Her gaze scanned the scenery they were passing and thought how much she belonged here. Emma said their marriage would work no matter how different she and Samuel were. She hoped Emma was right because she did love Samuel, but they had come from totally different backgrounds.

The Fletcher family believed in tradition and taking care of the land. Those values were instilled in her from an early age. She had a feeling her father sent her to finishing school because she spent most of her time working with the men on the ranch rather than with the ladies in the house sewing and keeping the house and staff in order. She went to the school, listened carefully to what an ideal wife should do and be, then came home with those things tucked in the back of her mind. She certainly could be a proper wife that Samuel and his family would be proud of, but they would also have to accept her background and love of the land.

Samuel's family concentrated on business, specifically banking, and she understood that. It was not how she was reared, but she could certainly understand his background. The two of them had talked about their differences, but they'd managed to find a common path together—or at least she hoped they could. It might be difficult but she knew they could blend their lives to make a good life.

Emma turned around again. "When we get closer to town, I'll have Douglas stop and I'll help you get your hair tucked in under your hat. You need to be as presentable as possible. I'm sure Samuel's family will be in church as they always are."

"Thank you." Caroline slumped against the back seat, closed her eyes and inhaled the clear air, letting her mind wander aimlessly until her eyelids felt heavy.

Before she knew it, Douglas stopped the carriage. "You awake back there?"

Caroline blinked and looked around and saw rooftops in the town ahead of her.

"You fell asleep, Aunt Caroline." Her nephew Oliver smiled at her.

"I did, didn't I?"

"Let's get that hat back on you so we can get to town. I don't want to be late for service." Emma placed the baby on the seat, and with Douglas's help, got on the ground. "Let's see what we can do."

Caroline got out of the carriage and allowed Emma to help her pin her hair back and to reposition the hat on her head.

"Now, you're as beautiful as you were when we left the ranch."

"Thank you, Emma." She held onto the hat with one hand and let Douglas help her into the carriage.

As they entered town, everyone seemed to know who they were and waved. She'd missed this familiarity while she attended finishing school. She eagerly waved back and spoke to several people she recognized on the sidewalk and also people in carriages heading toward the church.

As they neared the sheriff's office, Victor waved to them from the bench outside.

Douglas slowed the carriage. "Hey, Victor. Good morning to you. How are you this morning?"

"I'm great. I'm glad your family could get to town this morning. I'll see you in church. I'll be there shortly."

She could tell Victor was about to say more, but instead he seemed to look directly at her, then simply raised his hand in farewell. Douglas led the carriage toward the church.

She waved goodbye as well, then untied the ribbon holding her hat and was retying it when she stopped. On the other side of the street talking to two men was someone who looked very similar to Matthew. Could it be that he was back in Independence and no one mentioned it to her? Surely not. He would never be here and not visit the family at the ranch.

She looked closer. It had been over four years since he had left her crying at the gate of Fletcher ranch to find his stepfather who had been released from prison. Four years had added inches to his height and muscle to his body but she was sure it was him. His hat was pulled low on his forehead, and his dark wavy hair was a little longer than she ever remembered him wearing it, but as he talked to the man on the sidewalk, his gestures were the same as she remembered.

Closing her eyes to get control of her emotions, she inhaled deeply and glanced back toward the sidewalk. All three men laughed, then Matthew turned and headed in the direction they'd just come. She'd recognize his walk anywhere. She slumped against the back of the carriage seat.

"Aunt Caroline, what's wrong?" Oliver sat up and stared at her with his big brown eyes.

"Nothing, Oliver. Auntie Caroline is just fine." But on the inside, she knew she had told a little fib.

Douglas eased the carriage past the three men but obviously did not see Matthew. She remained silent. What would she have said to him had they stopped? Would she pretend he was just an acquaintance and talk about the weather? Would he recognize her, the girl to whom he had professed his love?

She squeezed her eyes and pretended seeing him did not matter to her. For four years she had worked hard to understand why he'd left her. She struggled with the idea that he had chosen the man who had killed his stepmother over her. Now, if that man on the sidewalk was actually Matthew, how would she ever face him?

And, more importantly, how would she ever pretend seeing him didn't matter to her when she sat next to Samuel in church? Glancing up to heaven, she prayed a silent prayer. *God, help me to know what to do. Samuel is a good man. I don't want to hurt him especially for a man who doesn't want me.*

CHAPTER TWO

Matthew pulled out his pocket watch. 11:30. Church services should be over by now and the congregation would gather under the trees for a meal together. Today might be the last time the church would eat outside. Sporadic days of cold winter weather reminded everyone that soon life would move indoors to escape the bitter cold ahead. He didn't look forward to that. The outdoors always had a pull for him, and now that he was an adult, it wasn't any different.

He turned the watch over in his hand. The engraving on the inside was from his mother to his father. He didn't remember them. When the fire took the house and the lives of both his parents, he was only a baby. The neighbor, Charlie Wright, pulled him out before the building collapsed. The watch was the only thing he had from his father before that horrible day. Charlie also gave him a ring with a small ruby that he pulled off the corpse of his mother. One day he hoped to pass that on to a woman he'd make his wife.

But, thinking about a wife was not his idea of spending a pleasant Sunday morning. At one time, maybe, but not now that Caroline would become the wife of Samuel Brown.

Straightening his shoulders, he got up from Vic's chair and shoved it back. "Joe, are you ever going to wake up?"

The cot creaked and Joe sat up. He put his head in his hands. "I don't feel so good."

"I can't imagine why. I'll get you a cup of coffee. That

might help." He walked to the pot bellied stove, grabbed a cloth, then lifted the pot. "You still want it black?"

Joe got up and leaned against the bars on the cell. He nodded.

Matthew walked over and handed him the cup of steaming coffee. "Drink this. Sheriff Sanchez will be back in a few minutes. Church is over, but I'm sure he'll be getting some food from the ladies at the church picnic. If you're lucky, maybe he'll bring you a plate."

Joe held the cup between both his hands, then backed against his cot to sit. "You and the sheriff are good people."

"You are, too, Joe, but no one knows it because they never see you sober when you're in town. You can do better, or this drinking is going to kill you."

Joe looked at the floor then sipped his coffee.

Matthew felt sorry for Joe. His last few years had been hard ones. He'd worked as a ferrier until he broke his shoulder and it didn't heal properly. He had to quit working, then his wife died suddenly and he was left alone. After Vic relayed Joe's story to him, he understood him much better and wished he could help him. Maybe if he took the job at the new jail, he could find something for Joe to do there. A productive job worked wonders for a depressed ego.

He let that thought settle. If he took the position, maybe he could help some of the other men in the community as well. Emma's brother, Edward, could use something productive to do. After getting involved with a bad group and actually shooting Douglas Fletcher, who in turn shot him, Edward seemed as though he wanted to walk the straight and narrow, but from the way Douglas and Victor talked about him, he had a ways to go. He'd have to talk with Douglas about him.

He thought about that new position as he walked outside and took a seat on the bench out front. His stomach growled thinking about the food under the trees on the church grounds, but Victor needed time away from this building. If he took Vic's place as sheriff, or rather County Deputy Marshal as the new prison warden would be called, would he be able to handle being inside every day? Of course, he'd done it at the prison in Jefferson City. The job wasn't as enjoyable as riding the ranges of Fletcher Ranch and tending to the animals, but he did enjoy working with the prisoners. They all had a story. He could see how some of them had taken the wrong paths in life and ended up in prison.

He could've ended up in a place like that also if Lucas Fletcher had not taken him in and given his life direction. He would always be grateful for that man.

The street heading toward the church was empty. A lot of the townspeople attended Pastor Smith's service, and he wondered if the Fletchers had come into town this morning as well. If they did, had they gone to the old church where Victor went or had they already become members of one of the newer churches in town? Would they still be enjoying the lunch and the company of fellow church goers? And the big question, would he have the nerve to walk up to them? The longer he waited, the harder it would be.

Standing up, he slapped his thighs. He'd never know if he could do it unless he actually tried. He locked the front door of the jailhouse and headed down the street. If the Fletchers were not in town, at least he'd get some food if anything was left.

He walked two blocks toward the church talking to several people leaving the outside picnic area, but as he neared the church property he realized quite a few people still sat around on blankets under the trees. The first group he recognized was the Fletchers and thankfully Caroline wasn't with them. Taking a huge breath, he walked up to the blanket.

"Mr. Fletcher, I was hoping you would have your family here today."

Lucas looked up, took a second to register who was standing over him, then jumped up and grabbed Matthew. "I heard you were back in town, but I said, 'No way would that boy be in Independence and not come out to the ranch.'" He shook his head. "But here you are." He hugged him tighter this time, then stepped back.

Abigail struggled to get to her feet holding a sleeping toddler, so Lucas took the child then helped her up. She threw her arms around Matthew. "Oh, my goodness, you're such a man."

"Yes, ma'am, four years will do that to a boy." He looked around. "Where's Grandmother Fletcher?"

"Mother took little Emma for a walk. She was getting bored sitting here with the adults."

"I'll try to find her while I'm here."

Lucas took his hand. "Sit and talk with us. As soon as you got to town Victor made a point of telling us you were helping him as his deputy. I haven't been to town since you came, but today I was going to walk over to the jailhouse after I finished this dessert. Are you hungry? If you are, you'd better hurry. The ladies are packing away their food."

"Yes, sir, I am. I'd love to fix a plate."

Abigail pulled out a tin plate from a picnic basket and handed it to him. "We'll be right here when you fill that plate."

Lucas took his hand again. "I'm so glad you're back. We have a million questions, but they can wait."

Matthew nodded and headed toward the food tables. Several women looked up. One recognized him and gave him a huge hug. Molly, Preacher Smith's wife and owner of the cafe, walked up behind him and hugged him, too.

"Matthew, I'm so glad you came out this morning. Give me a minute and I'll pull out some of the leftovers. Vic just fixed two plates for the jail, but you can fix your own."

"I'm sure Joe will appreciate eating my share."

She left him standing with the other women. He smiled at them and backed away from the table. He didn't want to search the dwindling crowd for Caroline, but he couldn't stop himself. If she had come into town, she'd probably be with the Brown family, but he wasn't even sure he'd recognize them. When he lived at Fletcher Ranch, he had no personal dealings with the banker or his sons. Why would he? He had no money to speak of. Even though his salary was sufficient, he kept the little he saved in his saddle bag. Several times, he'd gone into the bank to do business for Lucas Fletcher, but he talked with the tellers and not the Browns.

"Here we go." Molly handed him a plate loaded down with ham, vegetables, and potatoes.

"This looks delicious. Thanks. I'm going to go back by the Fletchers to enjoy this."

"I'll take a dessert to you over there. I know which ladies still have some left."

He gave her his best smile and walked toward the Fletchers and sat down next to Lucas.

"So, tell me, how does it feel to be a lawman in your old town?"

Matthew took a bite, chewed, then swallowed. "I really like being back in Independence. Vic is the greatest boss ever. I've always admired him."

"And now he says he's trying to get you to take his job so he can retire."

Matthew chuckled. "Yes, he is trying, and I'm flattered, but there's a lot to think about."

Lucas rolled his head on his shoulders. "Sounds like the ideal job for you, that is, if you're going to stay in Independence."

"That's the catch. I think I am, but I'm not really sure."

"Vic tells me the new jail will be finished in a few months and he wants to recommend you to run for the head position there. With your experience in Jefferson City, you'd be perfect."

"I'm flattered he thinks I can run a prison. My experience is limited."

"He sees a lot in you, Matthew. We all do. I, for one, will speak before the council to recommend you for the position."

"Thank you, sir. Again, I'm flattered."

"Don't be. We don't throw around compliments unless they're deserved." He looked around. "I guess you know Caroline is engaged to Samuel Brown."

"Yes, sir. Abigail wrote me a letter." He cleared his throat and hoped he'd sound sincere. "I'm happy for her. She'll make a beautiful banker's wife."

"Are you really pleased?" Lucas speared him with his dark eyes. "I seem to remember you and Caroline had a lot of good times together."

Matthew took another bite and hoped he could swallow it. This was not the way he wanted this conversation to lead. "We do have a lot of history, but we were kids back then. We're adults now. Things and people change."

"Yes, sometimes for the good and sometimes for the not-so-good."

Matthew looked at him, but didn't comment. Did Lucas not approve of Caroline's engagement to Samuel? He wanted to ask, but wouldn't dare.

They talked about Fletcher Ranch as he finished the plate of food. Finally, he stood up. "I'd better get back to the jailhouse, but first I have to find Molly. She's hunting a dessert for me. I don't want to miss that." He reached down and shook Lucas's hand. "I'm glad I got to see you and your family. I truly am sorry I haven't been out to the ranch, but I swear, I would have eventually. Vic keeps me pretty busy."

Lucas shook his hand hard. "You are welcome any time for as long as you want to be there. You're family. You know that."

"Thank you, sir." He walked away with a lump in his throat. The Fletchers were truly as close to family as he had. He was always amazed they took him in as they did. Now that he was an adult, he would try to repay them in some way.

"Matthew!" Molly waved to him from the side of one of the buggies. "I have a couple of desserts for you. I put them in one of my tins so you could get them back to me and not have to hunt the owners."

He took the plate covered with a red checked cloth, then peeked in. Two big slices of cake, one chocolate and one a pound cake lay next to what looked like rice pudding. "This is wonderful. I can't wait to get back to my room." He looked around. "Where's Preacher Smith?"

"I learned from the beginning of our marriage not to try to keep up with the man when there's a gathering like this. He takes his calling seriously and I'm not about to interfere."

"You tell him I said hello." He lifted the plate. "And thank you for this."

She smiled and kissed him on the cheek. "We're so glad you're back in town."

"And I'm glad to be here."

I just wish I knew if I could stay.

~

Caroline sat next to Samuel in the elaborate carriage the family had shipped in from the Boston area. Its deep brown upholstery and gold trim were exceptionally done. She ran her hand along the stitching.

"This is really beautiful, Samuel. I know you're family is proud of this carriage."

"Dad was ecstatic the day it came in on the rail. We all took a ride around town. Mother said it was a little too fancy for her taste but she liked the smooth ride and soft seats."

"It is quite fancy."

"I want us to use it when we leave the ranch after the wedding. Mother and Dad and the rest of our family can use the other two carriages that day."

Caroline smiled. "Won't we look special?"

Samuel looked at her with his deep blue eyes. "We will be special. It's not every day a couple gets married and vows to be together for the rest of their lives. I think that's very special."

She touched his arm. "You always say the right thing, Samuel." At moments like this she loved Samuel with all her heart and couldn't wait to marry him.

"I'm glad you think so."

"Always," she said and leaned against him. Silently she chastised herself for thinking about Matthew during the church service. Even if he were in town, he had not made the effort to see her. Obviously going away was his way of telling her he did not want to be with her any longer. *God, please let me forget Matthew. This man and I are about to be married. He deserves my entire love all the time, and I do love him.*

"You're in deep thought."

She blinked. "I guess I was. Planning a wedding takes a lot of thought and preparation. That seems to be all we talk about at the ranch."

He slowed the carriage down and looked at her. "I know you said you wanted a spring wedding, but Christmas is right around the corner. We could have a beautiful winter wedding."

"It's tempting to get married sooner rather than later, but it's too cold to be outside in December, and you know I want the ceremony to take place by my mother's rose garden at the ranch." Just thinking about it made her feel closer to her mother.

"I know you do, but I don't want to wait until spring. I want to make you my wife now." He put his arm around her and pulled her close, then kissed her sweetly on the forehead. "I want to take care of you and have children with you."

She put her head on his shoulders. "Again, you say the right things, but I'm not giving in on this one. I have my heart set on a spring wedding at the ranch."

Samuel chuckled and held her against him. "How's the new horse working out for you?"

"I love her, Samuel. She's a wonderful gift."

"Did you finally come up with a name?"

"As a matter of fact, I have. I'm calling her Lady because she always acts like a lady when I'm around her."

"I like that. I'm glad she's a good horse. I saw that horse's blonde hair and thought about you and how beautiful you'd look on her."

"I don't know how beautiful I look, but I love riding her."

"Are you ready to go see the progress on our house?"

"Yes, I'm excited about it."

They rode a few blocks to Liberty Street, one of the newer neighborhoods in Independence. Several houses were being built along the street. Samuel pulled the carriage up in front of a near empty lot with piles of wood and bricks.

Caroline looked, but couldn't distinguish what anything would be.

"This is great, isn't it?" he said with a huge smile on his face.

"Yes, I guess. The lot is really big, but where will the house go?"

"That's right. You haven't been out there since we took the trees down. Get down. We can walk around, and I'll show you what we're planning."

Caroline followed Samuel around the lot, stepping over lumber and other building supplies as he pointed out where the house would go.

"The porch will be really wide. I love a big porch." Samuel smiled down at her and pulled her next to him." We can have lots of rockers and a nice table so we can have our coffee out here in the mornings."

"That sounds wonderful. Is it still going to be two-story, or did you say three-story?"

"Right now it will be just two-story, but we're building a third story that can be finished as we need it."

"I can't imagine us needing three stories, but we'll see.

We're still painting it white, right?"

"I'm not sure. The newest fashion is adding lots of colors."

"I prefer white, but we can paint the shutters a different color."

"We'll talk about color later. Right now there are other major decisions to make."

"I can come to town anytime that the builders are here so we can work with them. I'd really like to have some input."

"Of course. This is your house and you certainly will be able to make suggestions."

Caroline made a mental note to make sure she came to town more often so she could have input.

They walked around the yard. She loved watching Samuel get excited about the house, and his excitement was contagious. By the time they climbed back into the carriage, she was bubbly.

"Do you think the house will be ready by the time we have the wedding?"

"The workers promised me it would be. They're the best carpenters in town."

"It's quite a lot to think about and take in."

He took her hand. "You don't worry about all this. You plan that beautiful wedding and I'll take care of this."

"With my suggestions, right?"

"Of course." He laughed.

She wasn't sure how to take that reaction, but she did have a lot on her mind, and she trusted him at this point of the building.

She sat up straight as they got back on the main street. "Samuel, can we pull over by the sheriff's office. That's my Uncle Vic sitting outside."

"Now, tell me again, how is he you're uncle?"

"My real mother was a sister to Uncle Vic's wife, Bettye." Did he really not remember her family connections?

She hid the sadness that his lack of interest in her family caused, especially when it came to her mother.

"Oh, I see. You did tell me that once. I was very young when your mother died as you were. That must've been hard on you."

"It was hard, and I think about her every day. I wish she'd be here for our wedding." She looked down, got her composure and continued. "My grandmother and father raised me and they were wonderful. Then Father married Abigail, and I couldn't have asked for a better lady in my life."

"I've seen Abigail in the bank with your father. She's beautiful and quite a lady."

"She is. She and Grandmother are helping with the wedding and they're really excited about it. Both of them are wonderful seamstresses and they're redoing my great grandmother's dress. All the Fletcher brides have worn it. I'm thrilled to be able to."

"You know I told you we could take the train to New York and buy you the dress you want. Mother wants to go with us and help you pick something out."

"I want to wear the family heirloom, but thank you for offering."

"If that's what you want." He looked at her. "Would you do me a favor? My mother would love to help with the plans. She knows it's not her place, but she'd feel so honored if you let her be part of the planning."

"Of course, Samuel. I had no idea she wanted to. You've never mentioned it before, but I'll talk to Abigail and Grandmother to see how we can include her."

Samuel flashed a gorgeous smile. "Thank you. That means a lot to me and she will be thrilled."

Samuel pulled the carriage off the road in front of the jailhouse.

Victor looked up, then stood up with a huge smile on his face. "Look who it is. I missed talking with you after service this morning."

"Yes, I missed talking with everyone after Preacher Smith's service, but I went with the Browns to that new church on the east end of town. It's quite an elaborate building."

Samuel got out and helped her down. Immediately she lifted her skirt and stepped up onto the sidewalk, then threw her arms around Vic. "After that service, Mr. Brown wanted to take the family riding in the new carriage, then we went to their home and had a fabulous dinner."

Victor looked closely at the carriage. "Nice. That thing is beautiful."

"It is. Samuel took me for a ride outside of town and then to our property to see what is happening with the construction."

"I've walked over to your lot several times. It will be quite the house when it's finished." He looked toward the jailhouse door, then back to her. "Sounds like a beautiful Sunday to me."

"It is, but I missed seeing you and Aunt Bettye."

Vic gave her a kiss on the cheek. "Bettye asked about you. We ate with your family at the picnic as usual, but I had to leave a little early. I'm so glad you've stopped in." He looked up. "Samuel, it's nice seeing you this morning."

"Yes, sir." Samuel reached out and shook Vic's hand. "It's nice seeing you as well."

"Have a seat and visit a few minutes." Vic sat down, but as he did the door to the jail opened and Matthew stepped out. He opened his mouth to say something to Vic, but stopped when he saw Caroline.

Caroline's breath caught. She cleared her throat. "Matthew."

CHAPTER THREE

For a long second, Matthew stared at the girl he once loved and hoped would spend the rest of his life with. She was the same Caroline he'd left on the ranch four years ago, only more mature and more beautiful— and she stood by her fiancé Samuel.

Finally he got control of himself. "Caroline." He nodded her way and forced a smile.

She responded with a smile and a nod.

His eyes locked on hers for another second, then he turned to Samuel. He held out his hand. "You must be Samuel. I never really got to know you when I lived here before, but I've heard a lot about you since I've been back."

Samuel shook his hand. "Same here, Matthew. I never got out to Fletcher Ranch when you were there, but I go as often as I can now." He looked at Caroline and smiled.

Caroline's face flushed.

Matthew swallowed. "I hear congratulations are in order."

"Yes, they are. This beautiful lady has agreed to marry me. I'm the luckiest man in these parts."

"Yes, you are." He speared Caroline once again.

Caroline cleared her throat. "I heard you were in town, but I said there was no way you'd be in Independence and not go see your family at the ranch."

"I saw Lucas this morning at the picnic and apologized

for not going out, but I certainly wasn't ignoring you, uh, your family. I've talked with Douglas and Emma in town at their practices"

"Douglas and Emma knew you were here? They haven't said a word to me."

He watched her think about that piece of information. He wondered why they hadn't said anything, but he didn't mention that. Instead, he looked at Victor. "This boss man has kept me busy, or I would've been at the ranch."

Victor laughed and shrugged. "Matthew is the best deputy I've had in years. I couldn't let him slip off to the ranch. I was afraid Lucas would steal him from me."

Again, Caroline cleared her throat. "I heard you were in law enforcement."

"Yes, I got into that in Jefferson City at the same prison where my stepfather had been."

"I'm sorry to hear about his death."

Matthew nodded, but didn't reply. Not sure how he really felt about the man's death, he never knew what to say to people when they voiced their sympathy for his losing his stepfather.

He looked at Vic. "If you don't need me for anything else, I'll head back to the boarding house, but I'll drop in later to give you some relief."

"Thanks, Matthew. With my other two deputies down with the some kind of stomach ailment, I need all the help I can get."

"That's probably from that awful coffee you make here." It was easier bantering with Victor than looking at Caroline with Samuel's arm around her.

"I don't see you refusing the coffee."

Matthew laughed. "You got me there." He turned to Samuel. "It was nice to finally meet you." Then he looked at Caroline. "You look as lovely as you've always been. Congratulations on the engagement."

"Thank you, Matthew."

As he stepped into the road, he glanced back at the girl-turned-woman who had captured his heart the day he'd met her. Today she still had a place there, but they were adults now with new lives and futures, and her future didn't include him. She'd chosen money over love—or maybe she really did love this man. He hoped so. He wanted to see her happy.

One thing he'd learned while taking care of his murderous stepdad was life was unpredictable, and to survive he had to deal with change.

Caroline had chosen Samuel Brown over him. He couldn't blame her. She deserved a good life. He'd live with her decision and deal with it as he had dealt with all the other unfortunate things he'd encountered in his life. He'd move on, but staying in Independence might be harder than he thought it would be.

He had a lot to think about.

~

"That guy is a fine lawman." Victor stood up and stretched. "I'm trying to convince him to take on this position so I can retire. Everyone on the city council who I've talked with agrees with me. He has quite the reputation for being in law enforcement for such a little time."

Caroline pulled her gaze from Matthew, who walked down the side of the road talking with several people with the confidence of someone who owned the world. She looked at her Uncle Vic. "Father said you wanted to retire. I wish you luck with that. I know Aunt Bettye wants you around more."

"Yes, she does. She has a list a mile long for me to do." He slapped his legs. "I need to go check on Joe." He gave Caroline a kiss on this cheek. "Samuel. Caroline. You two have a good afternoon."

Samuel took Caroline's hand, led her to the carriage, then helped her up. When he climbed in, he turned to her. "You sure are quiet today."

"Am I? I don't think so." She brushed her hair away

from her face and wished she'd be back at the ranch, alone in her room so she could think through the situation she found herself in. Seeing Matthew had been a shock, and she wasn't sure how to handle having him back in Independence.

Samuel took the reins but didn't have the horses move. Instead, he looked at her. "So you knew Matthew was in town?"

"No, not really. I thought I saw him on the sidewalk earlier, but I really couldn't be sure. It's been four years since he left town, and as he said, he hasn't been out to the ranch."

"You'd think that's the first place he'd go. I heard he was an orphan and your father took him in to get him off the streets."

She didn't like his tone, but what he said was true. Matthew had been a lost, starving orphan when Lucas brought him to the ranch. "Yes, he lived with us after his stepfather was put in prison. He's had a hard life. His mother and father both died in a fire when he was a baby. His neighbor saved him and then let him live with him and his wife. Unfortunately, his stepfather was not a good man. He killed his wife and that's when Matthew ran away. I'm glad Father was able to give him a place to call home."

"So you consider him a brother?"

"A brother. A good friend. We were very close." Caroline looked at Samuel. "Are you jealous?"

Samuel flicked the reins and laughed. "No. Absolutely not. I know you love me and are looking forward to the life I plan for you."

Caroline smiled and changed the subject. Seeing Matthew was hard enough. She didn't need to talk about him with her future husband.

Samuel led the pair of horses through town showing off the new carriage. Several people came up to them to admire it. She was cordial but wanted the afternoon to end. She needed time to think.

~

The next morning Caroline walked out to the barn as the sun's first rays peeked over the trees. She lit a lantern and headed to the barrel of oats. She filled the scooper, then took it to Sunflower's stall. "Here we go, Sunflower. You're always such a good girl."

Sunflower eased up to the railing and nudged Caroline with her nose.

Caroline scratched her between the ears. Sunflower had been her horse since she'd learn to ride. She was getting older, but still looked healthy. She looked over at Lady, her new horse that Samuel had given her. "I'll get you some oats in a second."

The barn door opened and Lucas stepped in. "You're up early."

"Good morning, Father. I woke up before daylight and got tired of lying in the bed."

"Did you have any breakfast?"

"No, not yet. I told Bonita I'd be back shortly. She's making hotcakes this morning."

"Sounds delicious." He walked up to the railing and gave Sunflower a pat on the head. "Any new plans for the wedding?"

"Not really or at least I don't think so. Emma and Abigail are quite the planners. I don't have it in me to tell them I'd rather have something simple."

"Abigail told me they are thrilled to be putting the wedding and the party together. I'm glad you want to get married by the rose garden. Both your mother and I and Abigail and I were married there."

Caroline turned and leaned on the railing with her back to it. "I've always loved that spot knowing Mother planted those rose bushes."

"It's special to me as well." He straightened up. "Are you happy with the way your life is heading?"

His question caught her off guard. "Of course, I am."

"That's good. I want you to be happy with your life's

choices. Marriage is a huge decision."

"You are okay with me marrying Samuel, right?"

Lucas placed his arms around her. "Of course I am. If you love him, then I'm thrilled."

She placed her head on his chest.

"You do love him, right?"

She laughed. "Of course, I do. Why would I be marrying him if I didn't?"

Lucas pulled her tightly to him. "I only want you to be happy, and when I see you with Samuel, you do seem happy. I'm not so sure you'll be able to become that perfect banker's wife though."

"Father, how can you say that? You sound like Douglas. I learned how to be a proper lady from Abigail and at Miss Porter's school." She pulled away, held her head high and shoulders back and sashayed around her father. "I can be as prim and proper as I need to be."

Lucas laughed. "I guess, but how will you live without all this?" He waved his arms around.

"I'm not sure, but I'll manage. I'm hoping Samuel will let me visit for a few days at a time. I can let my hair down and put on my trousers and hat and tend to the horses."

"I'm sure he will. I really am happy for you, Caroline. Your mother would be so proud of how you've turned out."

A wave of sadness swept over her. "I wish she were here. She would have as much fun as Grandmother and Abigail planning my wedding. My day would be complete marrying the man I love and having my mother with me."

Lucas pulled her into his arms again. "I know, honey. I wish she were here with us as well, but like Preacher Smith said, 'She's always with us in our hearts.' So she will be looking down on you walking out to the rose garden with a smile on her face."

"I know but I'd rather be able to see her."

Lucas let her go. "Me, too." He inhaled deeply.

Caroline knew he loved Abigail but still missed his

former wife deeply.

He cleared his throat. "I want you to know how much I appreciate your letting Abigail have such a big part of the wedding."

"I love Abigail. You know I do. She's like a mother to me, and I appreciate all she does for me. Still, I do miss my mother."

Lucas nodded, and Caroline spotted glassy eyes on her father as he turned.

"You're very good with the livestock around here. I'm going to miss you."

"You know how much I love the animals. I could spend my entire life doing nothing but tending to them. I wish I could've followed in Douglas's footsteps, but being a female probably would've stood in the way."

Lucas turned to her. "Really. I didn't know you ever thought about being a vet."

"Working with animals on a full-time basis would've been great, but being a girl was an obstacle. Of course, now that I've been to other cities, I realize I could've done anything I wanted to do."

Lucas pulled his daughter close to him. "Maybe Douglas would let you help in the office. He's always saying how he needs help."

Caroline blinked. "I've actually been thinking about asking him, but I didn't know how the family and Samuel would feel about me working."

"I can't speak for Samuel, but I know how all of us would react. We know how you love animals and are so good with them."

Caroline threw her arms around Lucas. "I love you so much, Father."

"I kind of like you, too." He laughed.

"I think I'll saddle Lady and ride to town to talk with Douglas?"

Lucas grimaced. "We still don't want you riding off

alone, especially all the way to town."

"Father, I'm almost twenty-three. I think I can handle myself on a horse."

"I know that. It's all the strange people you might run into on your way to town that I'm worried about. So many people have moved out here, we don't know half the people we pass on the streets in town."

"Must I remind you I lived away at school for four years? I can take care of myself."

Lucas shuffled his feet. "We have a lot of new people in this area since you left. It's not like it used to be when we knew everyone around."

"And I knew no one when I went to Connecticut." Caroline kissed Lucas on the cheek. "I do appreciate you still worrying about me, but I swear I'll be okay. I'll even take my pistol with me."

"I'll compromise with you. If you will wear a skirt and not those trousers and let our new boy ride along with you, I'll feel better. He can do some errands for me while he's in town, and you can do what you need to do. I'll tell him to give you as much time as you want, even if you want to go shopping."

Caroline thought for a moment. "I wasn't planning to wear a skirt if I ride a horse."

"But you will to make your father happy, won't you? And anyway, what if Samuel sees you in town in your trousers? He would not approve."

"You're right. I'll wear my riding pants. How's that? They're feminine and modest and no one could object to them."

Lucas laughed. "You know I can't tell you no."

She turned to go back inside, but stopped. "Did you know Matthew was in town?"

"Yes, Douglas mentioned it." Her father stuck his hands in his pocket, then pulled them out.

He was nervous.

"Matthew came to sit with us at the church picnic on Sunday. You were at the other church with Samuel so you missed him."

"Samuel and I saw him at the jail with Vic on Sunday morning. I couldn't believe everyone knew he was in town but me. Why didn't someone tell me?"

"To tell the truth, we weren't sure how you'd react. You two were so close for so long, and you were pretty torn up when he left."

"All that is true, but we're adults now, and I'm engaged. The shock of seeing him would've been a little less harsh for me had I known."

"I'm sorry, honey. I guess we all worry about your feelings."

"My feelings? Father, I'm not a child."

"You're right. You're a beautiful woman getting ready to be married. You'll have the finest house in the city, and before you know it, it will be filled with children."

She laughed. "Slow down. Let's get through the wedding first."

~

Johnny, the new boy Lucas had hired, rode his horse behind Caroline. She loved racing Lady down the road to town, but realized Johnny was having a hard time keeping up with her. She pulled the reins and Lady slowed down.

The boy rode up next to her. "Whew, you're quite a rider."

"I'm sorry. I didn't mean to leave you in my dust. I don't get away from the ranch on horseback very often anymore, and when I do, I love racing my horse. I missed this when I was away at school."

"Yes, I heard one of the guys say you'd just gotten back from Connecticut. That's quite a modern area of the country, isn't it?"

"It is. I loved every minute of it with its energy and excitement, but I can say I love this even more. This land is my life."

Johnny relaxed in his saddle after she slowed Lady to a slow trot. "I don't mean to speak out of place, but I hear you're marrying Banker Brown's son. Will you get to live out here away from town?"

"No, Samuel is having a house built for us on one of the newer streets in town. It's going to be beautiful. I'll take you by to see the land. You really can't tell much right now. They've only just begun working on it." She watched his reaction. His young face, still without facial hair, reminded her of Matthew when he was new on the ranch. Now Matthew was a man, strong and masculine. She shook her head.

Johnny smiled. "I'd like that. I'm sure you'll have fun helping with the design of the house."

"I am. I've never done anything like that before, but I saw some beautiful houses while I was away. I'd love to incorporate some of those ideas in it."

"Sounds fun. I hope one day I'll have a good enough job to afford to build a house for a wife and a family."

Caroline looked at the boy who probably wasn't over fifteen. "I hope so, too. Come on. Let's race."

Lady took off and surprisingly Johnny nearly kept up with her.

When they entered town, Caroline told Johnny she'd meet him at the sheriff's office about three. That way they both would have time to explore and take care of business.

After telling him goodbye she headed to the bank to tell Samuel she was in town. She thought about not telling him until after she wandered around alone, but then she assumed someone would see her and pass on that information to him. He would not be pleased if he hadn't been told first.

She was excited to talk with Douglas about helping out at the vet office, but she knew she should talk with Samuel first even though she was afraid he wouldn't be in favor of it. She'd have to stand her ground as she did with the location of the wedding.

As she walked through the door of the bank, she said hello to Murry, the guard, who had been with the Brown family since the bank had opened. "I'm going to the back to find Samuel."

"Yes, ma'am, he's with his father in his office."

She said hello to several tellers, then walked down the beautiful hallway with its marble floors and expensive paintings on the wall. She reached for the handle of the office door, but stopped in midair when she heard her to-be-father-in-law shouting.

"It's none of your business what your brother does, Samuel. Now forget you ever saw that."

"That's a little hard to do, Father." Samuel shouted as loud as his father. "What Richard is doing may not be legal. We could all be in trouble if he's caught."

Caroline stepped back and leaned against the wall. What could Samuel have seen his brother doing? She didn't know Richard very well. He seldom attended family gatherings and when he did didn't stay long.

The conversation inside the office got mumbled, but she was able to make out the word "embezzlement." She looked around hoping no one saw her, then turned and headed to the public area of the bank. Even though she hadn't intended to ease drop on their conversation, she'd heard what she should not have.

She headed back into the lobby where she stopped and talked with one of the tellers, hoping Samuel wouldn't know she had walked to the back. She wanted to see him, but decided to leave the bank and come back later. She left word with Murry to tell him she'd be at the dress shop and then Molly's restaurant, but would stop back by a little later.

"Is everything okay, Miss Caroline?"

"I'm okay, Murry. I didn't want to bother Samuel if he and his father are discussing bank business. I decided to get my shopping done before Samuel joined me. He's not one to shop in a lady's boutique."

"I can understand that. My wife tries to drag me in those stores, and I put my foot down."

"It was nice seeing you." Forcing a smile, she left the bank.

She hurried down the sidewalk hardly seeing where she was going or whom she greeted in passing. Her mind was in tangles. Was she marrying into a family with secrets that could ruin everyone involved? Would she be implicated just because she would be part of the Brown family?

Her heart pounded against her chest. How was she going to handle this piece of information? Should she ask Samuel what he saw? Should she bring it to the attention of the sheriff's office? If she told her Uncle Vic, he would surely involve Matthew.

She wasn't sure she wanted Matthew to be part of this new situation she found herself in, although talking with Matthew had always been easy.

No, this is my problem. I'll figure it out.

CHAPTER FOUR

Matthew entered Molly's restaurant. He'd skipped breakfast to help Victor get a prisoner ready to transport to Jefferson City. Now he was starved. He walked up to the counter and spoke directly with Molly, who took his order.

"I'll be at one of the window tables."

He headed to one of the smaller tables, but stopped dead in his tracks. Caroline sat alone at one of the other window tables with her head down. She looked as if she were in deep thought.

No way could he leave after having ordered, so he walked up to her table. "Caroline, you look lovely today." She did look lovely, but he'd known her long enough to know she was worried.

Raising her head, she blinked. "Matthew. I didn't see you come in."

"I stopped at the counter and gave Molly my order." There was so much he wanted to say to her, but words did not come. He wanted to tell her how much he missed her, and how much he needed her while he took care of his stepfather, but this not the time nor the place.

There never would be a time to tell her those things. She'd be Mrs. Brown soon.

"I'm waiting for Samuel, but you're welcome to sit with me until he comes in."

"Thank you, but no. I'll sit at this other table." He

started to walk away, but her sweet voice called him back.

"Matthew, how are you?"

Taking a deep breath, he turned. "I'm good. I like working with Victor."

"So you enjoy being a lawman?"

"Yes, I guess I do."

"Lucas and Victor both mentioned that your name is up to run the prison when it opens. That would be a wonderful job."

He nodded. "I'm sure it will be, but as I told Victor, I'm not sure I'll be in town for the duration. If I run, I've got to be able to guarantee the citizens if they vote for me they'll be electing someone who will be loyal to Independence."

"So you're thinking about moving back to Jefferson City?"

"I don't know, Caroline. It's not an easy decision to make. I have to consider a lot."

"So do I."

As soon as her words came out, her hands covered her mouth.

"Is everything okay? I didn't mean to upset you."

"No, no, you didn't upset me. I'm simply hashing over all the things I have to do."

She smiled big, but Matthew knew her smiles and this one wasn't sincere.

"Planning a wedding is sometimes overwhelming, not to mention having to make decisions about the new house Samuel is having built for us."

"Congratulations on both accounts. I heard about the house. It will be the talk of the town when it's finished." He was sure the wedding would be as well, but he left out that thought.

Caroline nodded. "Maybe. I think it's a little too big, but Samuel wants to fill it with children."

"That would be nice, Caroline. You'll make a wonderful mother." *A wonderful mother to my children.*

He looked around at the empty table. "I need to get my seat."

The front door opened and Samuel stepped in.

Caroline glanced up, then back at Matthew. "Please stay and say hello to Samuel."

Talking to Samuel was the last thing he wanted to do, but he smiled and nodded.

"Matthew, how are you today?" Samuel walked up to him and stuck out his hand.

"I'm fine but starving. Molly is fixing me a plate fit for a king, I'm sure."

Matthew didn't know Samuel very well, but he could tell the man was tense. His eyes darted. His jaw muscles twitched. *What's going on with these two?*

Samuel grabbed the back of his chair. "You can always count on Molly. She's a gift to our town."

"We're lucky to have her, that's for sure. I'm glad Preacher Smith doesn't mind his wife working."

"The town would rebel if she quit."

Samuel laughed, but Matthew felt it was a strained laugh.

Maybe he doesn't like the idea of finding me talking to Caroline. "It was nice seeing you, Samuel. You two enjoy your meal."

He walked to his table just as Molly brought out two plates of food piled high. Matthew chuckled. "Does Preacher Smith know what a fabulous wife he has?"

Molly put the food in front of him. "You know exactly what to say to a girl, don't you?"

"It's true, Miss Molly. You are a gem and the town is thrilled you kept the restaurant open."

"Thank you for saying something so sweet. I love what I do, and yes, he loves my cooking."

"He'd better treat you nice or I'll snatch you away from him."

Molly giggled. "You don't have to say such things. I'll

continue to feed you. Enjoy." She walked away, but stopped to talk with Caroline and Samuel.

Matthew dove into his food, but couldn't get his mind off Caroline. She'd looked so distraught when he'd first walked up, he wanted to put his arm around her and comfort her as he used to do. For years, the two of them confided in each other and helped each other get through problems. Today he wanted to do the same thing, but as he reminded himself, Caroline now had Samuel to confide in.

He hoped Samuel listened to her as he used to do, but then Samuel didn't look as though he'd be in a mood to listen to her problems.

Matthew ate his food without tasting it, and when he finished, he pulled out more than enough money for Molly. As he headed to the counter, he once again passed Caroline and Samuel's table.

"Did you enjoy your meal?" Samuel spoke up.

"I always enjoy what Molly piles on my plate."

"I totally agree. Have a good day, Matthew."

"Thanks, Samuel. Same to you." He looked at Caroline. "And you, Caroline."

"Thank you, Matthew."

Nodding, he walked past their table and breathed easier after he paid and stepped out the door.

Could he keep running into her and pretending that it didn't mean anything to him?

~

Caroline nibbled at her food and hoped Samuel wouldn't ask why she wasn't eating, but then she realized he wasn't eating either.

"Samuel, are you okay today?" She hoped he'd open up and tell her about his brother.

He snapped his head up. "Of course, I am. I just have a lot on my mind today."

"You know you can talk to me about anything. I might help if we share our problems."

Samuel shook his head. "No problems. The banking business is complicated and I'm sure you wouldn't understand. Sometimes it makes my head spin."

Especially when you find out your brother might be embezzling bank money.

She cleared her throat. She didn't like the fact he thought she wouldn't understand something about the banking business, but she let it slide. "I'm sure it is complicated, but I'd love to listen to the problems you're having. I know my mother always let my father talk about his day. It seemed to help him relax."

"Certainly. If you're going to be part of this family, you should at least know what your husband is doing every day."

"Exactly. I'd like that." It was obvious he was not going to direct the conversation to Richard. She wanted their marriage to be based on honesty and openness, but she could tell he wasn't going to tell her anything. She pushed around the food on her plate. If she told him she'd heard the conversation, he'd be embarrassed and probably be angry even though she had no intention of sneaking up on them.

She changed the subject. "Did you find out when the construction crew would start framing the house?"

His expression told her his mind was a million miles away. "Uh, no, not yet. I have to ride out to the mill this afternoon or tomorrow. They didn't deliver all the lumber order. I'm hoping it will be here to start construction this week."

"That would be nice, and so exciting."

"I'm glad you're happy about having the house built. I didn't think you'd want to live in the same house with my family after we're married."

"No, not at all, but we could've lived on the Fletcher Ranch. The house is huge, and you know Dad would've given us as much property as we wanted."

"Now, Caroline, we've talked about this before. You know I have to be in town to help with the bank. Anyway, I would have no idea how to manage more than a small yard around our house. Having hundreds of acres is not in my background nor is something I want."

"I know, and I thoroughly understand." She'd told a small fib. How could anyone not want to live on beautiful acreage and open lands like Fletcher Ranch.

"I hope so." Samuel concentrated on his plate of food.

Caroline did the same, but her heart hurt. Her future husband had a problem and he didn't want to share it with her. They had always been open with each other, but today was different. This problem was different. She wasn't sure what could happen if Richard were caught, but she had a feeling it might be a serious problem for the family and for their bank.

Samuel needed time to digest the information, she was sure. One day he would talk with her about it. He had to. She was going to be his wife and there should be nothing secretive in their marriage. Looking at him, she tried to determine if he was in the mood to hear she wanted to help out at Douglas's office, but since she'd just reminded herself that nothing should be kept a secret between a husband and a wife, she blew out a big breath and hoped he'd understand.

"Samuel, I had a wonderful idea. Really, it was Father's idea, but I think it's a wonderful suggestion. Since I'll eventually be living in town and not be around all the animals on the ranch, he suggested I ask Douglas if he could hire me to be an assistant."

"An assistant? You mean get a job to work with animals?"

"Yes, to work as an assistant to a veterinarian who happens to be my uncle. That way I could still be around animals doing what I love and yet living in town with you." Underneath the table she crossed her fingers, and hoped he'd agree.

"Caroline, what makes you think you need to work. You'll be my wife. You'll have anything you want, within reason of course, but you won't have to worry about money."

"I haven't even considered the money aspect of this. I just want to work around animals. When I was away at school, the worst part was being in the city away from my animals."

Samuel leaned against the back of his chair and stared at her. "You're really serious, aren't you?"

"Of course I am. I see no reason why I can't help my uncle in the office. Lots of women in the bigger cities have jobs and manage to keep their husbands happy."

"I don't know, Caroline." He shook his head.

"You're worried about what your family will think, aren't you?"

"Of course I am. We have a family image to think about."

Caroline sat up straight. "I'll have you know the Fletcher family is well thought of in this town. We've been here a lot longer than the Browns. If my father says he thinks I can help my uncle, I don't see why the Browns should worry." She reached for her bag. "I want to finish my shopping, and then go talk to my uncle about a job. One of father's hands rode here with me and I'm meeting him at three."

"Caroline, I've upset you, and I didn't mean to. Please don't leave mad."

"I'm not mad. I simply don't understand the obsession you and your family have with what other people think." Her voice was a little too loud. A man at the next table looked at them. She smiled at him and lowered her voice. "The way I was raised, you don't have to worry about your image if what you do is not something wrong."

She pushed her chair back, but he reached out and took her hand. "I'm so sorry I upset you. You go talk with Douglas and I'll break the news to my parents if he gives you a position."

"That's very kind of you."

He laughed. "Is this our first argument?"

She relaxed against her chair. "It wasn't an argument. I was simply sharing information with you so you knew what I was planning to do. I wasn't asking for your permission, though I certainly would've liked your blessing."

"Is this what they taught you in finishing school?"

"Do you mean the fact that I'm making a decision on my own? If so, no, they did not. According to them, wives are not supposed to go against their husbands or make major decisions without them. I listened and understood, but it doesn't mean I have to agree. There are some things in a marriage that doesn't take permission."

"Some things, maybe, but what you're planning involves both of our lives."

And embezzlement doesn't? She took a deep breath. "Samuel, the women in my family are all thinkers and doers. I see nothing wrong with that. If you can't live with that we might have to rethink our future."

He squeezed her hand he still held. "No, Caroline, we don't need to rethink anything. My love for you will get us through this."

"Thank you, Samuel. I appreciate it. I know I can do something to feel useful and still be a fitting banker's wife. It'll just take a lot of work, and I'm up for it."

"Yes, you are. You're a strong woman, Miss Fletcher. I guess that's why I fell in love with you."

She stood up. "Thank you for understanding. I'll let you know what Douglas says." She hesitated to leave without him talking about what she had overheard at the bank, but he didn't look as if he would say anything else, so she turned to go, then looked back at him. "You ought to see me wash the horses at the ranch. Hey, I can take care of your family's carriage horses."

His shocked look told her he didn't appreciate her humor. "I'm kidding, Samuel. I would never take away your stable hands' jobs."

She left him with his mouth hanging.

~

"You want to do what?" Douglas leaned back in his chair and stared at her.

"You heard me. I'd love to be your assistant. I know you're looking for someone to help in the office and with the animals."

"I do need someone, but not my niece."

She crossed her arms in front of her body. "And why not?"

"I don't know. Maybe it's because you're about to be Samuel Brown's wife. You don't need to be working."

"You don't even have to pay me. I don't need the money."

He stood up and walked around his desk and put one hip on it. "Then why do you want the job?"

"I want to be with the animals. You know I'm good at it, and believe it or not, Samuel didn't throw too much of a fit."

"What about Mr. and Mrs. Brown? I can't imagine them wanting their future daughter-in-law to be working with animals."

"They'll have to get over it." She plopped down in a chair. "Just let me help you when I'm in town and go with you when you're out on a call. You know I can do anything you need me to do."

He pushed away from the desk and walked around Caroline.

"Father is the one who suggested it." She added.

"He did, did he?"

"And let me remind you, your wife works and has her own office. As she said in the carriage the other day, it's not easy, but it can work if both of you try."

He shook his head. "I've got to be crazy, but okay. We can try it."

Caroline threw her arms around her uncle. "I love you

Uncle Douglas."

He hugged her back. "And I love you, too. Let's go in the back and I'll show you around and explain what some of the instruments are for."

"Don't teach me too much. I might become the town's next veterinarian."

CHAPTER FIVE

The next morning after a restless night, Caroline stood on a stool in one of the guest bedrooms at Fletcher Ranch with Abigail working on the wedding gown.

"Hold still, Caroline. If you keep moving, I'll end up pinning this fabric to your skin."

"I'm trying, Abigail." Caroline ran her hand down the front of the skirt. The intricate lace overlay came from Mexico where her great grandmother had worn it for early in the Twentieth Century. She thought about all the love that was brought together in this dress. She hoped it would be the same for her.

Abigail turned her slightly. "Are you okay today? You seem like you're a million miles away."

Caroline held the skirt up and stepped down from the stool. "I'm simply not in the mood to do this today. I'm sorry. I know it has to be done, but there's so much work to do on it. Maybe I'm too big for this tiny little dress."

"Caroline, you are not too big for this dress. Yes, your grandmothers were tiny women, but we were able to make it fit me so we'll do the same for you. You are perfect. Not big at all. We'll get this dress to fit."

"I have muscles."

Abigail laughed. "Of course you have a firm body because you don't sit around and do nothing. You're always outside and busy."

"Busy doing stuff with the ranch hands. I'm now realizing not all people think a lady ought to be doing things like that."

"That's true sometimes, but you also have learned to cook. You can sew if you had to, and you play the piano beautifully. Caroline, you are quite a lady and even more so since you returned from school. You might do things other ladies don't do, but you're certainly a lady. You'll make Samuel a lovely banker's wife."

"I'm trying to be, Abigail. I know men want a wife who can do all those things you said, but I really like being outside. You know I'd rather be wearing my trousers than some of those uncomfortable dresses."

"Yes, you do, and always have, but maybe you can find a compromise and do a little of everything that makes you a well-rounded woman."

"I'm glad you said that. I'm going to be Uncle Douglas's assistant at the office."

Abigail put down her pin. "When did this take place?"

"Yesterday, and yes, I told Samuel before I asked him for the job."

"And? What did Samuel say about that?"

"In the end he said he'd go along with it."

"But I don't imagine he was thrilled. Is he going to tell his parents before the wedding?"

"I'm sure they'll find out if he doesn't tell them so let's hope he will. I'm excited to help Uncle Douglas. I think I'll be good at it."

"I'm sure you will, and he needs help." She put her pins down. "You know that house Samuel is building is going to be gorgeous, and it will take a big staff to run it and a strong woman to oversee the staff. You won't be bored making sure everything is done, and then he'll want to fill those bedrooms with babies. You won't want to be away from the house then. You'll want to be by those children."

"I guess, but I'm not so sure I want children right now."

"That's something you and Samuel will have to discuss."

That and other things like embezzlement. She sighed.

"I can tell your heart is not into this alteration today. Let me help you out of the skirt." Abigail held her hand until she stepped off the stool. "Let's do this tomorrow. We still have a lot of time to get this sewn."

"Thanks, Abigail. I do appreciate all you're doing for this wedding."

"I'm thrilled you want your grandmother and me to help."

Caroline threw her arms around Abigail and kissed her on the cheek. "I love you so much."

"Watch out. Those pins in the top will get you." Abigail got quiet, then sniffled. "I love you, too, Caroline. You were my first daughter, and I'm so glad you allowed me to be."

"What will you wear to the wedding, Abigail? You have such beautiful dresses."

"My dresses are all old, but. . ." She clapped her hands and turned around to the armoire. "I bought this fabric at the mercantile the other day. Lucas loves me wearing green and when I saw it, I knew that's what I wanted to use to make my dress for your wedding." She pulled out a bundle wrapped in brown paper, then laid it on the bed. "I'm so excited over this fabric." She removed the paper and lifted deep emerald green linen.

"Oh, Abigail, it's gorgeous. You'll be more beautiful than the bride wearing this."

"Not hardly, but I can't wait to start working on it. After two pregnancies, I'm ready to get back into regular clothes, and I really wanted something nice to celebrate your special day."

"I'm excited for you. Lucas will love you in this. I still remember your wedding day. You were the most beautiful lady I'd ever seen. So sophisticated and pretty. When you walked out of the house toward the rose garden, I heard everyone whisper how gorgeous you were. I knew then I wanted to be like you on my wedding day."

"And you will. Samuel will be so proud of you when you walk out in this family's heirloom."

"Okay, you've got me excited. Let's work on the dress some more today." She stepped into the skirt of the dress and climbed back on the stool. "It's going to take a lot of work for you to make me look as good as you did wearing this dress."

Abigail picked up her pin cushion and smiled. "You have no idea how beautiful you are, Miss Caroline."

~

Matthew stood on the construction site where the new prison was being built. He had passed it many times, but had not stopped to talk to any of the workers.

"Matthew Jennings, I was wondering when you were going to come by to see this building."

"Sir, do I know you?"

"No, we haven't been introduced. I'm George Hasel. I'm the foreman of this project, and I've been told you might be the new county marshal overseeing this building."

Matthew raised an eyebrow. "Victor has been talking to me about running for the office, but I haven't made up my mind."

"The way I understand it, you don't have anything to worry about."

"That's to be seen. Do you have time to show me around?"

"Gladly. I'm proud of the work being done here. Let's start with the house where you or whoever runs this place will live. It's cozy but is well built and perfect for a new family. I hear you're not married, but that won't last long before you have a wife and six kids running after you."

"Slow down, George. You have me being the marshal, married and having kids. We're moving a little fast." He laughed.

"Maybe, but who knows? Come on in."

Together they walked into the bricked house.

"You'll love this place. We're proud of the way it has come out."

The kitchen, small, but efficient, would be where his wife or a hired lady could cook meals for him and the prisoners. Matthew took in everything in the house and could envision himself living here. He'd never had a place to call his own, and even though he would not officially own this, he would feel as if it were his if he became the new marshal. He stepped over wood and headed to what appeared to be two separate bedrooms. "This is amazing. There aren't many houses around here that have two bedrooms." *Except that huge house Samuel is building for Caroline.*

"I told you it will be perfect for you and your future family. You need to think about it."

George took him to another space that would be his office. "This has a separate entryway from the house. That way you can do the bookings and other prison business away from the family or the prisoners."

"I like it."

He followed them into the area where the prisoners would be housed. As soon as Matthew stepped in, he stopped. "Whew, this is great. I'm impressed."

Six cells filled the bottom floor. George explained there would be six more cells upstairs with two doors for each cell, one made of grated iron and one of solid iron. Each cell had one window covered with grated iron to allow light and air to come into the cells.

George put his hands on his hips. "Unfortunately, these cells will not have any means of heating or cooling."

Matthew nodded. "None of the prisons offer that luxury now. Maybe as the years go on, something can be done about it. How many prisoners are these designed for?"

"Each cell is six by nine feet and they can hold up to three prisoners, but I'm sure if the occasion arose, a lot more could be squeezed in."

"That sounds sufficient. Let's hope the prison doesn't lose any prisoners from the cold or the heat." He remembered how cold it was in the winter in the Jefferson City prison.

"If you ask me, if they don't want to die in prison, they need to stay out of trouble."

Matthew assumed most people felt that way, but he always hoped the men he saw in the Jefferson City prison would serve their time and leave better men. He wasn't sure his stepfather had changed his ways, though. Not once did he say he was sorry for shooting his wife. Maybe he was, but Matthew had a feeling he died still thinking he had done the right thing because as he put it, "that nagging woman deserved to die." That's not the way he remembered his stepmother. She'd always been kind and loving to him.

"So, what do you think? Is this a place you think you might want to run?"

George's words brought him out of his thoughts. "It's definitely an impressive building, and any lawman would be proud to have the position."

"We hope you feel that way, too."

Matthew simply nodded. He'd love to have the position, but was he ready to take on such an important job and did he really want to stay in Independence with Samuel and Caroline raising a family right down the street?

He thanked George for the tour and headed to Vic's office.

Independence and the ranches around the area had always been special to him. He'd love to settle down here and raise his own family, but things were so different now. He'd always assumed Caroline would wait for him.

How stupid was that?

When one year turned into the next and then the next and he was still in Jefferson City, he knew his time with her had come to an end. Her letters became less frequent, and then they stopped. Then a letter came from Lucas's wife, Abigail, who explained that Caroline was engaged to the son of the local banker. He couldn't blame her. She couldn't wait for him forever, and marrying a wealthy, upstanding man in the community would give her the life she deserved, one he never would be able to give her. Even if he got the job of Deputy County Marshal, he'd never be able to afford the life Samuel would give her. One day she'd live in the most elegant home in Independence. The only home he could offer her would be one in a prison.

No, she had made a good choice not to wait for him. Now he had to get her out of his system and move on with his life.

But, the big question remained. Could he live that life here in Independence?

He wasn't scheduled to work today, but Victor had asked that he stop in for a few minutes around the noon hour. As he opened the door to the office, he stopped. Six men sat or stood around Victor's desk.

Not wanting to interrupt a meeting, he turned to leave.

Victor stood up. "Matthew, come in. These men have been waiting for you."

Matthew closed the door. *Who are these men and why do they want to see me?*

One of the men stepped forward. "Matthew, I'm Harry Miller, former mayor of Independence. I'm now on the city council."

"Yes, sir. I do remember seeing you a few times when I came to town with some of the Fletchers."

Harry introduced the others in the room. "We're here to convince you to throw your name into the race to run for the County Deputy Marshal's position. We need someone like you to oversee our new prison."

"I'm flattered, but I'm not sure you've thought this through. First, I just got back to town. I've been gone a few years. Most people have no idea who I am so I'm not so sure

I could win the election."

One of the other men spoke up. "No, you have that wrong. Most people are aware of who you are and what you've done with your life. Everyone knows the Fletcher family, and they know you were part of them."

"We all know your story, and that's the kind of man we want for the job." Harry pulled out a chair. "Here, sit if you'd like. I know you have a thousand questions about the position."

Matthew stepped near the chair, but instead of sitting, he stood behind it and placed his hands on the chair back. He looked at each man. "You do know I don't have any experience running a prison."

"Your old boss in Jefferson City says differently. He said you were just a jailer, but you helped him in more ways than one. You were always ready to give a hand and offer suggestions, and he told us about the jailbreak that you alone put down. You may not have had the job title, but you did a lot of the job."

"I'm Cal. Besides all of what Harry says, we hear your reputation is one the prisoners don't want to mess with."

Before he could answer to tell them he did what all the other guards did at the prison when the prisoners waged a breakout, another man spoke up.

"We talked to Lucas Fletcher and he believes you would be excellent for the position. He said he'd personally campaign for you."

"Lucas said he'd campaign for me? He hates leaving the ranch and he especially hates talking to people."

"We all know that, but he said he'd do it because he has faith in you."

"I don't know what to say?"

"Say you'll put your name up for the position. We can't guarantee no one else will run, but as of right now we have not heard of anyone. Even if they did, we would throw our support behind you. What do you say? Independence needs someone like you in this position. You're young and energetic, experienced, and you're from the area."

"I have to say, you definitely know how to pump up a man's self-esteem. I'm totally flattered. Can you give me a couple of days? I'll give you an answer by next Friday."

"At least you didn't say no to us, so we'll definitely give you a few days. Did we mention the salary? The marshal will make $50 a month and, of course, you have that nice brick home to live in with your family at no cost."

"That sounds enticing. I promise I'll give it my total attention and get back with you."

"We'll be waiting and hoping you'll show your love of this area by running this jail and keeping law and order in our city."

All the seated men stood, walked to him and shook his hand. Matthew was flattered, but shocked at the same time. When the last one left the office, he stood staring at the door.

"I told you the council was behind you."

Matthew turned. "Vic, I know you've been saying that, but I don't know these men and they don't know me."

"Yes, they do. They know how you were raised, why you left town, and what you tried to do for your stepfather. It takes a real man to do what you did. When they spoke to your boss in Jefferson City, they were convinced you'd be perfect for the job. I've been saying that all along. I hope you'll give it some thought and let us get your name up."

"I'll think about it. I promise I will. I had no idea those men would be behind me as they seem to be."

"Well, they are. Now, get out of here. My two deputies are both supposed to come in to relieve me this afternoon. You're free to go do whatever you want."

"Thanks, Vic. You and those men drive a hard bargain."

"That was the point." He laughed and hit Matthew on the back. "You're a good man, Matthew. This town needs you."

CHAPTER SIX

Caroline sat in the saddle on Lady and listened to the ripple of the water in the river. She loved this spot and had vague remembrances of her mother and father bringing her here as a child. Mother always packed a picnic basket, and she'd play in the water while her parents sat on a blanket. The memories of her mother waned with each year that passed, but here and in the rose garden, those memories were the strongest.

Oh, Mother, I wish you were here so I could talk with you. I know you'd know what I should do with the information I overheard about Richard.

She looked up to heaven and smiled feeling her mother's presence. Taking a deep breath she stared at the grassy slope near the river. Memories of other things surrounded her here as well. She and Matthew spent many afternoons here basking in the warmth on that slope or playing in the frigid water. He had filled her younger life with joy and hope and expectation. Those years were gone, just as her mother was.

Those were the growing years, she called them. Now she was grown and she needed to look toward the future.

The river had not changed much. It rose and ebbed depending on the weather and the rainfall, but today it was the same gentle flow she loved. As soon as she was old enough to ride alone, she'd ride out here and enjoy the quiet.

Today she needed that quiet to get her thoughts together.

A few weeks ago her life seemed perfect. Engaged to a wonderful man, she looked forward to a wedding just as her mother and the other Fletcher women had celebrated, then to a fulfilling life in Independence with Samuel. Everything seemed to be falling into place.

Now she wasn't sure about anything. First, Matthew appeared in town and threw her off kilter. Why had he come back after all these years, and how would she handle his presence? Maybe she wouldn't have to deal with him at all. They'd seen each other a couple of times. He'd talked with her in the cafe, but he never seemed to be affected by being near to her. She had to forget him.

Then after overhearing the argument between Samuel and his father at the bank, she wasn't sure about her future at all. She couldn't shake the feeling that the Brown family wasn't as they appeared to be. She felt sure Samuel had no knowledge of what was going on with his brother Richard at the bank, but she wasn't so sure about Mr. Fletcher.

She needed to talk with someone. She wanted it to be Samuel, but it didn't appear he'd open up to her. Shouldn't he have confided in her since she was to be his wife? She wanted to hear his side of the story and needed to hear it from him. Maybe she had not given him enough time to think through his situation. Maybe he'd come to her soon and explain his problems.

Staring into the water, she let her shoulders slump. Maybe Samuel was old fashioned and "didn't want to worry her pretty little head" as she'd heard so many of the men around the ranch say about their wives. Samuel had been around the country. Surely, he had gained a different insight into life and into women than some of the men who had never left this area—or, maybe not. Maybe his father and mother and position in the community kept him in the past.

She thought about her father. She could talk with him about the bank and Richard, but he never condoned anything that wasn't within the law. If she told him, he might storm into the bank demanding to find the truth. His fatherly instincts might get him in trouble.

Uncle Vic was a sheriff. She probably should have gone straight to his office the day she'd heard the conversation, but he'd tell her father immediately.

She sighed and looked up into the heavens. *Why does life have to be so confusing and why doesn't Samuel talk to me?*

Then there was Matthew. He's the one she wanted to tell. He'd always understood her and together they'd talk through their problems, but could he be objective with a problem that involved her or the Fletchers or the Browns? He was a lawman, but the Fletchers were his family, and the Browns would be her future family. All of those reasons might make him act irrational, but the biggest reason had nothing to do with any of that. She had once been his love.

Had Samuel opened up to her, they could have faced this problem together. That day in the restaurant she could tell he was upset, but, of course, having an argument with his father would cause that. Maybe that was all it was. What if she'd misunderstood what she heard? That was the big "if." Did she really hear the word "embezzlement"? The more she thought about that day in the hallway, the more surreal it became.

She rubbed her hand down Lady's mane. "What should I do, Lady?" She laid her head on the horse's neck. "Life used to be so simple."

A crackle of leaves in the nearby bushes caught her attention as well as Lady's. The horse stomped her feet and jerked her head again and again.

"What wrong, little girl?" Caroline looked around, but didn't see anything, but her instincts told her something wasn't right. "We need to get back to the house."

Years ago she'd been thrown from her horse because a mountain lion scared her horse. No one had seen a cat recently that she knew of, but she wasn't taking a chance. It could be hiding in the brush.

Scanning the area once more, she turned the horse and slowly headed away from the peaceful river bank. Her dad was never comfortable when she rode off alone after that day he'd found her unconscious from the fall. After losing his first wife from a fall off a horse, he became overly protective. Today she needed the peace and quiet of the river, but she hoped that decision to come here had not been a mistake.

She'd always been good about sensing danger, and at the moment her body told her something wasn't right.

"Let's go, Lady."

Before the horse moved, a man jumped out from behind a tree and ran toward them. Lady reared up as the man grabbed one of the reins.

Caroline held on as tightly as possible to the other rein and kicked toward the man. He grabbed her leg. She screamed and twisted, but he was stronger. He pulled her and tugged at the rein at the same time. Again the horse reared up, but he stepped back before her hooves hit him. He never let go.

"Get down and I won't hurt you." He yelled and held on tighter.

"No! Leave me alone. Lady, run!" She tried to get the horse to run, but the man held onto her leg, making the horse go in circles. Fear gripped her chest. The man was young and strong. No way could she pull away from him.

Holding onto the horn with her left hand, she reached into the saddlebag with her right hand and pulled out a pistol. *Please let it be loaded.*

"Oh, no you don't," the man yelled. He jumped toward her and grabbed for the gun.

She screamed again. The gun went off in the air, scaring the horse. She jerked away from the man as Lady took off through the woods. Caroline hung on for dear life. No way could the man keep up with the horse, but if Lady got in trouble and threw her, she'd be at his mercy.

Turning around, she saw he was still running in her direction, but Lady ran faster. "Good girl. Run."

Please, God, let me get away.

It was hard to focus on anything but holding on, but in front of her coming across the north field there appeared to be a group of men. Panic set in. Were those men from the ranch or were they with the man chasing her. She tried to turn Lady away from them, but her horse was out of control. There was nothing for Caroline to do but hang on and pray.

The horse jumped over several logs. She slid from one side of the saddle to the other. Fear gripped her chest. A small ravine lay in front of her and she didn't think the horse would be able to make it across. She pulled at the reins to no avail. "Lady, please slow down. Please."

From the corner of her eye she saw a man break away from the group of men. He raced toward her on a huge horse. Praying it was someone from the ranch, she held on as Lady ran toward the ravine.

The man's horse caught up with Lady. Together the two horses ran side by side until the man reached out and grabbed Caroline and yanked her to his side. Lady took off alone.

"Hang on," the man yelled as he slowed his horse.

Caroline didn't have to be told. She threw her arms around the man's body and buried her head in his chest. Her body hung limp at the man's side, but she managed to wrap one leg around his leg.

Finally, the horse came to a stop.

"Caroline, are you okay?"

Shaking, she lifted her head and realized she was clinging to Matthew. "Matthew. Oh, Matthew. How did you . . .? Where did you. . .?" Her words were jumbled. Her thoughts scattered.

He lowered her to the ground, immediately jumped off the horse, then threw his arms around her. With both their feet on the grass, he pulled her to him and held her tight.

"You had me, all of us, worried."

She clung to him as if life itself depended on it and savored the weight of his arms around her. His heart pumped as fast as hers. Finally she lifted her head and looked into his face.

"I don't understand. Why are you out here? How did you know where I was?"

"We heard a gunshot."

At that moment another gun fired from the direction of the river.

They both looked.

"Vic and I and two other deputies were out hunting an escaped prisoner. Your neighbor pointed us in this direction. When your dad realized you had taken a ride alone, he came along." He pulled her even closer and rubbed her back. "You're shaking. It's over, Caroline. You're okay."

"That man tried to take my horse." She snuggled against him again with her face against his chest. She knew she needed to step away and stand on her own, but she didn't want the moment to end. She'd always felt safe in Matthew's arms.

At the moment he was all she needed.

"That man has a bad reputation. I'm glad you had your wits about you and were able to get away."

"He was so strong. I wasn't sure I could. Lady helped me."

"Whatever you did, I'm glad you're okay."

The beating of horse's hooves made them both look up. She stepped away from the security of Matthew's arms as the horse neared them.

Lucas's horse stopped inches from them. He jumped off and pulled her into his arms. "Caroline, are you okay? You had me scared out of my wits."

"I'm okay, Father. I'm sorry I caused you distress."

"Why were you out here alone?"

"I needed a little time to myself. I'm fine." She looked

around. "But I'm not so sure of Lady. She panicked and I couldn't stop her. She headed toward the ravine. I'm scared she'll hurt herself."

"We'll find her. I'm sure she'll head back to the house."

"Mr. Fletcher, we heard a gunshot. Did Vic shoot that man?"

"No, Vic shot in the air, and the man stopped. He knew better than to try to run." Lucas looked down at Caroline. "I'm so glad you're okay. I was terrified."

"I really am sorry. I simply needed a little ride and some time alone."

"I understand. We all do sometimes." He stepped away from her. "Who fired the shot we heard?"

"I did. I was able to get my pistol out of my saddlebag, but he grabbed my arm. That's when it fired and Lady took off. If it wouldn't have been for Matthew, I'd still be hanging onto Lady hoping I wouldn't end up on the ground somewhere." She kissed her father on the cheek. "It all worked out."

"But it could've gone in another direction. I'm glad you had the sense to do what you did." Lucas looked at Matthew. "Thank you for getting her off the horse. This horse I'm riding isn't very fast, nor as strong as yours. I could've never caught up with her. You probably saved her from a horrible fall."

"You know I would never let anything happen to Caroline."

She looked up into his eyes. For a second their gazes locked and Caroline knew what he said was true.

Matthew swallowed then looked at Lucas. "I need to go see if Vic needs help."

"I'd rather you take Caroline back to the house. I don't know if this horse can hold both Caroline and me. I'll go help Vic and the other deputy, then we'll get Lady back to the house."

Matthew looked at Caroline again. "Yes, sir."

Lucas gave Caroline another hug. "Don't ever make me go through that again." He jumped on his horse and headed back toward the river.

Matthew watched Lucas ride away then turned back to Caroline. "It'll be like old times." He held out his hand to her.

Caroline's heart thumped. Did she dare sit in the saddle with him? Would she be able to separate the boy she once loved from the lawman who had rescued her?

She was an engaged woman. Of course, she could, but even as she grabbed his hand and lifted herself into the saddle, she knew this man was the same one whom she'd dreamed about and loved for years after he'd left.

He hesitated, but eventually put his foot in the stirrup and swung his body up on the big horse.

She held her breath and squeezed her eyes as he snuggled behind her and put his arm around her body. She tried not to push against his body, but the saddle was only so big and Matthew took up most of it. Her back and thighs were jammed against his body. She tried to move forward but it didn't help.

"I'm sorry the saddle doesn't hold two people, but we'll be back at the house before you know it."

"I know, Matthew. It's okay. I'm not uncomfortable, but I'm afraid you don't fit at all."

"We're fine. It's like old times, isn't it? The only different is we rode bare back. I guess I could've taken the saddle off."

She laughed in spite of her feeling awkward. "I remember well those days."

Caroline relaxed against his body. It was going to be a long, glorious ride back to the house.

~

With his arms around her, Matthew closed his eyes and pulled from every ounce of self-restraint he had. This was Caroline, the love of his life, the girl who made him feel whole, but this was also the Caroline who was engaged. He would not do anything to interfere with her choice.

Realizing he still had her snuggled against him, but not moving, he took a deep breath and loosened his arms. "Are you ready?"

She nodded. "I think so." Her voice was soft, just as it was when they were young and carefree.

He wanted to hold her forever and kiss her until she forgot her banker, but that wouldn't happen today.

He swallowed. "You can trust this horse. His name is Morgan. He's big and fast, but he can be as gentle as we want him to be."

Caroline turned her head and looked directly into his eyes. "I'm not scared. I trust you, Matthew."

"You can, Caroline. As I said before, if it's in my power, I'll never let anything happen to you."

Her big blue eyes filled with tears. "I know I can. For as long as we've known each other, I've trusted you. You were always there to protect me."

He pulled her close, kissed the top of her head, then pulled away. "Hold on."

She settled down and tried to relax. Finally she looked back at him. "What kind of name is Morgan for a horse?"

He laughed. "Who knows? I bought him in Jefferson City. I tried some other names but this is the name his other owner called him, and he refused to respond to anything else. So Morgan it is."

For a moment the awkward moment passed.

Morgan pulled at his reins as if he knew they were talking about him and headed toward the ranch not realizing his riders had once been in love. Matthew tried to keep his body away from Caroline's but it was difficult sitting in the same saddle. She seemed to be sitting up straighter than normal, probably not wanting to touch him either.

Why had Mr. Fletcher suggested he take her back to the

house? *Doesn't he know I still love his daughter?*

No, he wouldn't know. He'd told Mr. Fletcher they had both moved on with their lives, but maybe her father sensed he had not told the truth. Maybe he knew he had loved her as a teen and still loved her now.

Again, he reminded himself she was engaged to be married. Her life would be filled with everything she could ever need or want. Her new husband could give her that. If he took the Deputy Marshall position, he'd be living in a house connected to a prison. What kind of life would that be for the woman he loved? No, he had chosen his path in life when he left to care for his stepfather.

He had made his choice. He'd have to live with it.

CHAPTER SEVEN

Caroline breathed a mixed sigh of relief when the house on Fletcher Ranch came into view. She needed to get off the horse and out of Matthew's arms, but when that happened, she had a feeling she'd never be there again. Being this close to him was more wonderful than she could imagine. If she closed her eyes, she could pretend they were young and carefree riding the ranges together, racing their horses, bickering about who shot the best, and lying on the grass by the river exchanging sweet kisses.

How had they grown so far apart and why?

That was an easy question to answer. Matthew left her. Plain and simple. He left her and never looked back.

She had to get him out of her system because she did love Samuel. Maybe it was a different, more mature kind of love than the exciting, young love she'd shared with the man who held her on the horse today, but it was love. Samuel would be a stabilizing, responsible husband. They'd have children who would have opportunities   for a good life. She was never impressed with material things, but he always said he would give her all the things that a good marriage should have. She guessed that would be good.

But would her marriage be exciting and carefree and fun-loving as the time she'd spent with Matthew? Of course, it would not. Grown people didn't need those things. They needed stability, something Matthew never had in his life and would never be able to offer that to anyone else.

No, the man sitting behind her, holding her against him, needed to be forgotten. The sweet kisses from the past needed to be shoved aside, and the wonderful times together needed to be tucked away forever. She could tell he didn't want her in his life.

As those thoughts materialized, Matthew did something totally unexpected. He pulled her close to his body and whispered. "Caroline, I've missed you so much."

Her heart skipped a beat. She turned and looked into his eyes. "I've missed you as well. Why did you leave, Matthew? You knew I wanted you to stay."

"You know why I left. I had to find forgiveness. I thought by taking care of my stepfather I'd be able to move on."

"And did you?"

"I don't think so." He stopped the horse. "I tried every day to forgive him, but I'm not sure I did. I waited for the sadness to set in when he died, but it never came. I think I was relieved that he was gone."

"I'm sorry, Matthew. I truly am. It's been hard on you. Nothing in your life has been easy."

"You're wrong, Caroline. Being with you was easy."

Tears welled in her eyes. "Don't say that. I'm engaged. You left. I couldn't wait for you forever."

"Yes, I know all that. I just want you to know I've never forgotten you, but I'm happy for you. Samuel will make you a good marriage."

What could she say? Yes, it would be a good marriage, but not the kind of marriage she'd dreamed of having with Matthew.

"Thank you, Matthew."

Neither said a word for a long second. She watched his chest heave up and down. So much needed to be said between them, but she couldn't get the words out.

Finally, he sat up straight. "We need to get you home."

She turned and through tear-filled eyes stared at the open range ahead of her. They did need to get home so both of them could start their lives without each other.

The rest of the ride was strained. She pushed back the tears, then realized another emotion surfaced—anger—that ugly emotion she never acknowledged when it came to Matthew.

Why didn't he want her? For all those years together, was he just having fun until he came to his senses and left?

He'd said he missed her, but had he really loved her? The answer was simple. If he loved her as she loved him, he would not have stayed away so long and would now try to win her away from Samuel. She knew that would never happen. He'd moved on and so should she.

Matthew led his horse toward the ranch. She had no idea where she was or how long she'd sat in the saddle with her body jammed against the man she used to love, but what she did know was she had been in the saddle long enough for her to realize she needed to wipe away all leftover feelings toward Matthew and appreciate the wonderful man who wanted her as his wife. She swallowed the lump in her throat. The chilly air blew through her hair taking with it the past she'd hung onto for too long.

Before she knew it Matthew led Morgan through the arched gates of the ranch then to the front of the steps at the house.

Abigail and Grandmother sat on the big front porch. Both of them stood up when they saw Matthew and Caroline ride through the gates. Abigail helped Grandmother Fletcher down the steps. Both of them stood with open arms as Matthew led Morgan near them.

"Caroline, we've been frantic." Grandmother Fletcher held a handkerchief up to her eyes.

Even from the top of the horse, Caroline could tell she'd been crying.

"I'm okay, Grandmother. I'm okay." she said.

As soon as Morgan stopped, Matthew jumped down and held up his hand to Caroline.

She didn't need his help, but she held out her hand. When he took it, her heart broke knowing this was their last time together.

Matthew nodded to her. Words were not necessary. His eyes told her everything. He did love her, but they needed to move on with their lives.

She nodded back, then slid out of the saddle into his arms. "Thank you for getting me home."

"This is where you belong." With those words he nodded to Abigail and Grandmother, then jumped back on his horse and headed back to the gate.

Abigail and Grandmother both grabbed her from behind. Grandmother buried her face in her hair and sobbed. "I was so scared. When those men took off today, I had a horrible feeling. I prayed and prayed and prayed asking God to help those men bring you home. He answered my prayers."

Caroline pulled her gaze away from the man who was riding out of her life and hugged her grandmother. "I'm okay. I'm sorry all of you were so worried." She looked up into Abigail's eyes then hugged her as well. "I have to admit I was worried, too. That man scared me to death."

"Come inside and you can tell us what happened. Bonita made pudding. We'll eat and listen. I want to know how you got away from him."

"Pudding sounds wonderful."

"Did they catch him?" Abigail asked as she helped Grandmother Fletcher back up the steps.

"Yes, Matthew saved me from my runaway horse. Lucas and Uncle Victor and the two deputies went after the man. I'm told they got him."

"Thank goodness," said Grandmother. "We don't need any escaped convicts roaming around here."

"No, we don't," Abigail said. "I'm ready for some

pudding.”

“That sounds wonderful.” With one last look toward the open field where Matthew had ridden through, Caroline put her arm around her grandmother to help her into the house. Matthew’s silhouette was almost gone. Her chest hurt, knowing her best friend and past love would never be back at the ranch as he used to be. As she got older she knew she’d have to put aside things from her past, but saying goodbye to someone like Matthew was harder than she thought it would be. She’d already told him goodbye once four years ago, but this time seemed final.

She turned her attention to her grandmother. “Thank you for being here for me.”

“We’re always here for you. Now I’m ready to sit with you. I want to hear all about my granddaughter’s traumatic adventure today.” She hugged Caroline.

Caroline smiled. This part of her past was always there for her, and she hoped Grandmother and her father and Abigail would be with her for years to come.

~

Matthew rode toward town with a heavy heart. Even knowing there was no other way for this unexpected meeting with Caroline to go, it still hurt.

Riding away from her crushed his heart even harder this time than it had four years ago. At that time, he thought he would be back quickly, but things never work out as they are planned, at least they never did for him in the past.

But this was now, and if he allowed it, his life could be different.

He wasn’t sure where Victor was with the captured convict so he headed back to Independence letting Morgan run as fast as he wanted. Even with the afternoon temperature falling and the cold wind hitting his face, he didn’t stop Morgan. He needed this wind and cold to wipe away the memories and the heartache.

“Run, Morgan. Give it all you have.” He held on and let

the horse run.

By the time the town appeared ahead, the sun was setting and the air was frigid. He eased up on the reins. "Slow down, boy. I can't have you falling out on me. You're the best thing I have in my life right now."

Between the waning light of day and the cold wind blowing, the streets of Independence were quiet. At least Victor didn't have to deal with trouble here after getting the prisoner back in jail.

He took Morgan to the stable.

"Deputy Jennings, come on in. I was worried about you when you weren't here before dark." Stuart put his bucket down and walked toward Matthew. "Whew, you and Morgan must've flown here. He's pretty wet."

Matthew got down and patted Morgan's head. "I let him run. He's been in here too long this week. He enjoyed his run. Didn't you, boy?"

Morgan nudged Matthew.

"You go on and give Sheriff Sanchez a hand. He and his deputies came in a few minutes ago. I'll rub Morgan down and get him comfortable for the night."

"Thanks, Stuart. You're the best."

He left the stable and headed back to the jail, but not before looking down the street toward the new prison being built. He might not be able to do anything about Caroline getting married to someone else, but he sure could do something about bettering his life. Being the County Deputy Marshall was more than he'd ever thought he could accomplish in this life. He might not win the election, but he'd never know if he didn't run.

He turned and headed to the jail. At least Victor would be happy with what he was about to tell him.

CHAPTER EIGHT

Caroline brushed her hair once more. Samuel would be at the ranch any minute to take her to town to spend some time with his mother. She wanted Mrs. Brown to come to the ranch to meet with Abigail and her grandmother to talk about the food for the reception, but Mrs. Brown refused. Samuel had asked Caroline to try to involve his mother, so she felt obligated to go to town to talk with her, but she wasn't looking forward to the afternoon with her future mother-in-law.

Someone knocked on her bedroom door and eased it open. "May I come in?"

"Abigail, you're always welcome in my room. Please come in and tell me what I should do about this meeting with Mrs. Brown."

"This meeting will be simple, Caroline. If she wants something special for the wedding, let her do it, as long as she takes care of it and it blends in with what we are doing. We'll have our hands full preparing what we want to serve." Abigail handed her a piece of paper. "I wrote down what you, Carmella and Grandmother and I have come up with. Grandmother wanted the traditional wedding foods, and I certainly agreed, but we also added our usual party foods. I remember my wedding. Everyone loved what we served."

Caroline took the list, glanced over the food, then laughed. "Yep, love all the bar-b-cue. Our friends will love it. Can't guarantee the Browns' guests will, but they'll have to adapt to our ways if they come to the wedding hungry."

"You're right. I'd give the list to Mrs. Brown and let her add to it, but don't let her change what we want to serve." Abigail took a long, deep breath. "If she is really against something, tell her we'll talk about it. Better yet, she ought to come out to the ranch to sit and talk with us. That would be the polite thing to do."

"I totally agree, but she didn't want to come out. I'll extend another invitation. I'm proud of our ranch. I wish she'd come out to see what we have here. I have a feeling she thinks we live in a rundown shack or something."

Abigail hugged Caroline. "We'd love to have her come out to meet us. Good luck today. I'm sure she will be very cooperative."

"I hope so."

"I hate to ask, but are you going to tell Samuel about your harrowing experience at the river?"

"I have to. He might have heard about it in town already. You know how gossip spreads."

"Oh, yes, but I hope he hasn't. It would be best if it came from you."

"Definitely. You know how stories grow in town." Caroline looked toward the window. "I think I hear Samuel's carriage. I'd better go down."

"I'll go with you if you don't mind."

Just as they stepped off the bottom of the staircase, Samuel knocked at the front door. Caroline opened it with a smile on her face.

"Don't you look lovely today, Caroline?"

"Thank you, Samuel. You look pretty good yourself."

He laughed. "Mother insisted I wear my Sunday best since I was picking you up in the new carriage. Not sure why one would matter to the other, but I shook out my good pants to make her happy."

"I wish she would've come out here. Maybe we can

convince her to do just that the next time."

Samuel shook his head. "Don't count on it. Mother hates to leave town."

"Then we'll have to work harder on convincing her to take a ride out."

He looked up. "Abigail, how are you today?"

"I'm fine, Samuel. Thanks for asking. You two enjoy the ride. It's pretty warm right now, but, Caroline, you should take your coat anyway." She took one from the coat rack and handed it to Caroline.

Samuel helped Caroline out onto the porch, then into the carriage.

She settled on the cushioned front bench and thought about how she'd tell him about her experience with the escaped prisoner.

He hopped in and took the reins. "Ready?"

"Yes, looking forward to it. It's such a lovely day." *But not looking forward to opening up about what happened to me or talking with your mother.*

She decided to get it out in the open immediately. "How was your week?"

"Pretty good. Things never get too exciting in the banking business."

"Unless there's a bank robbery."

"Don't even go there."

"I was joking about the bank robberies, but, you're right, that's not a good subject." She took a big breath and crossed her fingers. "My week has been quite interesting."

"Really, what happened?"

"I needed a break from all the decisions that have to be made about the wedding and house, so I took a ride out to the small river on our property. It's really not more than a creek, but I love being out by it. It's so peaceful."

"You rode out alone?"

"Yes, I've always ridden out there alone. It's not too far from our house. I keep telling you to spend more time out here so you can see more of the ranch. You'd like my special place by the water."

"And I keep telling you it's hard for me to leave the bank." He looked at her, but his face told her he was worried.

Caroline smiled. Samuel was such a handsome, kind man. She didn't want him to worry about her or about his brother, but she had to tell him what happened. Holding anything back from him was not the way to start a life together.

Even as she tried to find a way to tell him without making it sound too horrible, he did it for her.

"You said your week was interesting. Did something happen on your ride?"

"Not on the ride, but at the river itself something did happen." She blew out a big breath. "I was getting ready to leave when this man jumped out from the bushes and tried to take my horse."

Samuel snapped his head toward her. "What?"

"It's okay, Samuel. I was able to get away from him and the gunshot alerted my father and the sheriff and his men where I was."

"Gunshot? Who shot the gun?"

"I was able to grab my gun from my saddle bag, but in the scuffle, it went off. Thank goodness. That's how the men found me and captured him."

Samuel slowed the horses. "Scuffle? That man put his hands on you?"

"Not really, just my legs. I was on Lady, and he tried to grab the reins, but I fought him off. Lady spooked and took off. Now that was a little scary."

"Caroline, I can't believe this. You could've been killed."

"I realize it could've turned out differently, but everything is okay. The deputy saved me from having an accident on Lady, the sheriff captured the escaped prisoner, and I'm safe and sound."

"I'll have to go by the sheriff's office and thank the men and the man who got you off Lady before you were thrown. Which deputy rescued you?"

Caroline groaned. "Matthew Jennings." She tried to sound casual as if the ride back to the ranch, jammed up against him, wasn't a big deal.

"Matthew." He frowned. "The guy who used to live at the ranch with the Fletchers,"

"That's him. Luckily his horse was faster than Lady and he was able to pull me off before she threw me or fell into the ravine."

"I hope Lady is okay."

"She is. The men found her grazing under a tree. She didn't wander off."

"And you're okay, too?

"Yes, Samuel. I'm okay. No harm for wear." *Except for my heart being torn out again by my first love.*

"I don't like you off alone away from the house. There are too many unsavory men coming into this area."

"I do know that, Samuel." She gave him her best reassuring smile. "I've never had trouble before, and I promise I'll think twice about riding off alone in the future."

"When we're married and we live in our new house, you certainly won't want to ride off into the wilderness alone."

His words hurt. "Our ranch is not wilderness. You'd know that if you'd spend a little time there."

"We'll see."

Caroline didn't respond even though she knew she was right. Fletcher Ranch was beautiful and as safe as living in town. Accidents could happen anywhere and bad men roamed the countryside and in towns.

From the side of her eye she watched him, deep in thought. Was he thinking he'd made a big mistake asking her to marry him, or was he thinking he'd have fun changing her into a city girl?

Life was going to be interesting.

The rest of the ride was rather quiet. Twice he mentioned Matthew's name and wanted to know more about the rescue, but she skimmed over some of the details— details she'd have to wipe out of her memory forever.

Much too soon he pulled up in front of the fence of the huge Brown home.

A young man ran from behind the house. "Mr. Brown, I'll take care of the horses."

"Thank you. We'll be using the carriage again in probably an hour or so."

"It and the horses will be ready, sir."

Caroline gave the young man a sweet smile, then followed Samuel up the steps.

Mrs. Brown opened the door as soon as they stepped onto the porch. "Come in, Caroline. You look lovely today."

"Thank you, Mrs. Brown. You do, too, as usual." She wore a beautiful grey dress with a huge white collar and cuffs along the sleeve. Caroline could tell it was a store bought dress, probably shipped in from New York. For a second she wished she'd worn one of her nicer dresses, but then realized this dress was perfectly okay for the kind of morning they would spend. She wanted Mrs. Brown to like her, but she'd have to like her as she was.

At least she didn't choose to wear her favorite trousers. She almost giggled at the thought of Mrs. Brown opening the door and seeing her in her ranch clothes.

"I have refreshments being brought into the parlor. We can enjoy a little food and talk about the wedding at the same time."

Samuel led her to the door of the parlor. "I have some business at the bank. I'll leave you two ladies for about thirty minutes or so."

Mrs. Brown kissed her son on the cheek. "I'm sure we'll have exciting plans when you return."

Caroline accepted a quick kiss on her cheek from Samuel.

"See you soon." She hated being stuck here alone with Mrs. Brown, but this lady would be her future mother-in-law. She needed to get to know her better.

Caroline took a seat at a small mahogany table with two straight-backed chairs with deep blue velvety cushions. "I'm glad you want to have some input into the wedding. Abigail and Grandmother look forward to working with you. In fact, they want you to come out to the ranch the next time we get together."

Mrs. Brown sat across from the table. "I think they should come into town. We would have the stores here if we need to check out something."

"True, and I'm sure they can do that, but since the wedding is taking place at the ranch, we think you should see the venue and what we have planned. I think you'll be happy with it."

"About that. Is there any way I can convince you to use the beautiful new church in town and have the reception here at our house. Our back area is ideal for outdoor events and, as you can see, the interior rooms are big enough to hold as many people as we want to invite."

"I do appreciate your offering your beautiful home, but Samuel and I have discussed this. I want a traditional Fletcher wedding by my mother's rose garden. Her roses will be in bloom in May and I have my heart set on that."

"I can understand that, but wouldn't you want to walk down the aisle in that gorgeous new church with your gown flowing behind you?"

"I'm sure that would be beautiful, but that's not exactly me. I'm wearing the dress that three of the other Fletcher women have worn. It's a beautiful Mexican lace. It's not flowing at all."

Mrs. Brown stared at Caroline. "Honey, I would be glad to take you to one of the bigger cities and we could buy something more modern."

Caroline held her hands up. "Ma'am, I appreciate it, but

I know what I want, and this dress and my mother's rose garden suit me perfectly."

Mrs. Brown's shoulders slumped. "You think about my offer. I would love to help you find a dress. Wouldn't that be fun?"

Caroline smiled. "Yes, ma'am, but totally unnecessary." She took a huge breath, knowing her future mother-in-law would not like the meal that her family planned to serve, but it had to be done. "Let's talk about the food for our special day."

By the time Samuel helped her into the carriage for the ride home, Caroline longed to be home alone to think about all that had taken place. Caroline soon realized Mrs. Brown was used to getting her way and did not care for Caroline's ideas or strong will. She left the house on a cordial note, but Samuel's mother probably wished her son had chosen someone else to marry, someone who had not grown up on a ranch with cows and horses.

While she waited for Samuel to climb into the carriage, she giggled to herself. What would Mrs. Brown say if she had mentioned she was going to help her Uncle Douglas with the animals at the vet office? Samuel probably had not mentioned it to her.

She also had a feeling neither Samuel nor his father had confided in her about the trouble her son Richard might be in. Mrs. Brown was a strong woman, but Caroline could tell she knew her place in her marriage. It appeared she ran her home with a firm hand, but had no input in bank business. Her future mother-in-law projected the kind of image the finishing schools taught. Caroline understood those lessons, but didn't believe they suited her.

Her life on Fletcher Ranch had taught her a different life. She'd include what she thought was important to be a banker's wife, but she would never give up her independent thinking and belief in the land and tradition.

As soon as Samuel slid onto the carriage seat, he turned

to her. "So, how was your meeting with my mother?"

"Very interesting."

He chuckled. "That's a nice way of saying you thought it was awful."

"No, Samuel, not awful. Your mother is very nice, but quite used to having people do what she says. I tried to include her ideas into my family's plans, but I'm not sure she approved."

Samuel held the reins but didn't have the horse move. "Could you and she agree on anything?"

"Very little, but I think she has a better understanding of the kind of girl her son is bringing into the family."

"And?"

"And I don't think she's very excited about it."

He turned his attention to the horses and had them move down the street very slowly. "Mother is set in her ways, that's for sure, but she'll come around. She knows how much I love you so she'll relent and let you plan this wedding."

"But will she welcome me into the family?"

"How can you ask such a thing? Of course, she will." He waved to a few pedestrians, and didn't elaborate on their discussion. She decided not to force him to keep talking. What she wanted to do was find a way to direct their conversation to Richard. She closed her eyes and took a chance.

"How's Richard? I never see him in town."

The muscles in Samuel's face tensed. "He stays pretty busy at the bank, as we all do. Father keeps us on our toes."

"Yes, I'm sure running a bank requires hard work from those who manage it."

"That it does."

"I have a confession to make."

He turned and looked at her.

"I went into the bank last week. I walked to the back to find you, and before I knocked, I heard you and your father yelling at each other."

The frown on his face told her he didn't appreciate her snooping into family business. "You listened to us?"

"No, I didn't hang around to ease drop. Your voices were loud so I wasn't about to interfere. I do think the two of you were talking about Richard though and something that he did."

Again, Samuel turned to her. "Sometimes my brother and I don't see eye to eye, that's all. Father usually takes his side, but we figured it out, and I left his office with everything okay."

"That's always a good thing." She smiled, but didn't totally believe him. "I would hate for there to be a rift in the family I'm going to be a part of."

Samuel swallowed. "No rift, just little family disagreements."

Caroline didn't respond. Her family never argued, or if they did, it was done where she had never heard it. Her father didn't appreciate her and Matthew going off alone when they were friends years ago, but he was usually quite civil about it. Maybe her family wasn't normal, but if they weren't it's the way she would want her own household to be run.

Samuel turned the carriage onto the main road. For a Monday, the shops seemed to be quite busy with people walking along the sidewalk and going in and out of the different stores. As they passed the jail, Matthew was not out. Relief spread through her, but she still wondered how he was doing since he left her at the ranch a few days ago. Did their ride together on his horse bring back memories for him as it did for her?

Her thoughts scattered. She had a lot on her mind, including Matthew, but she would have to push his memories aside. She loved Samuel. Making a life with him would be different and sometimes hard, but she wanted it to work.

As they eased down the main road, she put her hand over his. "Samuel, would you convince your mother to come out to the ranch. I don't think she has any idea how beautiful it is."

"I'll give it my best shot."

"She'd like my family. They're wonderful people."

"Yes, they are." He turned his hand over and squeezed hers. "Just like their daughter."

~

Matthew headed to the jailhouse door, but something caught his eye as he passed the window. The Brown family carriage eased down the road with Caroline sitting next to Samuel. As they passed, she put her hand over his and smiled up to him.

He pushed away from the window and clenched his jaws. No way did he need to watch her enjoy an afternoon ride in the most expensive carriage in Independence.

Victor looked up from his paperwork. "You okay, Matthew?"

"Yeah, I'm fine." He glanced back to the window but the carriage had moved on. He tried to loosen the tension in his shoulders.

He wasn't a kid anymore. Living in the same town with Caroline and her rich family would be hard, but he could do this.

A new life awaited him.

"Yes, I'm fine and ready to face the day."

CHAPTER NINE

Two days later, Matthew said goodbye to Vic at the jail and picked up his things to head to the boarding house. Mrs. Hagerty was preparing roasted pork for dinner and he didn't want to be late. As he stepped out onto the sidewalk in front of the jailhouse, a young man approached him.

"Sir, are you Deputy Jennings?"

"I am." Afraid he'd miss the meal he'd thought about all day, he almost told the guy he wasn't, but then he wouldn't feel right about not asking why he wanted him and not the sheriff. "What can I do for you?"

"I have a note for you from Miss Fletcher."

Matthew's heart skipped a beat. "A note?"

"Yes, sir. She was quite specific. She said to give it to you and no one else, and then I had to promise I wouldn't tell anyone else about it."

Matthew's interest was piqued. Surely the Miss Fletcher would be Caroline, but he had no idea why she would send him a secretive note. "Thank you for riding out here to find me."

The boy stuck his hand in pants pocket and pulled out a piece of paper that looked as if it had once been neatly folded. He handed it to Matthew.

Matthew, in turn, reached into his pocket and pulled out a coin. "Thank you for doing this." He handed the boy the money.

The young man looked at the coin. "Thanks, sir. This is great."

Matthew smiled, remembering how happy he always was when he was that age and had the opportunity to be given any little bit of money.

"I have some errands to run for Mr. Fletcher before the stores close, then I'll be back for your answer." He tipped his hat.

"You need to hurry so you can get on the road before dark."

"Yes, sir, but I have to get your answer before I leave."

"I tell you what, why don't you go do Mr. Fletcher's errands, then stop by the boarding house at the end of the street. I'll be sitting on the porch and I'll have your answer."

"Thank you, sir."

The paper felt warm in his hand and it was all Matthew could do not to open it on the sidewalk and read it. He headed for his room at the boarding house and would read it in private. It had to be important if Caroline chanced sending it to him.

As he opened the door to the common room at Mrs. Hagerty's, his stomach growled. The aroma from the dining area was heavenly.

The swinging door from the dining room opened and Mrs. Hagerty stepped out. "Matthew, I was afraid you wouldn't make it. The other guests are already seated, and I can't promise they'll leave you any if you don't take your seat."

"Ma'am, I have some business to attend to in my room. Would you mind if I came down a little later."

"Not at all, but as I said, I can't promise you food will be left. I have two new guests and they're pretty big guys." She looked back through the doors. "I tell you what. You go to your room and I'll bring you up a plate. You can eat up there. If you want more and there's food left down here, you can get another helping at the table."

"Thank you, ma'am. That would be wonderful. I'm starving."

He turned and went up the stairs taking two steps at a time. His heart pounded as he opened his door. Before sitting down, he unbuckled his holster and removed his gun and placed it on the bed. He hated wearing a gun all day, but in this job it was a necessity.

Finally, he sat down in a chair by the window and opened the letter. Instantly, the beautiful cursive writing told him it was from Caroline. His heart pumped.

Dear Matthew,

I'm sure you think this is strange receiving a letter from me when I could have easily ridden into town to speak with you. Circumstances, however, prevented me from doing that, but I need to speak with you. The matter concerns the law, and I don't know who else to turn to help me decide what to do.

Could you meet me by the river at Fletcher Ranch tomorrow morning about nine? At the moment I would ask that no one else know about this meeting. After we talk, you can direct me to whom I should tell and how to proceed.

I know you are a busy man at the sheriff's office, but if you can break away for a little while, I promise not to keep you away from your duties too long.

Please let Johnny, the young messenger, know if you can make it.

Yours sincerely,
Caroline

The knock on the door told him Mrs. Hagerty was outside in the hall. No way did he want to answer it. He needed time to reread and to think about this note from Caroline, but he couldn't let Mrs. Hagerty stand in the hall.

He jumped up and opened the door.

"Here's a plate as I promised, and just as I suspected

those men are cleaning the plates. They act like they haven't eaten in a week."

"It's okay, ma'am. Whatever you brought me will be wonderful. Thank you."

"You enjoy." The middle aged lady smiled at him, then turned and walked away.

For a second, Matthew held the warm plate in his hand and stood in the doorway. Finally, he closed the door and sat back down by the window. When he removed the cloth from the plate he smiled big. Mrs. Hagerty had piled his plate high with a huge chunk of pork, vegetables, hot bread and a pile of potatoes.

He lifted the fork and took a bite, then groaned. This was as good as any of the meals he'd had at Fletcher Ranch.

As he ate, he reread Caroline's note two times. Something was wrong in her life. He hoped he could help her with her problem.

~

Caroline threw the saddle on Lady and prayed no one came into the barn. She didn't want to tell a fib, but no way would she tell anyone she was meeting Matthew. After several nights of lying in bed not able to sleep, she decided someone with knowledge of the law would be able to tell her what to do next. Samuel would not share what he knew about Richard, and she had no idea what to do about what she'd overheard.

She hoped she was overreacting, but her gut told her otherwise.

As she pulled the last cinch around Lady, she stopped and listened. Outside behind the barn she could hear her father talking with Mason, the ranch supervisor.

Please don't come inside. Please.

She held her breath and leaned against Lady. The talking got louder as they walked closer to the barn. She cringed. Never had she lied to her father. What would she tell him today if he entered the barn?

Both men laughed.

"Come on, Mason. Let's go grab a bite of breakfast before Carmella throws it out to the hogs."

"Sounds good to me. We can work with those two other horses when we finish."

Caroline listened to their footsteps head toward the house. Their talking got softer until she heard nothing.

She dropped her head against Lady. "That was close." She knew if Matthew had ridden out to the river and she wasn't there, he would be worried and probably angry since she pulled him away from his job.

Lady threw her head up and whinnied. "I know, girl. You're ready to go, but we have to wait just a few minutes more. At least I hope it's only a few minutes."

She strained to hear her father's voice. Had they gotten to the house yet? She'd give them a little more time before she tried to peek out the door.

With fingers crossed, she led Lady toward the back door and cracked it ever so slightly. Her father and Mason were almost to the back steps of the kitchen.

"Thank you, God. Thank you."

She closed the door and led Lady toward the front door. She stepped out, checking every angle around the barn and toward the house. Everything looked clear, but she didn't get up on Lady. Not yet. She walked her horse across the corral, then toward the small trail through the trees. When she was certain no one had seen or heard her, she jumped on Lady and headed toward the river.

Knowing it was close to nine, she let Lady run as fast as she wanted. Even aware it wasn't safe to ride through the trees this fast, she didn't slow down, afraid Matthew would leave if she didn't appear near nine.

A brisk, cold breeze blew around her, but under her jacket she broke out in a sweat. She'd braided her hair, but the braids hit her back as they flew out the bottom of her hat. Finally, she eased on the reins.

"Whoa, Lady. Let's slow down a little."

The thick bushes around the clearing along the river sent chills up her back. The last time she was here, the escaped prisoner jumped out from the bushes and could've hurt her had Lady not taken off at the sound of the gunshot.

The chills up her spine turned into warmth as she remembered leaning against Matthew's body as they rode together toward the house.

She shook that feeling away. Engaged ladies were not allowed to think of other men. Isn't that what the instructors at the finishing school told their students?

Yeah right. Getting Matthew out of her mind would not be easy, but she knew it had to be done.

Before Lady stepped into the clearing along the river bank, she saw Matthew get up and stand by his horse. As she neared, he came to her and held out her hand.

She took it. "Thank you, Matthew."

Without a word, he helped her down, but held onto her hand.

"Thank you for riding out here. I hated to ask you to leave your job, but I need some advice."

He nodded and let go of her hand, taking his warmth away.

She stepped away.

"You can drop Lady's rein. She's okay here. She won't run."

She knew that, but holding the reins gave her something to do. Her insides twisted, but she did as he said.

He pulled a small blanket from the back of Morgan's saddle and threw it on the ground. "Let's sit and you can tell me what's got you so concerned you had to get me and not your fiancé out here."

His words hurt. She inhaled deeply before starting. "I know this seems strange, but you'll understand when I tell you." Glad she was wearing her riding pants, she sat on the blanket and stretched her legs out.

Matthew sat as well, but not on the blanket.

She understood. He didn't want to be too close to her.

"I'm listening, Caroline. What's wrong?"

"I'm not even sure how to go about this." She clinched her hands together in front of her. "Maybe this is a bad idea. Maybe I shouldn't have come."

He reached out and took her hand and looked straight into her eyes.

She melted. It was the same look he always gave her when he wanted her to know he understood how she was feeling. She relaxed.

He pulled his hand back.

She looked out over the river. "I went into the bank last week to meet Samuel. He didn't know I would be there, but I went toward the offices hoping he'd be in his office. As I passed his father's, I heard him and his father shouting at each other."

She stopped and squeezed her eyes.

Matthew waited.

She looked at him. "They were talking about Samuel's brother Richard. I tried not to listen, but before I could back away, Samuel said something about Richard pulling the entire family and the bank down, and then he used the word 'embezzlement.'"

Matthew frowned. "That's a serious accusation. Are you sure you heard that word?"

"I've played that moment in the hall over and over in my head. I was so sure I heard that. That's what made me turn around and nearly run out the hallway, but now I second guessing myself and think maybe I really didn't hear it. I'm afraid if I say something to Samuel, he'll deny it and I can't prove anything." She looked into his eyes. "You're a lawman. What should I do?"

Matthew stood and walked to the river's edge. He turned to look at Caroline. "I might be a lawman, but I'm not an attorney. I do know that nothing can be done about what you heard unless it can be proven. There are laws surrounding bank business that govern how to go about an investigation. I really don't know that much about it. I've read up on it recently though. Just last year a Mr. Jones was arrested for embezzling $75,000 from a bank in Connecticut. He escaped to New York where he was arrested and eventually returned to Connecticut. It was quite the scandal and the story went national."

He walked back to the blanket and squatted down. "I can check around to see how the case was proven and that might give us some idea of how to go about this."

Caroline breathed a sigh of relief. "Thank you so much. I didn't know where to turn. We're talking about a family that I'm supposed to marry into. From what I heard of the conversation, I don't think Samuel had any idea of what Richard was doing so I'm sure he is innocent."

"That might be, but if Richard has embezzled money one way or the other, the entire bank could go under and Samuel would have to face the consequences of what his brother did, assuming he did anything."

"And if I marry Samuel, I could be intertwined in all this mess."

"You're right, but let's not jump the gun. Whatever Samuel found out about what Richard is doing may not be anything big. It might only be family money, not general funds in the bank." He stood up and shook his head. "I'd hate for you to be mixed up in all this. Something needs to be done quickly and get it resolved." He looked as if he wanted to say more, but he looked down, then simply took a deep breath.

Was he going to say the matter needed to be resolved before she married Samuel? She mwaited, but he said nothing more.

"It does need to be resolved quickly," Caroline said. "I agree. Thank you for listening. I didn't want to pull you into this, but I was afraid if I went directly to Uncle Victor, he'd tell my father and he'd do something stupid. You know how protective he is of me."

"Yep, you don't need to remind me." He laughed.

Caroline loved to hear him laugh. His smile was beautiful. She looked away to get control of unexpected emotions. "I do remember how he didn't approve of some of the things we did."

"Even though we didn't do anything bad." He smiled again. "I thought we were pretty good kids."

She looked down at the ground.

Matthew cleared his throat. "Independence has a new attorney. I met him the other day and I really like him. If it's okay with you, I'll talk with him and see what he says."

Caroline got up and took his hands. "Thank you again and again."

He looked down at their intertwined hands, then pulled his out and stepped back.

She realized what she'd done. "I'm sorry. I didn't mean for this to be awkward."

"It is awkward, but this is business, and I'm glad you came to me. We always could discuss our problems." He smiled, then walked to Morgan and Lady who had been grazing peacefully near the water.

Caroline did the same and took Lady's reins. "If Samuel voluntarily tells me anything I'll let you know, but I don't look for that to happen."

"I understand. I'm sorry he hasn't shared his problem."

He stepped near her and lifted her into the saddle before she could tell him she could get in the saddle by herself. He knew that, of course, but he'd always helped her mount.

"Be careful riding back."

She nodded and turned Lady toward the trail. With a heavy heart she left him standing near Morgan watching her.

CHAPTER TEN

"Are we going to celebrate with a Thanksgiving dinner this year?" Caroline sat at her usual spot at the dining room table at Fletcher Ranch surrounded by Grandmother, Douglas and his family, along with her father and Abigail and all the children.

Lucas put down his fork and looked at Caroline. "We give thanks at all our meals, Caroline. Why do we need a dinner just for that?"

"I'm aware we give thanks every day, and I think it's wonderful we do that, but the celebration of Thanksgiving on one particular day of the year is becoming the thing to do."

"Where may I ask is this taking place?" Lucas put his fork down and looked at his daughter.

"Most of the big cities do it in November toward the end of the month. Some families share meals with lots of folks they know and some prepare meals for people in the community who are not as fortunate enough to have a big meal."

Douglas took a sip of water, then spoke. "When I was in New York studying, some of the students talked about their families doing something like that."

"They do it as well in Boston," said Abigail. "I think the gesture is a wonderful one."

Caroline nodded toward Abigail. "Whether it's a real

holiday or not, I think we ought to get all the family, including Carmella's family and the ranch hands, and have a big meal to give thanks and to enjoy each other."

Grandmother Fletcher placed her napkin on the table. "I'm always in favor of a party. I think that sounds wonderful."

Lucas looked at Abigail. "If that's okay with you and Emma and Mother, we'll plan a big dinner a week from this Saturday. Would that suit everyone?"

Everyone around the table agreed on the following Saturday.

"Thanks, Father. I'll ask Samuel to come out. I want him to get to know all of you. He's always so busy he rarely has time for himself."

"That would be wonderful. We should invite his family as well." Lucas looked at Abigail. "Would you write an invitation and have Johnny take it to Mr. and Mrs. Brown. I'll pass the word to the ranch hands and to Victor and his family."

Caroline listened to the excited chatter around the table as they planned what they wanted to eat for this Fletcher Thanksgiving.

"In the East quite a few families eat turkey to remember what the Pilgrims did," Abigail threw in.

"I saw a flock of turkeys in the trees by the north pasture," Douglas said. "We could easily get us several and have enough meat for as many people as we want."

Lucas nodded. "We haven't been hunting together in quite a long time. I'd like that. Let's plan on a turkey hunt next Thursday."

"Thank you, everyone." Caroline squeezed her father's hand. "Our family has a lot to be thankful for, and this is a wonderful way to express it."

When the meal was over, Caroline went into the parlor and sat at the piano. Times like this when families got together, she missed her mother the most. She opened the piano and tinkered with the keys until she put both hands up and played one of the songs her mother had taught her. Tears wells in her eyes, but she didn't wipe them away. Sometimes tears needed to be shed to cleanse the soul.

Lucas walked into the room and sat by her. "That's beautiful, honey. I heard the melody and had to come in. Your mother would be so proud of you." He put his arm around her.

Caroline finished the song then leaned into her father's hug. "I miss Mother so much. Sometimes I can feel her next to me and hear her voice, but then sometimes I have a hard time remembering a lot of things about her."

"That's normal. I do the same thing, but we'll both always have a place in our hearts for her."

"I wish she could be here for my wedding."

"I, too, wish she could be with us."

She sat up straight. "Don't get me wrong. I love Abigail and am so thankful she came into our lives."

"I know you do and she knows how you feel as well. As she says, you were her first daughter." He kissed her on the top of her head and stood up. "I talked with Douglas about you helping out at the vet's office. He seems excited."

"I am, too. I'm hoping I can start going into town regularly to help out."

"We can plan something so you can go. Johnny would make a good riding companion."

"Father, you're treating me like a little girl."

"Yes, I know, but I also know things happen."

"And they would happen if Johnny is with me or not." She stood up and kissed him. "I can ride alone, and if it gets too late to ride back to the ranch, I can stay at Douglas's office."

Lucas groaned. "We'll talk about it."

She laughed and left the room.

~

"Mr. Fletcher, come on in." Matthew sat behind the

desk in the jailhouse, but stood up when Lucas walked through the door.

"How're you doing, Matthew." Lucas pulled out the chair in front of the desk and sat.

Matthew sat back down. "What brings you to town? It must be important for you to leave the ranch."

"It is important. I wanted to talk to you and Victor about coming out to the ranch next Saturday. The family is planning a get-together. Douglas, Abigail, and Caroline ganged up on me to have a Thanksgiving dinner."

"While I was in Jefferson City, I heard about families doing that. I never attended any, but I was told some of the people coming in from the East were doing a gathering to give thanks. There's nothing wrong with that."

"Then we can expect you to come?"

Matthew fidgeted. "I'll probably need to stay in town if Victor leaves."

"He has two other deputies. He can make sure they are here. You haven't been out to the ranch since you came back to town. We're setting a place for you at the table. I won't take no for an answer."

"Sir. . ."

"Matthew, you are part of our family. Please, for my sake, come."

"Who will be there?"

"If you're asking if the Browns will be there, I'm not sure. We sent an invitation, and their response was they didn't think they could make it." He stood up. "It'll be safe to come." He laughed.

Matthew stood up as well. "Thank you for the invitation. I'll do my best to get to the ranch."

"I'll go by Victor's house before I leave town, but would you mention it to him in case I miss him."

"Certainly."

"And, Matthew, I told the council I'd back you wholeheartedly for the new position at the prison. I think it's a good opportunity for you and a wonderful thing for the community. You'll be excellent at the position."

"I thank you for your support. I told the council I'd let them know by Friday whether I'll throw in my hat."

"You realize that's tomorrow, right?"

"Yes, sir. It's on the foremost of my mind."

Matthew watched Lucas leave the office. He would never refuse to give thanks to the man who saved his life years ago, but being at the ranch with Caroline and Samuel would be difficult. Of course, he might get an opportunity to give her the information he'd gotten from the attorney concerning bank scandals.

Mr. McCarthy, the newest attorney in town from New York, gave him some great advice about how to proceed, but he wanted to talk with Caroline before he reached out to Victor or anyone else at the state level. It wasn't a mission he wanted to be on since it was Caroline's future family involved, but since she'd brought it to his attention, he couldn't ignore the situation.

He walked to the jail window and watched Lucas cross the street, stopping to talk with several people. The man was a devoted rancher and was content never to step into town. It was nice seeing him today and being invited to the family gathering, but he wasn't sure he was thrilled about going out to the ranch. He'd go, of course, but he'd pray that Samuel and his family would not be there.

The next day, Matthew walked into the jail a little early for his shift. "Morning, Victor."

"Morning to you, Matthew. You do know it's Friday, right?"

Matthew sat down in the chair in front of Vic's desk. "I do know it's Friday, and I'm ready to give you an answer about the job."

Vic sat up straight. "And?"

Matthew nodded. "This might be a decision I'll regret for the rest of my life, but I'll run."

Victor jumped up and hit the desk with his hands. "That's the best news I've heard in a long, long time. You won't regret it."

"Let's hope not." Matthew stood up with a smile on his face. "I have to tell you I think I'm excited about starting this adventure. If I lose the election, I can move on, but if I win, it's an opportunity I never thought I'd have. Thank you for all you've done."

"You're a good man, Matthew Jennings. We wouldn't be pushing you into this if we didn't think so."

He nodded. A lump formed in his throat. He might not have a blood family, but this man and the Fletchers accepted him for what he was. He'd always be thankful.

~

Matthew thought about the Browns quite a lot during the week before the Fletcher dinner. He sat with the attorney several times to ask questions. He'd wanted to start a bank account, and now he had a reason, not just to put his money in a safe place, but to have a reason to go into the bank.

While in Jefferson City, he'd made enough money to actually start a bank account. Now, he'd take that money, as well as the money he was making working for Vic, and do the same here in Independence.

He'd been in the Brown bank several times to do jail business. On one occasion he met Mr. Brown. The man had an air about him that shouted business but was friendly at the same time. Matthew hoped he was not involved in the financial mess, but from what Caroline overheard, it appeared he at least knew what Richard was doing.

The day he opened his account, he walked out of the bank with newfound confidence. He even allowed himself to think about the possibility of buying a house. One day he'd have a wife, or at least he thought he might, and he'd have to give her a place to stay and to raise a family.

His thoughts went to Caroline. She'd be living in the biggest, newest house in Independence. Whatever he could afford in the future would look meager compared with hers, but he was happy for her. She deserved to live in a grand house. He could imagine her sitting at her piano in a huge parlor playing songs for their children.

He pushed those thought aside. Caroline was in his past. He could now look forward to working in Independence if he actually won the election for the deputy marshal position with the jail. If he did, his room and board would be free and he could concentrate on saving. Today, he planned to splurge. He headed for the General Store where he would invest in a new hat. If he made it to the Fletcher dinner, he would at least be presentable.

Feeling good about himself, he walked down the sidewalk. Not bad for an orphan whose stepfather was a murderer.

~

His job at the jail kept him busy the week before the Fletcher dinner. Several fights took place at the saloon. Both cells were filled, so he wasn't sure he should leave town on Saturday. On Friday he told Victor he thought he should stay in town to help the other deputies.

"My deputies will be fine. Don't try to come up with excuses not to ride out to the ranch tomorrow."

"I'm not coming up with excuses. I feel bad leaving Roy and Malcolm with all these guys behind bars. You know how easy it is for trouble to start."

"Yes, I do, but I also know my guys are capable of handling whatever happens." Victor picked up his things to leave the office. "Try to get some sleep tonight so you can enjoy yourself tomorrow."

"Sure. You go home and get some rest. I'll be fine." He patted Victor on the back. "I'll see you tomorrow."

The next morning he left the jailhouse at daybreak when Roy came in to relieve him. He had grabbed a couple hours of sleep during the night, but not enough. He hurried to his room and hoped to get a couple more before he had to leave.

At ten o'clock he brushed off his nicest trousers and shirt, made sure his boots didn't have mud stuck to them, and plopped his new dark brown hat on his head. He wished he was going someplace besides the Fletchers because of Caroline, but they had included him in the family. He wouldn't miss this.

The ride to the ranch was peaceful, giving him time to think about his life and how it had changed in the last few years. Thanks to Lucas Fletcher and now Victor, he was able to move on with his life. He smiled. He liked the direction it was taking.

As he led Morgan through the ornate gate of the Fletcher Ranch, nostalgia pulled at his heart. This had been the only home he ever remembered. After watching his stepfather shoot his stepmother, he'd run away from the man he feared. Being only nine years old, he quickly realized he had no idea how to live alone on the streets. Scared and hungry, he tried to take food from the general store only to be grabbed by the owner and hauled off to jail.

Lucas Fletcher happened to be in the sheriff's office that day. Matthew remembered sitting in the big chair behind the sheriff's desk and telling his story. By the time he finished, he was sobbing. He'd loved his stepmother. Now he had no one.

He'd watched Lucas pull the sheriff to the side. Later he found out he promised Victor if he could take the boy to the ranch, he'd keep him out of trouble. That's exactly what he did. Matthew owed Mr. Fletcher his life.

He flicked the reins. "Come on, Morgan. You'll be impressed with the barn and pasture they'll put you in."

He rode toward the big house. Several wagons were near the barn, and the corrals were filled with horses he was sure others had ridden in.

"You'll have lots of company, Morgan."

Lucas and his wife and sister-in-law sat in rockers on the big front porch surrounded by several men and ladies. He waved to them and headed toward the barn. A young boy met him at the door and introduced himself as one of the stable hands.

"I'll take good care of your horse, sir."

Matthew got off and shook the boy's hand. "I'm Matthew Jennings. I used to be the stable hand here."

"Really? You lived here on the ranch?"

"Yes, I did. Best years of my life. The Fletchers are the salt of the earth. You're lucky to be here."

"Yes, sir, I know I am."

The boy took Morgan's reins and led him inside. Matthew left, knowing his horse would be fine.

"Matthew, up here." Lucas stood by the side railing of the porch. "Come, join us."

He nodded and headed toward the front steps. By the time he got to the top, Abigail and Emma both grabbed him and kissed him on the side of the face.

"Whoa, had I known I'd have these beautiful women around me, I would've gotten here much sooner." He pulled each of the ladies toward him and returned their hugs. "You ladies look wonderful."

"And so do you," Abigail said. "You're not the same boy who left here years ago."

"Let's hope not," he said, and let them go. "Where's Grandmother Fletcher?"

"She's sitting in the parlor with some of Carmella's and Bonita's family. It's a little too cold for her out here."

"I'll be sure to go in to see her."

"Matthew, I'm so glad you could make it." Lucas walked up and shook his hand. "I was afraid you'd get tied up at the jail and not join us."

"I did, too. We have two cells filled with men, but Vic assured me his deputies had everything under control. Thank you again for coming into town to invite me."

"I wouldn't have done it for just anybody. Let's go in and see Mother then we can go check out the grills. We're having turkey today, but some of the hands insisted on throwing beef on the grill as well."

As they walked side by side toward the front door, Lucas turned around and groaned.

Matthew turned to see what he saw. Coming through the front gate was the Brown's new carriage carrying Mr. and Mrs. Brown, Samuel and his sister.

He looked at Lucas. "What happened to being safe today?"

CHAPTER ELEVEN

"I swear I didn't know the Browns had decided to come." Lucas shook his head. "What can I say? You'll have to grit your teeth and bear it."

"Thanks, Mr. Fletcher, you know how to throw a guy under a bucking bronco."

"First, of all, you need to stop calling me Mr. Fletcher. You're not a kid anymore and you're bigger than I am. Please, call me Lucas."

"I'll try."

"Try hard. You're family and a friend. No more Mr. Fletchers. Why don't you go in and see Mother. I'll welcome our new guests since they were actually invited and I'm the host."

"Gladly." Matthew went inside expecting to find just Grandmother and Carmella and Bonita's family, but as he stepped into the parlor, his heart fluttered. Caroline sat next to her Grandmother looking as beautiful as ever. The blue dress she wore made her fair skin shine and her blue eyes sparkle.

She stood up.

Except for the sweet smile, there was no emotion on her face. It was clear to him she saw him only as an old friend.

"Matthew, Father said you were going to join us today. I'm so happy you could make it."

"Thank you, Caroline. I've missed coming out to the

ranch." *And I miss being with you.* He wanted to hug her and never let her go, but instead he bent over and gave Grandmother Fletcher a quick hug. "You look wonderful, Grandmother."

Her smile was huge as she hugged him back. "I don't know how wonderful I look, but I thank you for making an old lady happy. I'm thrilled you joined us today. I've had you in my thoughts and my prayers since you left here."

He nodded. "Thank you. I need all the prayers I can get." He looked at Caroline. "The Browns were coming through the gate when I was coming in."

"Ladies, you'll have to excuse me. I should go welcome the Browns." Caroline took a step but then stopped and looked at Matthew. "You have a nice visit with Grandmother. I'll see you at the meal."

No one said a word as she left the room.

Finally, he turned his attention to the other ladies in the room and introduced himself.

"We remember you, Matthew. You were that young boy who helped us so many times when we needed it."

"Yes, ma'am, I do remember riding out to your place several times. How are things going with that beautiful garden you used to have?"

He sat next to Grandmother who took his hand and listened to the ladies talk about their harvest before the cold weather set in, but his mind wandered outside to the Browns and Caroline. Was she excited to see Samuel? Did she get along with Samuel's family and dream of giving them a grandchild?

He hoped so because if she were to become Mrs. Samuel Brown, she needed to have all those feelings for it to be a good marriage.

He listened as the ladies told their stories. He didn't want to be rude after so many years away, but he longed to be lost amongst the men outside.

It was going to be a long day.

~

Before walking out onto the porch, Caroline straightened her hair and smoothed her skirt, then lifted a shawl from the coat rack near the door. Mrs. Brown would be dressed to perfection, and she didn't want to embarrass Samuel. Otherwise, she would have worn her pants.

She took a second to inhale deeply. Seeing Matthew in the parlor was unexpected. Lucas had told the family he was attending today, but having him walk in nearly took her breath away. Tall and handsome and filled with confidence, it was hard to remember him as the awkward, shy boy from years ago.

Squeezing her eyes tightly, she swallowed and headed outside.

Samuel met her at the door, took her hand and squeezed it. "You look beautiful. I've missed you so much. If all these people weren't watching, I'd give you a kiss"

She squeezed his hand back. "You're making me blush."

"I like that." He cleared his throat. "We're glad we could make it today. For a while we thought we'd be tied up at the bank. Things got hectic on Thursday and Friday and we weren't sure we'd be able to finish."

She let go of his hand. Were they busy at the bank trying to fix the mess that Richard created? She prayed Samuel would open up and tell her about his problems. She wanted their marriage to start on the right note.

Pushing thoughts of Richard aside, she smiled. "I'm thrilled you and your family are here." She looked around him. "Let's go make sure they have what they need."

"We brought along my sister Margaret. I hope that was okay."

"Of course, it's okay. The more people we have to celebrate our thanks, the better. I wish your brother would've joined us, as well."

"Richard said he had business to attend to, but he passed

on his regrets. Maybe the next time we come out, he can join us."

She doubted he would ever come here to visit, but the invitation would always be open.

Samuel led her down the steps where Lucas was shaking hands with Mr. and Mrs. Brown. Caroline stepped near them and welcomed the group, as well, then introduced herself to Margaret.

Mrs. Brown hugged Caroline, then whispered. "Is there a place Margaret and I could go to freshen up? The dust on the road was awful."

"Certainly, but let me introduce you to the some of the family on our way in." She took Mrs. Brown by the hand. Margaret followed without saying a word. Caroline led them to where Abigail and Emma sat surrounded by their children playing on the porch or out in the front yard."

When the introductions were over, she turned to Samuel. "We'll be back shortly."

As they passed the parlor, Caroline glanced in. Matthew still sat with the ladies.

"We'll stop in to meet Grandmother Fletcher and the other ladies after you two freshen up." At the top of the stair Caroline opened the door to a spare bedroom. "I'll be downstairs when you're finished. You'll find everything you need in here. If you don't, I'll be at the bottom of the steps. Just call."

Mrs. Brown and Margaret hurried into the bedroom. Caroline turned and took the stairs slowly. As she took the last step, Matthew walked out of the parlor. Startled, she held onto the railing.

"Caroline, I didn't know you were inside."

"I led Mrs. Brown and her daughter to a guest room to freshen up."

Matthew shifted his weight from one foot to the other.

Was he as nervous as she was?

"I'm going to find your father to see if anyone needs

any help with the food." He stopped talking, turned to go, then turned back to her. "Do you think we can find a few minutes to talk later? I spoke with the attorney and I'd like to give you the information."

"Certainly, but I don't know how long the Browns are staying. I need to be with them."

"Of course, you do. We'll see how the meal goes and what happens afterwards."

"If we don't find the time to talk, I should be going to town periodically now to help out at Douglas's clinic. When I do, I'll go by Victor's office to see you."

He looked at her so intently, she caught her breath.

"I'm glad you're going to help out at the clinic. You've always been so good with animals. I think it's great."

"Thank you for saying that. I'm not so sure everyone feels that way about me working with animals."

They both looked up at the same time. Mrs. Brown stood at the top of the staircase holding onto the railing watching them. Margaret stood by her grinning.

"Mrs. Brown, come down and meet Matthew Jennings. He used to live on the ranch and work for my father." Her words came out much too quickly as if she'd been caught doing something wrong.

Mrs. Brown started down. At the bottom she held out her hand. "I'm Georgia Brown, Samuel's mother."

Matthew took her hand and held it. "It's so good to meet you. I met your husband in the bank a few days ago. I'm glad your family was able to join the Fletcher's Thanksgiving dinner."

"We are as well. I'm hoping we'll find time after the meal for the ladies to sit and talk about wedding preparation."

"It would be the ideal time." Matthew nodded but showed no emotion. "I'm sure I'll see you and Margaret at the dinner."

He left Caroline and Mrs. Brown at the bottom of the

stairs. Caroline wasn't happy with the lady. Why she mentioned wedding preparations to someone she just met was beyond her, except for the fact that she wanted Matthew to know Samuel and Caroline would be married.

Finally, Caroline forced a smile. "Let's go into the parlor. Grandmother Fletcher would love to meet you and I'm sure you two can talk wedding. I think I'll go outside to find Samuel. He's been so busy this week we hardly had time to talk."

Probably trying to figure out how to stay out of prison and keep the bank open if his brother is caught doing whatever it is he is doing.

~

Several of the old ranch hands corralled Matthew and dragged him to the grilling area. He met several of the newer hands and realized how at home he felt here on the ranch, even with the new men. Two grills were smoking. Mason opened the biggest one with two huge turkeys on it.

"We put the turkeys on at six this morning and we're cooking them slow."

"They smell delicious. I can't wait to taste them."

"How do you feel being back in Independence?"

"I love it. I've missed this area and the people here."

Mason pulled him to his side and gave him a quick hug. "Lucas talks about you all the time, especially since we heard you were back in town."

"I should've gotten out here sooner, but things kept getting in the way."

"Yeah, like a banker's son."

"What can I say? Life moves on. I'm happy for Caroline. She'll get the life she deserves."

"Nobody at the ranch believes that. Don't get me wrong, Samuel seems to be a good guy, but he's not who any of us thought she'd end up with."

Matthew didn't like this conversation. "As I said, life moves on. I hear you and Emma's mother hot hitched."

The smile that spread across Mason's face told the whole story. "I'm the luckiest old man alive. I've had two wonderful women to love me and put up with me. I couldn't be happier." He got serious. "We all want *you* to be happy, too."

"I appreciate that, but I'm happy with the way things are going for me. I've decided to throw my hat into the race for County Deputy Marshall at the new jail. I love being back in Independence, and I think that job will suit me. What more can I ask for?"

"I can think of one more thing, but you already know that." Mason nodded toward the house. "Lucas is walking over here with Mr. Brown."

Matthew groaned. He wanted to walk away from Samuel's father, but he made himself stay. With the possible problem at the bank looming, he needed to find out as much about the man as he could.

~

Caroline walked out on the porch to find Samuel talking with Abigail.

"Come sit by me, Caroline." He stood up and pulled up a chair next to his. "Abigail and I are enjoying watching the children."

"They're the best kids ever." She sat next to Samuel. "I love little Emma and William."

He took her hand. "We'll have some wonderful children, too, one day."

"Why certainly. They'll be beautiful and sweet, just like all my nieces and nephews."

Samuel looked toward the door. "Where are my Mother and my sister?"

"They stopped in the parlor to talk with Grandmother. I'm sure the conversation will end up about the wedding."

Abigail stood up. "Then I'd better go in there to reel them in. Grandmother wants to invite the entire state." She laughed. "I enjoyed talking with you, Samuel."

"Same here."

Caroline's attention was drawn next to the barn where the grills were set up. Matthew, her father, and Mr. Brown stood with the other men. She wondered what was being said and wanted to be with them, but then Samuel was next to her. She wouldn't dare suggest going over to the grills. She'd have to wait until later to talk with Matthew about the attorney's suggestions.

"I'd love for us to go to the rose garden where you want us to get married."

Caroline's attention was drawn back to Samuel. "Yes, I'd love to take you there and before you leave I want your mother to see it as well."

He stood up and took her hand. "I'll step inside and get both of our coats."

The rose garden was on the opposite side of the house from the barn. As they walked through a grove of walnut trees Samuel took her hand. When they were far enough away from the house, he stopped, lifted her face to him and gave her a light kiss on the lips.

"I've wanted to do that all day."

Caroline smiled up at him. "I'm glad you waited until we were away from our families. I'd hate for Father to go in to get his shotgun."

Samuel chuckled. "He knows I love you. He doesn't care if I steal a few innocent kisses."

She reached up on her tiptoes and kissed him sweetly. "You're a good man, Samuel Brown."

"Then why can't we get married before the spring?"

"We've talked about this before. I want a spring wedding when the roses are blooming. Anyway, our house wouldn't be ready. We'd have to live with one of our parents and that's not a good way to start a marriage." *Especially if it had to be with your parents.*

She took his hand again. "Come on, Mr. Brown. I want you to see where you'll make me your wife." She took his hand and led him down a well-trimmed path, until they stepped into an opening. Her mother's rose garden had been kept up even after her death. She'd found her father here one day, weeding it and trimming the bushes. From then on, she helped him.

"This is beautiful, but why is it so far from the house? You'd think your mother would've wanted the garden where she could enjoy it from the porch."

"I asked Father the same question. He told me Mother wanted it tucked away so the two of them could come out here and sit together alone."

"That's very romantic. I understand now." He looked around. "I can see this decorated into a beautiful spot for a wedding." He smiled. "I agree with this area for the wedding, but you do know Mother still wants us to use the new church in town. It's very grand."

"I'm standing my ground on this, Samuel. I have no connection to that big church. You know our family attends the small, older one in town with Preacher Smith. If I had to get married in town it would be in that church."

He nodded. "I know when I've lost an argument. Let's hope Mother will, as well."

~

Three huge makeshift tables lined the front yard of Fletcher Ranch. Since the weather cooperated and turned out sunny and cool, the family wanted to enjoy the outdoors before the bitter cold winter days took over. Abigail and Emma helped Carmella and Bonita cover the tables with beautiful hand-embroidered cloths that had been passed down for several generations. China and everyday settings from the Fletchers as well as dishes from Carmella and Bonita's families were put out. Caroline added big bouquets of fall flowers on each table.

When the turkeys were ready to be set on the table, the ladies brought out bowls of dressing, potatoes, beans, corn, and three kinds of bread.

Samuel led Caroline and Margaret to the table. Mr. Brown helped his wife. Lucas and Douglas helped their families, including all the children, find places.

Matthew let all the others sit before he chose to sit with some of the ranch hands. Lucas glanced in his direction and frowned, then motioned for him to pull a chair up to the family tables. Matthew smiled but shook his head. He was perfectly content to sit away from the Browns.

Lucas asked the blessing, giving thanks for his family and friends, especially for Matthew joining them and being home in Independence, and then he turned to the Browns. "We have a special thank you for the Browns joining us today and for our Caroline having Samuel in her life. Amen."

The dinner lasted for over an hour. Everyone talked and ate, then ate more. When the main meal was finished and the dishes removed, large bowls and platters of different desserts were set in the middle of the table. Everyone oohed and aahed at the dishes.

Matthew helped himself to a big slice of chocolate cake and wished he had room to eat some of each. Several times during the meal he glanced in Caroline's direction. She and Samuel talked quietly together, laughed softly, and seemed to be enjoying each other's company.

His heart hurt, but he refused to let the situation ruin this beautiful day.

By the time some of the families were packing up to leave, Matthew hoped the Browns would leave early as well so he could talk with Caroline.

Victor walked up to him. "I hate to ask you this, but Bettye wants to stay longer. I was wondering if you could go back to town to check on the jail and let the deputies leave if they want. Bettye is packing up some food for you to take them."

"I don't mind leaving. As soon as the food is ready, I'll head out."

Matthew figured the Browns were staying so leaving

would be no big deal. He'd have to wait until Caroline came to town before he could tell her what the attorney recommended.

CHAPTER TWELVE

On the following Monday, Carolyn rode into town alone on Lady to start work at the vet clinic. Excitement flowed through her. If she couldn't be a veterinarian, helping out in the clinic was the next best thing since soon she'd be leaving the ranch and its animals to live in town with Samuel. As a child she assumed she'd always live on Fletcher Ranch, but now that she was older, she knew she had to make a life of her own elsewhere.

The streets of Independence seemed to get busier each time she came. Today was no exception. She waved to several people she knew and even some she didn't know. Since wagon trains didn't leave during the winter months, she assumed most of the people in town today were those who were settling near here. Like her father, she loved the solitude of the ranch, but there was something about the chaos of the city that made her smile. Maybe living here wouldn't be as hard as she thought it would be.

She considered riding down the main road toward where their new house was being constructed, but decided against it in case Douglas needed her help. She took Lady to the stable riding past the jail. No one sat outside. She wasn't sure how she felt about that, but she continued down the street and passed the bank where several people stood along the sidewalk. Finally she passed the street on the side of the clinic. Emma's office was in front of Douglas's. She'd make sure she stopped in to say hello to her.

After getting Lady checked in at the stable with Stuart, she walked down the sidewalk toward the clinic, but as she passed the bank, she knew she had to go inside to tell Samuel she was in town and what she was doing. It wasn't a task she wanted to do. At the Thanksgiving dinner on Saturday she avoided the conversation about her working at the clinic knowing he did not approve. Today she had no choice.

"Good day, Murry." She greeted the security guard as she walked into the bank. "Is Samuel here today?"

"He just stepped out. He said he'd be back in about an hour."

She wrinkled her nose. If she didn't tell him before going into work, he'd really be upset, but at least she tried. "Would you tell him I'll be back later, maybe around the lunch hour? I'll be at my uncle's office."

"I certainly will. You have a good day, Miss Caroline."

Smiling, she left the building. She had avoided the issue once more, and now it would be worse when she finally told him.

As she passed the jail, she hesitated. She needed to hear what Matthew had learned from the attorney, but she knew it would not look good if Samuel saw her going in. Still, she needed to know. Throwing her shoulders back, she stuck her head in.

"Hey, Caroline, what brings you to town?" Victor stood up. "Come on in."

"No, I was just seeing if Matthew was working. Would you tell him I'll come back here before I leave town."

"I can do that. You doing some shopping today?"

"Oh, no. I am Douglas's new assistant." She felt the smile spread across her face.

"Fantastic. You'll be excellent. He's a lucky man to have you."

"Thank you for saying that. Not everyone thinks it's such a good idea."

Victor raised an eyebrow. "Sometimes we need to do what's right for us." He smiled back at her. "Go have a wonderful first day at work."

She walked down the street with a lilt in her step. At the veterinarian's office, she tapped on the door, then opened it.

Douglas sat at the front desk. "You did come."

"I said I would." She looked around. "No animals today?"

"Not at the moment. I was swamped earlier."

"I knew I should've ridden out sooner."

"Don't look so discouraged. There's work for you to do. How are you with numbers? I need to balance these books for the month. I hate doing stuff like that."

"I'm good with numbers, but I really hoped I'd be working with the animals and not the books."

He stood up. "There's more to running a veterinarian's office than treating the animals. You'll see. I'll show you what needs to be done, then I'd like to walk to Emma's."

"Sure. I'll run over to get you if anyone brings in a patient."

"Thanks, Caroline. I won't be long, but if you need me, we put a gate between our two offices. It will save you from going all around the block."

He took a few minutes to show her how he'd set up his books, then he left. For the next thirty minutes she worked diligently organizing and transferring information from slips of handwritten papers. Before she finished, the door opened and Matthew walked in. She couldn't believe he'd come to the office. She swallowed.

"Are you busy? I had a few minutes and thought I'd drop in."

"No, please come in. Douglas walked over to Emma's a little while ago. He asked me to help with his books. They're a total mess."

"I'm sure he's too busy tending animals than to deal with books." He pulled up a chair in front of her desk. "I wanted to tell you what that attorney told me."

She sat up straight. "Please, I've been eager to hear, but I didn't expect you to come over. I know Victor needs you at the jail."

"One of the other deputies stopped in to see if we needed anything, so I took a few minutes to walk down. I hope this is okay."

As long as Samuel doesn't come in, it is.

"Certainly, it is. You're always welcome to come here."

He started explaining the procedure of finding out if a bank and its money had been compromised, how and who to contact at the state level, and what to expect if something was found that wasn't correct.

"And if something is found, what happens?"

"Someone has to pay for the crime, because it is a crime if someone is taking money from the bank. We can only hope nothing has happened, but if it has I hope it is only Richard involved and not his father and definitely not Samuel. What I've seen of Mr. Brown and Samuel, they're both good men."

"Thank you for saying that. I hope they are not connected in any way to the problem." She relaxed a little in her chair. "So, are you going to talk with Victor to see how and when we should proceed or do you want me to do it?"

"I'll talk with him. I was waiting for your okay before I did anything." They both stood up.

Caroline walked around the desk and took his hand. "Thank you for helping with this. I really didn't know what I should do."

Matthew squeezed her hand just as the front door of the clinic opened.

Samuel stepped in. His frown told Caroline everything she needed to know. He saw them holding hands. As innocent as it was, he didn't know that.

"Samuel, please come in." Realizing she still held Matthew's hand, she dropped it and stepped toward Samuel.

"Matthew and I were talking about how nice the dinner was yesterday."

"Yes, it was nice." He looked at Matthew. "You have a sick animal?"

"No, my horse is my only animal, and he's perfectly okay. I heard Caroline was in town at the clinic and wanted to tell her hello." He looked at her. "If you need anything while you're in here, I'll be at the jailhouse. Victor or I can always help. I know Samuel is kept busy at the bank." He nodded to Samuel. "Have a good day."

As he left, Samuel stared at his back then at the door that he closed behind him.

Caroline swallowed. This was her fault. Without thinking she'd left word for both men that she'd be at the clinic. "Samuel, you weren't very nice to Matthew."

He shook his head as he turned around. "I'm not sure about that man. First of all, he was holding your hand. You're engaged, Caroline. Does that mean anything to you?"

She took Samuel's hand and pulled him to her. "Of course, it does. It means everything to me. Matthew and I are dear friends. That's all."

"That may be all it is for you, but I can tell when a man has feelings, and that man still has feelings for you. I saw it at the dinner and now today."

"You have that wrong."

"I'm not so sure about that." He stepped away from her. "I guess you're here at the clinic working."

"I am. Right now there aren't any patients, so I'm helping with the books."

"I thought we talked about this, and you knew how I felt about my future wife working in an animal clinic."

Caroline inhaled to keep from saying what she really wanted to say. She got control of herself and spoke in a calm voice. "Yes, we did talk, and you did indicate after we were married I wouldn't have to work, but, Samuel, this isn't about money. It's something I really want to do. If I could've figured out a way to attend the kind of classes needed, I would've become a veterinarian. I love animals, especially big animals like horses and cattle. I've been around them all my life and I want to work with them. This is the best way I can do it."

"I don't like it, and I know my parents will not approve."

"Then they will have to learn to live with it because I'm going to do this with or without your blessing." She stopped talking, took a breath, then continued. "I don't like us not agreeing on things. I would think you'd want me to be happy. I have agreed to live in the city so you can be by the bank. Since I'll be away from the ranch and the animals, this will be my way of doing a little something that I love."

"And what about our babies? Have you thought about how you'd raise children and work here?"

"That's in the future. I may not want to do anything outside the home after we have children, but until then I do."

She stepped away from him to calm herself.

"I'm going back to the bank." Samuel stepped back, as well. "If you can pull yourself away from here before it gets too dark for you to ride back to the ranch, would you please stop in to say goodbye."

She nodded.

He stared for a moment, then turned around to leave, but as he opened the door he turned back to her. "And I'd appreciate it if you refrain from holding that deputy's hand in the future."

He slammed the door.

She plopped down in her desk chair. She had never seen this side of Samuel. He'd always seemed to understand, but today he was not himself. Had something gotten him upset at the bank before he'd come here? Even though he didn't approve of Matthew being in the office with her and holding her hand, he could've handled it differently. Was he that jealous of Matthew? Maybe she needed to have a talk with him about how Matthew had left her and didn't want her in his life.

But, then he would probably ask how she felt about her old friend. How would she answer that? Her feelings for Matthew ran deep, but as he'd told her, "life moves on," and so should she.

She'd buried her love for Matthew long ago. It was still there, but she would never allow it to surface as long as Samuel was in her life. Samuel was a good man and deserved to have a wife who loved him and only him.

She wanted to be that kind of wife for Samuel. Why did Matthew have to return to Independence now that she had buried his memories? How had life gotten so complicated?

Small sheets of paper and the open ledger lay in front of her. Since Douglas had allowed her to come to work, she needed to get her act together and concentrate on numbers, not the dark haired deputy.

The door flew open, and Douglas ran in. "I met Thomas Hansing outside. He was on his way here. He has a horse that needs help." He ran to the back room.

Caroline followed. "I'm coming along. I have Lady at the stables."

"I don't know…"

"Uncle Douglas, I've been with the ranch horses all my life. I can help. I'm not taking no for an answer. Is your horse at the stables?"

He nodded.

"I'll have Stuart get him ready for you." She turned and left. No way would she let Douglas leave her at the office. She hurried to the stables, asked Stuart to get Douglas's horse ready, then saddled her own horse.

Glad she wore her riding skirt Caroline swung herself in the Lady's saddle, then reached for the reins of Douglas's horse. "Stuart, thanks for the help."

She rode Lady and led Douglas's horse down Main Street, trying not to glance at the jailhouse as she passed. She and Matthew might both be in the city of Independence, but she would learn to live her life without him in it—and without looking for him every time she passed on the same street.

When she got in front of the bank, Samuel stood on the sidewalk talking with another man. He stepped out into the street and headed towards her.

She eased Lady to a stop.

"Where are you going?" he asked as he held onto the reins.

"Douglas and I are riding out to the Hansing ranch. He has a horse in trouble."

Samuel frowned. "Shouldn't you stay at the clinic and take care of the paperwork?"

"Why would I want to do that? Samuel, I want to work with the animals, not do paperwork or cook for Douglas."

Samuel dropped the reins. "I was going to the clinic to tell you I was sorry I got upset with you. I don't like us to argue, but you've got to know I do not like this job you've taken on."

Caroline looked in the direction of the clinic. Douglas stood on the sidewalk with his hands on his hips.

"Samuel, thank you for the wanting to apologize, but it's not necessary." She looked up again. "I really have to go. Douglas is waiting for me and we need to get to that horse."

"Then go, Caroline. Go do whatever it is that you envision you should be doing. Obviously, it is not becoming a good wife."

Caroline's heart raced. "That's not fair, Samuel." She squeezed her eyes before she said something that she'd regret.

When she opened them, Samuel had his arms crossed in front of his body.

"We'll talk about this later," she said as she nodded to Douglas. "I have to leave right now." Before she flicked Lady's reins, she looked back down at Samuel. "I'm sorry you don't approve of my choices, but if we are to be man and wife, we need to come to some understanding."

She flicked the reins and headed to the clinic with tears in her eyes. Did her future husband not know she loved the open ranges and animals? She would try to be the kind of wife he expected, but he couldn't expect her to change everything about herself even though that's what the instructors insinuated at finishing school. She was a Fletcher and would always be that girl from the ranch, no matter what her last name was.

Douglas met her in front of the office. "Are you ready?"

"Yes, I am." She tossed the reins to him.

He fastened his bag to the saddle, but before he got up, he turned to her. "Are you okay?"

She nodded.

"You don't look so good."

"I'm okay. I promise."

He nodded. "We'll talk on the way out, but are sure you want to do this?"

"Of course, I do. Why else would I want to work for you if I can't help with the animals? I'm not a bookkeeper."

"If you insist, but if you pass out or vomit, this will be your last house call."

She swiped a tear that rolled down her face and laughed. "Have you ever seen me sick while I helped at our ranch? I told you I know what I'm doing around animals. I had a good teacher."

Douglas laughed. "Yep, I was a pretty good teacher." He got up in the saddle and headed out.

She followed. The Hansing ranch just east of town. Compared to the Fletcher Ranch, Mr. Hansing's operation was small, but he was well respected among the ranchers and had a reputation of taking good care of his farm animals.

She kept up with Douglas as he raced toward the outskirts of town. When they left the last building and noise behind, she rode alongside of him. "What's wrong with the

Hansing horse?"

He looked at her. "A lion attacked it last night. The dogs put up a raucous and his ranch hands were able to run the cat off before it killed the horse, but it sustained a lot of wounds. Hansing wants us to try to save him. The horse is his daughter's."

"I hate to hear about the cat. I know how they can cause trouble. Thankfully, we haven't had problems with them at our ranch in quite a while."

"We've been lucky. I've heard of several ranches being attacked. We might have to form a group to go out and kill it or run it off. I have a feeling it's a female with a kitten to feed."

She remembered how one had scared her horse and threw her when she was much younger, but the men were able to run that cat off. She hated to see any wild animal killed, but the ranch animals were their main concern.

They rode through the gate of a modest wooden fence and headed toward the corral farthest away from the barn where several men squatted down by a horse. Caroline jumped off Lady and followed Douglas. The horse lay on its side with bloody hay surrounding it.

"Poor thing," she said as she ran to its side.

"Dr. Fletcher, thanks for coming out." Mr. Hansing looked at Caroline. "And I see you brought some help. Caroline, you're all grown up."

"She's my new assistant." Douglas squatted down by the horse and first examined its eyes, then moved to the deep wounds on its body. "That cat wasn't fooling around."

"That's what I thought when I saw the cuts. Do you think you can clean the wounds enough so they don't fester up? I was afraid they were too deep for me to try to do it myself."

"I think so." Douglas reached into his bag, then asked Hansing for a bucket of clean water and some rags. "I brought some, but I'm going to need a lot more than I have."

Caroline squatted as well and rubbed the horse's head. "You're in good hands, boy. We'll get you better."

For the next hour, Caroline assisted Douglas with cleaning each wound, stitching up the deep ones, spreading ointments, and bandaging. Finally, she leaned back on his legs. "I think we tended all of them unless there's some under his side where we can't get to."

"It's possible there are more, but it looks like the cat attacked from this side. I think we got them all. I'll tell Hansing to send someone to get one of us if he finds more wounds when the horse turns or gets up."

His words did not go unnoticed. She caught the fact that he would let her come out alone to tend to other wounds if they were found. She was thrilled.

Before leaving the ranch, Douglas took time with Mr. Hansing explaining how the wounds should be cleaned. "Don't hesitate if you think we need to come back. If I can't come, Caroline will. She's worked with horses all her life and I trust her completely."

Mr. Hansing smiled and nodded. "Caroline, we'd love for you to come out any time and tend to my horses. I like to see a lady not afraid to do what she wants to do and not just what our society thinks she ought to be doing."

"I thank you for saying that. I wish everyone felt that way, but maybe over time I can convince the men and women of Independence I can do more than just cook and clean."

He nodded. "Thank you both for coming out."

"One of us will come out in the next couple of days to check on him. You need to get him to stand as soon as you can. We don't want him to get too weak."

As they rode back through the gate and down the road to town, Caroline thought about Samuel. What would he say if he'd heard Mr. Hansing's comments? Would she ever be able to convince him to let her do what she loved?

Maybe she wasn't meant to be the kind of proper lady

he needed as his wife. Could she be the hostess of teas and dinners as Mrs. Brown was?

Should a successful marriage be based on more than love? She did love Samuel, but maybe that wasn't enough.

She inhaled the fresh, crisp air blowing around her head. Today had been wonderful. Could she give this up?

CHAPTER THIRTEEN

Two weeks later bitter winter cold blew in from the north and snow covered the Missouri landscape. Matthew pulled on a heavy coat before he left the boarding house heading for the jail. He stepped through the door and grimaced when a strong, cold wind hit him.

Pulling his fur-lined coat tighter against his body he headed down the steps, careful not to slip on the thin coat of ice reflecting the waning light of the moon. Daylight would lessen the danger of falling, but the sun wouldn't be up for another hour or so. Normally his day started a little later, but today Victor needed him early to help get three prisoners ready for transport.

Days like today proved to everyone that the new bigger jail was needed. Transporting prisoners was always dangerous, especially when there was more than one.

He stepped onto the sidewalk, but before heading towards the jail, he surveyed the road and the dark alleys between the buildings. Nothing seemed amiss, but his gut told him not to take any chances. The three prisoners were part of a larger gang hitting trains along the route from Independence to Jefferson City. One prisoner was the younger brother of the leader of the gang and Matthew felt sure his brother would try to break him out.

With the street seemingly quiet, he headed toward the jail. As he passed Dr. Fletcher's office with Douglas's behind it, his thoughts turned to Caroline. But he forced his gaze away from the clinic and scanned the surrounding areas once more before he walked into the darkness. Several times a sound from the alleys made him put his hand on his gun, but nothing materialized. Finally, he got to the jail. The warm glow from several lanterns lit the entire jail.

"Good morning, Matthew." Victor poured a cup of coffee. "Thanks for getting here early. Come grab a cup before things get too hectic."

"Thanks, Vic. No one was up at the boarding house. I could use a hot cup. It's freezing out there. If I remember right, weather this cold usually happened in January and not the beginning of December." He rubbed his hands together to warm them, then headed for the coffee pot sitting on an old pot-bellied stove. He took a moment to hold his hands over the heat radiating from the stove, then grabbed a tin cup and poured himself a cupful.

"I heard some of the ranchers talking. They said the almanac predicted an early, colder winter."

"Great." He took a sip. The hot coffee warmed his insides as it went down.

"Did you have any trouble getting here?"

Matthew took another sip and walked near Victor's desk. "No." He laughed. "I think I'm a little paranoid. I thought I heard noises coming out of several alleys."

"Maybe not paranoid at all. I'm waiting for the rest of the gang to try to stop this transfer. I put out word the transfer would happen in two days, but I'm sure they are onto our tricks. They'll be waiting."

"Let's hope they're not as smart as we give them credit for."

"They're smarter than you think," one of the guys from the cell yelled.

"Go back to sleep, Bull. We don't need your input." Victor stared at the cell.

"You'd better listen. You and your deputy won't get far

when we leave here."

"We'll see about that." Victor walked toward the window and signaled Matthew to follow. "I've deputized three other men who have agreed to help. One will ride alongside of us. The other two will ride a short distance back for an element of surprise. We need as much advantage as possible."

"Sounds good, but I hope the effort is a wasted one."

Victor spoke low. "Yes, me too, but knowing this gang, there's a good chance we'll need more than these three men."

"Still planning to leave at day break?"

"As soon as the other men come in, we'll leave whether the sun is up or not. Do you have everything you need?"

"I do. I packed my saddle bags last night. They're at the stable already."

Movement in the cells told them the other prisoners were awake.

Matthew downed the rest of his coffee. "I'll get them each a cup." He walked toward the coffee pot once more. In his head, he went over the plans he and Victor had made earlier. Transporting these men was not a job he looked forward to.

Just before the sun came up Matthew, Victor, and the three additional deputies left the jailhouse with the prisoners. Victor's two other deputies stayed in town. As planned, one newly deputized man stayed with Victor and Matthew. The other two waited a few minutes before riding out. The three prisoners were handcuffed to their horses and tethered to each of the other men. With his rifle lying across his lap, Matthew's senses were on high alert.

Victor led the procession. Matthew took the rear. The farther away from the safety of town they went, the higher the risk of an attack. He knew the danger they faced, and all the other men did as well. Still, this was the job he wanted to do. He'd fallen into law enforcement by accident while his stepfather was in prison. They needed guards and he took a position. Soon after that, the sheriff asked him to be a deputy. Taking the job was the best decision he'd ever made. Now with the deputy marshal position about to be established in Independence, he knew he could do the job well, that is, if he won the election.

Victor raised his rifle. Everyone stopped. Bull said something. He couldn't hear the words, but he saw Victor hush him and direct the deputy to gag him.

Bull put up a fight as the deputy wrapped the handkerchief around his head, but in the end, the deputy won.

"If you other two say anything, you'll be gagged, as well."

Neither said a word, and Victor rode around the men towards Matthew.

"There's a narrow area in the road where the river comes in. I'd like for you to ride closer to the prisoners."

"Will do. I have both my guns ready."

"Good deal." Victor headed back to the front of the procession stopping to talk to his new deputy Thomas.

Before he got to the front a gunshot rang out, hitting Thomas. He grabbed the horn of his saddle but didn't fall off.

"Off the road," Victor yelled as he headed to help Thomas with the prisoners.

Everyone headed to the trees. Matthew rode up to the wounded deputy and helped him down, then tied his horse to a tree. One of the prisoners tried to get the horse to run, but Matthew grabbed the reins. "Stay put or you'll never see your new prison cell."

Bull tried to do the same thing, but Victor and Matthew grabbed him, threw him to the ground, then tied him to a tree.

"Is Thomas okay?" asked Victor.

"Yeah. He can still shoot." Matthew pulled the rope tighter around Bull's arms. "Could you see where the gunfire came from?" he asked Victor when the stood.

"Just south of us. I'm sure they're planning to pick us off one at a time. I'm sure the other two deputies heard the shots. They'll get here soon, and I hope they can come up without being seen."

"Hope so." Matthew checked his gun. "Maybe we can pick them off first." He chuckled. "If it's okay with you, I'll go through these trees to get behind them."

"Perfect, but wait until you think the other two have gotten here."

Matthew nodded. "When they get here, start shooting. I'll try to surprise them from behind."

"Be careful."

Matthew checked his rifle and pulled out his handgun, then slid behind a clump of bushes then into a thick section of trees. With snow covering the ground, his footsteps were silent, giving him a nice advantage.

Several gunshots startled him, but the bullets were nowhere near him. Confident they had not seen him, he edged closer to the gang, then stopped abruptly. Directly in front of him on the other side of the road he caught the glimmer from the barrel of a rifle. The man holding it lay on the ground with the gun pointing toward Vic and the others.

"Perfect," he whispered to himself. He continued through the trees until he knew he was behind the group, crossed the road quickly, then eased up closer to them. He counted four men with their backs to him, but he waited for Victor and the deputies to start firing before he did anything.

He didn't have to wait long. Gunshots blasted from the clump of trees where he'd left Victor's group. He moved closer, fired, and hit one of the gang in the arm. The man's gun flew out of his hand. Immediately, he spun around then raised his arms.

Two of the others turned on Matthew. He hit one in the leg, but the other fired simultaneously hitting Matthew in his left arm. He hit the ground, but pulled himself up and aimed at the guy who had turned back on Victor. He was an easy target, but he didn't want to kill him. He fired and knocked the gun from his hand, but the man didn't surrender. He threw himself on his weapon, aimed at Matthew, but Matthew was quicker. He fired and hit him in one of his hands. The man screamed and the gun flew out again.

With Victor's group still firing, he carefully kept his gun aimed at the two. "Tell your other men to drop their weapons, and I won't shoot you in the heart."

At first Matthew thought the man on the ground was not going to cooperate so he raised his rifle and pointed it directly at the man's chest.

"Drop your weapons," the man yelled toward the other gang members.

One guy turned, surprised to see Matthew behind him. Immediately, he threw down his gun. The other one followed suit.

"Victor, get over here. It's safe."

Within seconds, Victor and one of the other deputies barged into the clump of trees where Matthew stood holding his rifle on the other men.

Immediately, Victor grabbed one of the men and tied his hands. The other two deputies did likewise. The ambush was over.

"Nice job, Vic." Matthew stood up straight but grabbed his arm. Now that the shooting was over, the pain in his arm radiated into his shoulder. Blood flowed down his arm and onto his left hand.

"You're hit."

"It's just a scratch. Before we get on the horses, I'll let you tie a scarf around it." He looked at the gang members. "This was easier than I thought it would be."

"Yeah, these guys aren't as smart as the brother thought they were."

"Let's get these four on their horses and back to the others. That prison in Jefferson City will be surprised to have seven more inmates."

"I hope they'll house them there before the trial. I'd hate to have to transport them back."

Now holding his left arm with his right hand, Matthew agreed. "I know the warden. I think he'll take them."

CHAPTER FOURTEEN

The warden at the Jefferson City prison shook Matthew's hand after the prisoners were checked in and locked in their cells.

"I'm glad to see you stayed in law enforcement, Matthew. It's where you need to be. Did the clinic take care of your arm?"

"Yeah, they did the best they could. I'll have it checked out in Independence."

"Hope it won't keep you from running for that new position at the prison they're about to open. I've talked with Sheriff Sanchez several times about you."

"Yes, he did," said Vic. "He's the one who recommended you for my deputy. Best advice I ever got."

"I even sent word to some of the councilmen and gave you great recommendations. They all agree you're the man for the job."

"Thank you for the good words. You know how to make a man feel good. I'll certainly let you know if I pull off the election."

"I'm sure you will, but if you don't, you always have a job here."

"Thanks, I'll remember that."

The warden and Victor talked a little more, then the men headed out. Matthew was glad to be heading home. He loved this job, but he knew when he needed a little down time to heal, and his arm was screaming for a little rest.

Matthew rode alongside of Victor as they entered the main street in Independence. "I'm glad to be back home."

"And I'm glad to hear you call this town home. We need you here, Matthew."

"Thanks for saying that. It has always felt like home. Now that I've thrown my hat into the race, I really do hope I win. I'm looking forward to working in that new prison."

"And I'm looking forward to sitting at home doing nothing."

Matthew laughed. "You'll never be able to just sit and do nothing. I'll find you an easy, safe job at the new facilities to keep you out of Bettye's hair."

Victor laughed. "I'm sure she'll appreciate that." He raised his eyebrow. "You *are* going to stop by Dr. Fletcher's and let her look at your arm, right?"

"Definitely. It is aching."

"I'm sure it is. Most gunshots do." He laughed. "Now git. Take care of yourself. I don't want to see you at the jail for a day or so."

"I don't know about that."

"My other two deputies are booked for the next two days and the new deputies said they'd help me out while you take care of that arm."

"Thank, Victor. I could use a little rest, but you should do the same. With the cells empty, you can stay home for some of Bettye's tender, loving care."

"I've already planned that, and it wouldn't hurt if you thought about finding someone who would give you some loving care, too." He nodded toward the clinic. "Here's your stop. Thanks for the work. We couldn't have done it without you."

"I'm not so sure of that, but I was glad to help."

He said his goodbyes, then hitched his horse to the post in front of the clinic. He'd made light of his wound, but he knew it needed a little more attention before it would heal.

With a quick knock, he opened the clinic door, but stopped in his tracks. Emma stood in the middle of the lobby talking with Caroline. Both women turned and stared at him.

For a second he considered leaving, but knew that would be worse than going in with Caroline there.

"Ladies, how're you doing today?"

"We're doing great, but that blood on your sleeve tells me you're not."

"It's just a graze, but Victor insisted I come in for you to look at it. There's another deputy with a gunshot wound. It's not too bad, but he'll be in to see you. A doctor at the Jefferson City prison cleaned both of our wounds, but we need you to check both of us. They didn't stitch mine up. I wanted you to look at it first." He left out the part that the aching was getting worse.

"Come in the back and let's take a look at it."

He looked at Caroline, who had not said a word.

She swallowed. "I heard you and Victor were transporting prisoners. I'm so sorry you were hurt."

"We got the three prisoners to Jefferson City, and on the way we were able to capture the rest of the gang. It was quite a haul!"

"Congratulations, Matthew." Emma took his hand. "We need to look at your arm."

"I'd better go," Caroline said.

"Caroline, you don't have to run off, do you?" Emma still held Matthew's hand. "I could use the help and in the process you could learn a little about treating gunshot wounds. Vets are called to do all kinds of wound care."

Matthew looked at her, not sure what to say. Finally, he pulled his thoughts together since she hadn't said anything. "I'm sure Emma could use the help, Caroline."

Caroline nodded. "I'd be glad to help you, Emma."

Matthew's heart melted knowing she'd be in the room in close proximity to him. At the same time he berated himself for inviting more heartache having her in the room.

What he needed to do was to tell her to go back to Douglas's clinic so they wouldn't be close together.

He didn't.

He wanted her with him.

Emma never let go of his hand. "Come on, you two. Let's get this wound cleaned. I've seen too many arms amputated because they weren't cleaned properly."

"Thanks for that input, Emma." Matthew chuckled. "That makes me feel really good."

"A dirty gunshot wound is nothing to joke about."

"Believe me. I'm not joking." He followed her into her examining room never looking back at Caroline, but he could feel her presence.

"Sit on that table and take off your shirt."

Matthew hopped up onto the table, but when he pulled his shirt over his arm, he grimaced. Even though the doctor had bandaged it, blood had seeped out and dried on his shirt.

"Here, let me help you." Emma hurried to the table. "I'm sorry. I should've known it was dried and wouldn't come off easily. Caroline, would you grab that clean cloth by the basin and wet it?"

Again Matthew wouldn't let himself watch Caroline, but he felt her movement and heard the cloth splash into the basin of water. When she walked his way, he looked up into her eyes. For a second, their gazes locked. Matthew's heart pounded.

"Let's soak the sleeve around the wound," Emma said as she placed the soaked cloth over the area, "and I think it will be easier to remove the shirt."

Matthew nodded, half hearing what she was saying. He felt the cool cloth on his upper arm, but his attention was on Caroline. Her blue eyes showed sadness. Maybe confusion. Was he the cause of that? Leaving her had been hard for him, but maybe it was harder on her.

But looking into her eyes today, he wasn't so sure he had done the right thing.

No, don't think like that. Your love her too much to interfere with what she has with Samuel. They were the same thoughts he'd had many times, but it was getting harder and harder to believe them.

"I think the sleeve should slip off now." Emma placed her hand on his upper arm and loosened the fabric. There. It shouldn't pull too much now." She smiled at him, then concentrated on the arm.

When she lifted the bandage away from the wound, Matthew saw her grimace. He looked at the wound. "That doesn't look or smell good."

"It'll be okay, but it's starting to fester. Why don't you lie down? I might need to lance it before I clean it."

Matthew groaned as he tried to lie down.

Caroline stepped near his head and put her hand under it.

Again, he looked into her eyes. She had bent down to help, but her closeness unnerved him. She was inches from his face. Had Emma not been in the room getting her instruments together, he would've pulled Caroline down to him and kissed her just as he had done so many times in their past.

"This shouldn't take long, Matthew. It might hurt a little, but you'll feel so much better by tomorrow with all that nastiness gone." She walked up to the table, but stopped as she looked how close Caroline was to him.

Caroline stepped away. "What can I do to help?"

Emma looked from Caroline to Matthew, pulled in a big breath, and laid her instruments down on a tray. "Get a clean dry cloth and another wet one, as well. After I lance the wound, you can use the wet one to clean the area. I'll use the dry one to get it ready for a new bandage." She looked up at Caroline. "Can you do that?"

"Yes, Emma. I can certainly clean a wound."

"Good. Let's get started."

Matthew pulled his gaze away from Caroline, then

closed his eyes as he felt Emma lean over him.

"Try to stay very still. This will only take a second," she said. With that she lanced the wound.

He gritted his teeth and hoped he hadn't made a sound.

Caroline immediately pressed the wet cloth around the wound.

Again, he gritted his teeth.

"I'm sorry," Caroline said. "I didn't mean to hurt you, but we need to get all the drainage wiped away."

He opened his eyes and nodded. "It's fine. It wouldn't be like this today if the prison doctor in Jefferson City had done a better job. Do what you have to."

He lay still as both Caroline and Emma ministered to his arm. Finally, Emma covered the wound with an ointment, then wrapped it.

"You'll feel a hundred percent better by tomorrow. I'm going to give you a little something to help with the pain and to help you sleep tonight."

"I don't need. . ."

"Yes, you do. Now take what I give you and use it."

He smiled. "Yes, ma'am."

"Caroline, can you help him get his shirt back on while I get the laudanum?"

She nodded, then looked at him.

"I think I can get it." He tried to get up, but groaned.

"Would you please let the lady help you?" Emma turned and scolded. "I don't want you to start bleeding again."

Matthew smiled at Caroline. "Guess you need to help this poor old guy sit up so we can get the shirt on."

She put her arm under his head and took his hand with her other.

It was all he could do to sit up and pull away from her.

She stepped away and picked up his shirt. "This is pretty bloody. I hate for you to put it back on."

"I'll change as soon as I get to the room. I'm sure Mrs. Hagerty has a bowl of fresh water for me to use." He looked into her eyes. "Thank you," he whispered.

She only smiled and positioned the shirt so he could slip his bad arm into it.

With her help, he pulled the shirt around and pulled it over his other arm, then snapped the front. He slid off the table.

Emma walked over to him and handed him a bottle. "Please take a spoonful of this before bed. Sleep will be the best thing for you right now."

"Believe me. I don't need this to sleep. I'm exhausted."

"Matthew, please do as I say. You're going to hurt tonight and this will help you stay asleep."

"Yes, ma'am. I'll take it." He took the bottle from her. "I really do appreciate all you've done. I'm glad you're here in town. I'll come back in a day or two when I have some money on me."

"You're family, Matthew. There's no charge."

"We'll talk about it."

The back door opened and Douglas stepped in. "I heard you and Victor were back in town and have a lot to be congratulated about."

"Yep, we're back, and those thugs are in the Jefferson City prison. We couldn't get them there fast enough." He walked up to Matthew and shook his hand. "Sorry you had to take a bullet to get it done."

"It was only a graze."

"A graze that was turning bad." Emma walked up to Douglas and touched his arm. "I'm glad they got back when they did."

"We are, too."

"I see my assistant was here helping. Good job, Caroline."

"Douglas, it's not my first time to help out with a wound that wasn't on an animal. You know what it's like on the ranch. Someone is always getting hurt."

"You'd better watch out." Emma spoke up. "I might

take her from you. I can't find a nurse around this town."

"Oh no, she's mine."

Matthew took the opportunity to say his goodbyes. He gave Emma a quick hug. "Thanks, Emma, you're a wonderful doctor. This town is lucky to have you." He looked at Caroline. "Thank you for helping."

He left the clinic as confused as Caroline looked.

Life was not getting any easier.

~

Caroline stood in the middle of the examining room floor and watched Matthew walk out.

Douglas crossed his arms in front of his body. "What's up, Caroline?"

Caroline looked at her uncle. "What do you mean?"

"You know exactly what I mean. What's up with the two of you?"

"Nothing. There's nothing up and nothing ever will be."

Emma took Caroline's hand. "Neither of us believe that. Honey, you can't hide the love you have for that man. We can't choose who our hearts belong to. It just happens, and you and Matthew happened a long time ago."

"But it's over, Emma. It's over. He wants it this way."

"That might be what he says," Douglas said, "but that's not what's in his heart. The man loves you and he'll always love you."

Caroline pulled her hand out of Emma's and walked to the side window. "He might love me, but he doesn't want me."

"Have the two of you talked about your feelings?" Emma walked up to her and put her hands on her shoulders. "You have to talk."

"And what about Samuel? I know you say you love him," Douglas said as he walked up alongside of Emma, "but is it the same kind of love you have for Matthew?"

Caroline turned to face them. "Yes, I love Samuel, and, yes, I still love Matthew. I know that sounds crazy, but it's true. I love them in different ways, but my love for them is in my heart."

"But is it the same?" Douglas took her hands in his. "Talk to him. Tell Matthew how you feel. You don't want to spend the rest of your life wondering what would've happened if you had told him. He needs to know. And so does Samuel."

Caroline pulled her hands away, then walked to one of the chairs and sat. "It's not easy to be rejected. Matthew made it clear he does not want me."

"He says that, but that's not what he feels." Douglas put his arms around Emma. "It wasn't easy getting this lady to accept me, but I didn't give up. I'm the happiest man in the world because I spend every day knowing she's in my life."

"You two and Father and Abigail are all so happy. I want what you have."

"Then don't let it pass you by, Caroline." Emma bent over and kissed her on the forehead.

"I'll think about what you've said. Thank you. I really do appreciate both of you."

CHAPTER FIFTEEN

Caroline slept in the back room of the vet clinic for the next two nights. Both nights Douglas stayed with Emma in the back room of her clinic. Quite a few people in Independence had come down with the flu, and Emma wanted to see as many patients as possible before going back to the ranch.

Each night Caroline had dinner with Samuel, but each night as she climbed into bed, she knew something was wrong with him or with the two of them together. The dinners were strained. Their conversations were forced, and the night kiss he gave her was anything but passionate.

Was he falling out of love with her, or was he worried about what was happening at the bank?

And more importantly, was she falling out of love with him? That thought saddened her. She'd thought the two of them were good together and would build a great life in Independence, but maybe the love between them was not enough to carry them throughout life. Those thoughts and questions bothered her each night.

This morning she fixed a cup of coffee and went out to the small front porch of the vet office where Douglas had placed a rocker for her to use. The cold December air nearly took her breath away. She stepped back in, grabbed a small blanket, then snuggled into the rocker. The coffee warmed her hands and felt good going down her throat. The vet clinic faced a small street off the main one and was lined with about ten houses. Several windows were lit as people were getting up.

From the main road where Emma's clinic faced, the rumble and rattle of wagon wheels and the clapping of horses' hooves told her the town was coming alive. The activity in the city excited her, but she still loved the quietness of the ranch. Could she live here if she and Samuel went through with the wedding?

She was resolved to that fact when she agreed to marry him. The huge house he was having built for them pointed to the comfortable life she would have, but was that the important part of a marriage?

A man with his coat pulled close to his face and his hat down low stepped around the corner. She sat up straight ready to go inside, but to her surprise Matthew walked up to her gate.

"Mind a little company this morning?"

As always, seeing Matthew sent a warm streak through her body. "Certainly. Can I get you a cup of hot coffee on this frigid morning?"

"I'd love some. Victor has a pot going, but it hardly classifies as coffee."

He put his foot up on the first step, then stopped.

Caroline stood up, bundled the blanket in front of her and turned to the door. *Why was Matthew here this morning? Please, Samuel, don't show up on your way to the bank.*

She heard Matthew follow her into the front lobby. "Maybe I'd better wait on the porch while you get the coffee."

She turned. "I hate to make you sit in the cold, but I guess it would be the proper thing to do." She hurried into the back room, found a second cup and poured his coffee, then added a little bit of sugar.

When she stepped back into the lobby, he was already on the porch leaning against the railing. If Samuel happened to come by, at least they would be outside.

"Here we go." She handed him the cup. "I hope you still like it with a little sugar."

"Perfect. You remembered. I like that."

"It's hard to forget all those breakfasts we ate together at the ranch."

"Yes, I could use some of those meals that Bonita and Carmella cooked. I've been eating most of my meals at the boarding house and at the café in town, so I'm not going hungry, but nothing beats those meals at the ranch."

"You don't have to convince me."

Matthew took a sip of coffee. "This is great. Thank you."

Caroline took her seat in the rocker once more. "Is there a reason you're on this back road this morning besides hoping to get a cup of coffee?"

"As a matter of fact, I do have a reason. I wanted to let you know an auditor from the state level is supposed to come in today on the stage."

Caroline inhaled a ragged breath. "Oh, so soon. I had no idea he'd come this quickly."

"Action doesn't always happen that fast, but he said he's had his eye on this bank and few others for quite a while. When I wrote him and told him what you had heard, he was ready to drop what he was doing and come down."

Caroline put her hand on her chest.

Matthew took a step closer to her. "Are you okay?"

"I'm not sure. I'm scared of what will happen if he finds anything amiss."

"Yeah, I've been thinking about the consequences if Richard or Mr. Brown is involved in anything wrong. I hope you're not backing out of letting this happen—not that we could stop it. Mr. Dawson, the auditor, will come in and do his thing whether we want him to or not."

Caroline stood up and placed her cup on the railing. "If Richard is into something illegal, he needs to be stopped, but

I would hate for Samuel's father to get pulled down in the investigation." She put her hands up to her mouth. "Could they lose the bank?"

"I don't know, Caroline. I guess in the worse scenario it could happen, but we won't think like that. It's been a good bank for a long time. That has to mean something." He took her hand.

She looked down at her hand in his and remembered Samuel seeing them do this before. She knew she should pull hers away, but she couldn't. At the moment, she needed Matthew's strength to help her face what might happen.

He didn't let her hand go. "You did the right thing. We can't have someone using that money illegally. The money belongs to the town and its citizens, not the Browns."

"I know, but I hate I was the one to bring it to your attention and get things started." Finally, she pulled her hand out of his. "Thank you for coming by to tell me about Mr. Dawson's arrival. If you hear anything, will you keep me informed?"

"Certainly I will. This is your future family. You need to be kept up on everything that happens." He handed her his empty cup. "Thank you for the great coffee. Now I can face the day." He started down the steps, turned and waved to her. "Be strong. If you need to talk, you know where you can find me,"

She hated for him to leave, but she watched him walk away without calling him back. Plopping back down in the rocker, she squeezed her eyes. Her future family. Had she ruined everyone in it by telling what she had heard? *Please, God, watch over the Browns..*

For the rest of the morning she helped Douglas with several patients, one was a small dog run over by a wagon. His broken leg was braced, and his other cuts and scratches were cleaned and bandaged. She smiled at the owner as he carried him to his wagon, knowing that puppy would be fine. The other two animals were out on close-by ranches. They, too, would be back on their feet soon.

Douglas seemed to be appreciative of her help and with each patient, he allowed her to do more and more on her own. She had a hard time keeping the smile off her face, knowing her uncle finally remembered how good she was with the ranch animals and respected her abilities.

This job would be perfect for her.

As they rode down the main street into town, Caroline's breath caught in her throat. The stage coach was already unloaded and taking on new passengers. Had Mr. Dawson come in as Matthew said? If so, was he already at the bank?

"Caroline, what's wrong?" Douglas stopped his horse and stared at her.

"I hope nothing." She tried to smile, but she was sure her face didn't cooperate.

"Okay, I've known you long enough to know when you're about to cry or scream or do something stupid."

At those words she did laugh. "I'm not going to do anything stupid or scream. Now, I can't guarantee I won't cry."

"Do you need to go somewhere else besides the clinic? You know you're welcomed to do whatever it is you need to do."

She thought a minute. "I might take you up on that. I won't be long."

He stared at her again. "No explanation. Okay. I'll wait until you're ready to tell me what's going on in that brain of yours."

"Thanks, Uncle Douglas. I love you. You know that, don't you?"

"Yes, Caroline, I know that. Now go where you need to go. Check in when you have time, but take as long as you have to."

She nodded, then headed to Vic's office. No way would she go to the bank until she knew what Mr. Dawson was going to do.

She got to Victor's office much too fast. Her mind was spinning. With a quick knock, she opened the door. "Can I come in?"

Victor looked up. "Caroline, sure. Come on in."

She looked around. Neither Matthew nor Mr. Dawson was in the office. Her heart sank. Was he already inspecting the books at the bank?

"Is something wrong?" Victor stood up and walked toward her.

"I'm not sure. Do you know where Matthew went?"

"He left with Mr. Dawson. He said he was going to get him checked into the boarding house, then they'd head for the bank."

She blew out a big breath and nodded. "So I guess he told you about the audit."

"He did before he wrote the letter to him, and if what you heard is correct, he'll find it out when he sees the books."

She plopped down in the chair in front of his desk. "Do you think I did the right thing by telling Matthew?"

Victor walked closer to her. "Definitely. I'm sorry about the whole affair, but we can't turn our heads and let something like that happen—if there's something happening. We both hope you didn't hear the word 'embezzlement.' Mr. Brown and his wife are both well respected in Independence. So is Samuel. Now, as for Richard, we can't be so sure. He's never been one to let anyone get too close to him."

"I hope I'm wrong about what I heard, but I'm afraid I heard right. We'll have to pray Mr. Brown and Samuel have nothing to do with it. I feel sure Samuel knew nothing was going on. I heard it in his voice." She looked up at her uncle. "Does anyone else know about this except the new attorney?"

"No, neither I nor Matthew has told anyone but him. Matthew and I both agreed no one needs to know until we understand what's going on, especially if nothing has happened. As far as anyone is concerned, Mr. Dawson is here on a routine inspection."

"Thank you. I'd hate to have the Browns' reputation ruined if I'm wrong."

"We all feel the same way."

She stood up. "I'm going back to the clinic, but might take a little detour and head to the boarding house. I'd like to talk with this Mr. Dawson."

"I think you should."

She left the office not sure how she felt about the whole affair, especially her involvement in it. A thought struck her. What if Samuel found out she was the one who told Matthew about what she heard? He'd hate her, and she couldn't blame him, though as her uncle said, if anything illegal was going on with the town's money, something needed to be done.

The boarding house sat on one of the busy side streets. She turned and headed toward the ornate fence and cluttered porch with far too many rockers and chairs. As she stepped up onto the first step, the door opened and Matthew walked out.

She stopped. He did as well, but then regained his composure and headed toward her.

"Caroline, I was heading to the clinic to see if you were still there. I want you to meet Mr. Dawson. He wants to ask you a few questions."

"That's why I was stopping in here. I wanted to see him."

"Come sit on the porch. He won't be long. He wanted to freshen up a bit before heading to the bank."

"He doesn't waste any time." She sat in one of the big rockers.

"He wants to get started immediately. As I told you earlier, he's had his eye on this bank and several others."

"So he thinks something is really going on?"

He nodded. "Yes, he feels sure it is, but he won't know

for sure until he examines the books."

"Does Mr. Brown know he's coming?"

"No, and that's a little different. Usually an appointment is made to do these inspections, so I'm sure Mr. Brown will be a little leery."

Matthew reached over and put his hand over hers. "You did the right thing, Caroline. If you had not brought it to our attention, something would've happened eventually and things would have come down to this anyway, but it may have taken longer and more money would've been lost."

"But I would not have been the one pointing fingers at my future family."

He pulled his hand back, taking with it the warmth and strength she needed right now.

"No, you wouldn't have, but I've asked Mr. Dawson to try to keep your name out of the investigation. He couldn't promise, but he did say he would try."

"Thank you for doing that. It means a lot to me."

The front door opened and Mr. Dawson stepped out. Both Matthew and Caroline stood up.

"You must be Caroline Fletcher." He stuck out his hand.

"Yes, sir, I am. Thank you for coming to Independence."

"No. Thank you for giving us a head's up. If we don't catch these affairs in the beginning, a lot of people can lose their savings and it's difficult to get it back for them."

"I hope that's not the case. In fact, I hope I am totally wrong and nothing is being done illegally."

"That's what we all hope." He took a seat. "Do you have a few minutes to tell me exactly what you heard? Matthew has told me, but I need to hear it from you."

Caroline was going to sit back down on the porch, but two men walked along the sidewalk and waved to them. One she recognized from the bank. She didn't know the other.

Matthew waved back.

Caroline cringed. "Could we go inside? I don't feel

comfortable sitting here for all the world to see."

Mr. Dawson looked up at the two men who slowed their pace and seemed to be talking about them.

"Certainly. I should have thought about that."

They walked inside the boarding house and found seats in the corner of the large parlor, where she began telling him exactly where she was in the bank, why she was there, and what she heard.

He asked a few questions, but mostly he listened and took a few notes. In just a few minutes he took her hand. "Thank you, again, Miss Fletcher. I appreciate what you've done, and I'll try to keep your name out of all this mess."

"Thank you, sir."

Matthew helped her up. She looked into his eyes and wanted so badly for him to hold her, but that was impossible. He was the deputy taking the inspector to the bank where the reputation and the future of the bank might be in jeopardy.

Matthew squeezed her hand. "We'll keep you informed."

"Thank you, Matthew." She turned to Mr. Dawson. "I hope you are here to give the bank a clean bill of health."

"I do, too, ma'am."

She watched them leave. Instead of going back to the clinic, she went to the stables and saddled Lady. What she needed was a bit of fresh air alone before she could face the world again.

About an hour later Caroline took Lady back to the stables and headed to the clinic. She hated leaving Douglas alone, but she needed time to clear her mind. Riding alone always did that, and today was no different. After handing Lady over to Mr. Stuart, she headed out the door, then stopped. Should she go to the bank? Should she see how Samuel was holding up?

She hesitated, but decided she didn't need to be involved at the moment, so she turned to go to the clinic, hoping her uncle wouldn't ask her any questions.

As she walked up the steps and into the clinic's lobby Douglas looked up from his books. He stretched his back. "You okay?"

"Yes, I am now."

"You look a little pale. Are you feeling okay?"

"I think so. I'm a little tired, but I've had a full day and it is only early afternoon." She looked around. "Did you have any patients while I was gone?"

"No. I did get a note asking me to stop by the Loften ranch tomorrow morning just to check out some of the cattle. Mr. Loften has had a couple to die and not sure why. We need to make sure the herd hasn't been exposed to something."

"Do you want me to go with you?"

"No, I think you ought to stay here and keep the clinic open. If we get patients, you could examine them and maybe start whatever needs to be done."

"I can do that. Thanks for trusting me with your patients."

Douglas stood up and stretched again. "I do trust you, Caroline." He hesitated. "Would you feel okay staying at the clinic alone tonight? Emma and I want to be home with the kids."

"That's exactly where you need to be."

"Or, you could ride out to the ranch with us."

"No, I'm perfectly fine right here. I like your little room in the back."

"Okay, but let's hope my brother doesn't have a fit because I've left you here alone."

Caroline laughed. "He knows I'm not a child any more. He'll have to accept that fact one day."

"Maybe. I'll tell Victor we'll be at the ranch and to have his deputies to walk by on their rounds. That'll make my brother feel better."

Caroline lifted up on her toes and gave her uncle a quick kiss on the cheek. "You always know the right thing to do.

Now, go get Emma and get out to those boys."

The winter sun set early, leaving the town in darkness. Caroline settled down in the rocker that she'd dragged inside. She had a slight headache and thought maybe she shouldn't strain her eyes, but the office was so comfortable and warm, she opened a book and read by the lantern.

About six-thirty she heard footsteps on the porch then a hard knock on the door.

Even though she knew the door was locked, her breath caught in her throat.

"Caroline? Are you in the office?"

"Samuel, is that you?"

"Yes, can I come in? It's freezing out here."

She pulled her robe tight around her body and unlatched the door. "Samuel, what are you doing here after dark?"

He stepped in, bringing in a big gust of cold air. He pushed the door shut. "I was hoping you were here. I needed to talk with you." He blew on his hands.

"Come by the fireplace and warm up." She followed him to the small fireplace in the corner of the lobby, wondering why he was here and if he knew what was happening at the bank.

After a minute of rubbing his hands together over the fire, he turned to her. "We have an auditor from the state level at the bank."

"Really?"

"Yes, and don't act surprised. I know you knew he was here."

She clasped her hands in front of her body, not knowing what to say and how much he knew.

"Well, do you?"

"Why would you ask that?"

"Seems he was with your friend the deputy this morning. They were both talking with you at the boarding house where that deputy stays."

"His name is Matthew. Matthew Jennings."

"Are you going to deny you were talking with them?"

She stared at him.

"That's what I thought. What's going on, Caroline? Why were you at that boarding house in the morning?"

"What are you implying? Are you asking if I stayed at the boarding house over night?"

"Well, did you?"

The wind left her body. "I can't believe you'd ask such a thing. I shouldn't even answer that, but I will. No, I did not stay at the boarding house over night. I slept right here in this office with my uncle and his wife next door just as I always do when I'm in town."

Samuel swallowed and drew in a big breath. "It wasn't proper for you to be with those two men alone that early in the morning. And why were you talking to the auditor?"

She turned to go back to her rocker. All of a sudden her head felt as though it would explode. Her body ached all over. She sat down. "I guess those two men who passed this morning couldn't wait to tell you I was standing with Matthew and Mr. Dawson."

Samuel crossed his arms in front of his body. "Yes, they told me when they realized the man who is inspecting the bank was the man they saw with you and the deputy. I think I need an explanation."

"Maybe you do."

"You're dang right I do. My fiancé shouldn't have been anywhere near that boarding house. It doesn't look good, then knowing the man who was with the deputy was the inspector, I have a million questions. I'm not leaving until I get some answers." Samuel's face turned red. His vein in the side of his neck bulged.

"Mr. Dawson wanted to ask me some questions."

"What? Why would he do that?"

Caroline's chest ached. Her thoughts tangled. No way would she lie to this man, but she didn't want to tell him why Mr. Dawson was here.

"Caroline, what's up?" He stepped toward her rocker.

For the first time in her life, she felt threatened by a man she knew. She jumped up and stood behind the rocker.

"I want answers. I deserve answers."

"Yes, you do, but don't come near me."

Her words seemed to startle him. "Are you afraid of me?"

She hesitated. "I've never seen you angry like this. I don't know."

He stepped back. "I'm sorry. I'd never hurt you, you know that."

She nodded though she wasn't so sure. "I told you that morning I went to the bank and heard your father and you arguing, I tried to leave as fast as I could, but before I did, I heard you say the word embezzlement."

Samuel frowned.

"I didn't know what to do."

"So you told that deputy?"

"I didn't right away. I thought about it a long time. Finally, I did tell him because I didn't know what to do. I needed advice."

Samuel turned around and hit the bricks on the fireplace. "You told your old love that your future family might be involved in embezzlement? I can't believe this."

Caroline thought about turning and running out the door. The man was livid. His face was even redder now. His body tense.

"You had no business telling our family business to that man."

"And I wouldn't have, had you told me what was happening. We're engaged. We're about to be man and wife. I wanted you to share your concerns, but you held back. I gave you several opportunities to open up to me, but you wouldn't. What was I to do?"

"You could've asked me?"

"No, I wanted you to tell me on your own volition.

You're supposed to be my future husband. We should have no secrets."

"You kept a secret about telling the deputy and talking to the inspector. What's the difference?" His shoulders slumped

"There's a lot of difference." Still standing behind the rocker, she relaxed a little. "I needed advice. No one else knows except Sheriff Sanchez and the new attorney in town."

"What? You told the sheriff and the attorney? This is unbelievable." He walked in circles.

"No, I didn't tell anyone else. Matthew did. He needed advice as well so he went to the attorney before even going to the sheriff. He didn't want to call attention or make false claims about the bank unless there was a reason."

"You have ruined our lives, Caroline."

"No, Samuel. I didn't ruin your life or your families. Richard did. If he did do something illegal, he'll have to pay. If you or your dad is not involved, you have nothing to worry about. If Richard has done nothing, the audit will show it and life will go on as normal. Nothing will change."

"No, you've got that wrong. Everything will change. I will not marry someone who is willing to bring down my family and its good name."

Caroline was not surprised by his words, but they stabbed deeply hearing him say them. "I'm sorry you feel that way. Maybe we both need to move on."

"No maybes about it. I'm moving on, and you can move on as well, right to the side of that deputy. That's what you've wanted all along, isn't it?"

"No, Samuel. You have that wrong. I love you, but I've loved Matthew all my life. I was willing to push those feelings for him aside to marry you, but not now." Tears welled in her eyes. "Please leave."

He pushed away from the fireplace. Not sure what he was going to do, she held onto the back of the rocker staring at the man whom she believed would've been the perfect husband, but no more. The veins in his neck stuck out pumping blood to his red face. His eyes, squinting and darting from side to side, scared her.

Except for the man at the river who grabbed her, she had never been threatened by a male, but now her once-future husband put her body on alert. Without moving, she looked for something to defend herself, but the only thing she saw was a fountain pen on the desk not too far from her. It wasn't much, but it would be her only hope. She prayed she was overreacting.

This was a man she had loved, not some fugitive escaping the law, but she had seen men on the ranch lose their control when pushed into a corner. Had Samuel reached that point? Could she possibly keep herself safe if he charged her?

She didn't have to think for long. Samuel stepped toward the rocker.

She stepped back closer to the desk and the pen.

He pushed the rocker, but instead of getting any closer to her, he shoved it, spun around and grabbed the handle on the door. "Mother was right. You would have never fit into our family."

The slamming of the door sent shivers down her spine. Immediately, she ran to the door, latched the lock and leaned against the wooden barrier.

CHAPTER SIXTEEN

Caroline didn't move from the door. Her body shook. Her head spun. Squeezing her eyes, she let the tears roll down her face.

What had just happened? How could the calm, sophisticated man she was going to marry become so out-of-control? Had he intended to hurt her?

She crossed her arms in front of her and looked up to heaven. *Please help me to understand this mess.*

She looked around the small front lobby and realized everything was as it always was. A couple chairs lined the wall and Douglas's desk sat against the other wall with another chair behind it. A few simple paintings from the children who brought their pets were tacked on the walls. Nothing had changed, but she knew she'd never be the same again.

Samuel had shown her a side of himself and a side of humanity that she had not faced before. Had her family sheltered her too much? Did they keep her life safe and sound because she grew up without a mother? Now that she was older she understood how protective her father was of her. She understood why, but she wasn't a child anymore. Bad things happened to people. She'd have to face the truth and the world with that knowledge.

The Browns had gotten themselves in trouble and they would have to find a way to resolve it. She hated to have been the finger pointer, but she had no regrets if Richard did what they thought he had done.

She did feel horrible that Samuel would look at her differently now. He had ended her love for him by his actions, but she knew she had tried to love him with her whole heart and would have worked every day to be the wife he deserved.

Now her life had changed in a matter of minutes. Glad she had this assistance job with her uncle, she knew she could find happiness again.

Her thoughts turned to Matthew. Would she dare tell him Samuel had frightened her? Samuel had not done her any harm so she probably shouldn't tell anyone about how he acted. Did all men show only a side of themselves that they wanted to project, then turn into their real selves when the life didn't go as they wanted?

Matthew had always been her protector, but even he had not kept his word when he'd said he'd love her. He rode out of her life much too easily.

She'd have to think twice before she gave her love to any other man again.

She rubbed her hand across her forehead. The headache that started earlier today now pounded. She hoped it was only from the confrontation with Samuel that caused it, but even as she thought that, she knew her forehead burned.

"Surely I'm not getting the flu like everyone else in town,"

She headed to the back room. The bed called her name, and she wouldn't fight it. Her entire body ached. She washed her face, then headed to the bed. Maybe if she slept, she'd wake up refreshed and able to think about what she would do now.

Right now she couldn't even put a thought together.

She curled up on the lumpy mattress. Her body shivered. Reaching for the cover, she pulled it up to her chin and buried her face in the pillow.

The confrontation with Samuel had taken everything out of her, but what she felt now worried her. She couldn't ever remember being sick with anything but a cold. This wasn't a cold.

She tried to pray, but the only thing she could do was to close her eyes and drift into a deep sleep.

~

"Thank you for the coffee, Mrs. Haggerty. It'll feel good when I hit that cold wind outside."

"You be careful out there, Mr. Jennings."

"I will, ma'am." He took his hat from the coat rack and straightened it on his head, then opened the door. He grimaced as the cold wind hit him in the face.

Pulling his scarf up over his mouth, he walked down the steps and out the gate. On the sidewalk, he headed to the jailhouse. He'd told Victor he'd take the night shift even though the cells still remained empty. He could sleep in his chair if he needed to.

He walked in front of Emma's office. All the lights were out. He'd heard Douglas say they were going to the ranch to be with the children tonight. What would it be like to have a family like theirs? Would God see fit to have someone like himself be a husband and a father? If so, he hoped he could find the kind of happiness he saw in the Fletcher family

Maybe one day.

As much as he tried to not look around Emma's building, he caught a glimpse of Douglas's office. Light shone through the window in the front office. He assumed Caroline was there alone. He made a mental note to pass by the office on his routine rounds tonight just to check on her. He pulled the coat closer to his body and his gaze away from the vet office and hurried toward the jailhouse.

The inside lanterns lit the windows in the front of the sheriff's office. He smiled. The more he thought about entering the race for the County Marshall, the more excited he became. The longer he was back in town, the more he wanted Independence to be his home.

He knocked on the door of the office and heard Vic's chair scrape the wooden floorboards. Keeping the door locked and lights on seemed the safest way for Vic and his deputies to stay the night. If anyone wanted in, their knock would alert whoever was on duty.

"It's me, Victor."

He heard the key turn and the door opened. "Come in. You're the best thing I've seen in hours."

"Things must be pretty slow tonight. That's not a bad thing."

"You got that right. A slow night in the sheriff's office is a good night." Victor stretched and yawned. "I think I fell asleep. I can't wait to crawl into my warm bed with Bettye. Thanks for relieving me."

"No problem. Have a good night."

Victor waved, then turned. "You should get relief by daylight. When you do patrol, bundle up. It's horrible out there."

"You don't have to tell me. I just walked from the boarding house. Goodnight, Victor."

Matthew sat at the desk and pulled out papers that he'd been working on for the last few days, papers that listed his past work experience and his qualifications for the office he now wanted. He read over them, changed a few word, then when he felt confident that he'd put down as much as he could, he slid them back into the desk drawer. Tomorrow he'd get the papers to the city office to officially join the race. He hoped no one else threw in their hat to run. He was confident he could do the job, but not so confident he could win a race.

He didn't like the humdrum hours in the evening. Several times he laid his head back and tried to sleep in the chair, but that didn't work. Close to midnight he pulled out his watch and decided to do his rounds early. He knew no one would be out in this cold, but he wanted to do rounds anyway. At least the cold air would make him appreciate the warmth of the office when he returned.

He pulled his gun belt off the rack and buckled it around his body. He wrapped his scarf around his neck then slipped into his coat and gloves and stuck his hat on his head. "Here we go." When he opened the door, the cold air took his breath.

"Yep, this ought to get me going." He chuckled, then pulled the scarf over his mouth.

Just as he expected, the streets of Independence were empty. No one, except someone up to no good, would be out tonight in this cold, and that's why he and the other deputies walked their beat every night. He checked the door to the mercantile and several other businesses, then headed for the bank. He wondered how things were going with the audit. Mr. Dawson hadn't come by to see him, and he didn't want to bother him. Maybe tomorrow he'd try to see him at the boarding house.

He checked the bank's front door to make sure it was locked. Feeling good that everything was okay on that side of the street, he crossed and walked toward the other end. He shook the door to Emma's office. It was locked. He went around the back to check that door, as well, but as soon as he turned the corner, he realized the light in Douglas's office was still burning.

He frowned. "That's strange and dangerous. No one sleeps with a lit lantern." He wondered if Caroline was still up, or maybe she wasn't there at all.

Instead of going back to the main street, he walked through the fence that Douglas had put in between the two offices so he could visit Emma when he wanted. The curtains at the back window weren't closed all the way so he peeked in. He couldn't see much, but the light from the front office lit the back room enough for him to see the examining table and a few cabinets. He took a step to the side and strained to see the sleeping area to make sure no one was there.

He couldn't see much, but he could definitely see the outline of someone in the bed. He wasn't sure what to do, but he'd never forgive himself if the building caught on fire so he knocked, first lightly, then harder.

Whoever was in the bed did not move. He shook the handle on the door and realized it was not locked. For a second, he stood still. Why would they leave the door unlocked?

He took a deep breath and opened the door. "Caroline? Douglas?"

Whoever was in the bed did not move. He stepped in. It was freezing in the room.

Not taking any chances, he unlatched the strap on his holster, then pulled out his gun. Before going by the person in the bed, he stuck his head into the front office. It was empty. He breathed easier and slipped his gun back into his holster. The lantern still burned, but the fire in the fireplace had gone out. He walked over to the desk and picked up the lantern. He carried it into the back room and went straight to the bed where Caroline's blond hair spread across her pillow.

"Caroline. Wake up, Caroline. It's Matthew. I don't want to scare you."

She didn't move.

He placed his hand on her arm. "Caroline." Still no movement. Something was definitely wrong with her.

He stooped down by the bed and put his hand on her forehead. She was burning up. "Oh, no. That's why you forgot to turn out the lantern."

He knew no one was at Emma's office to help him. He stood up and looked around. First, he turned the lantern higher so he could see, then he found a clean cloth, wet it with the cold water in a basin, then went back by the bed. Even when he placed the cold cloth on her head, she didn't stir.

Matthew's insides clinched. Caroline looked so lifeless. He was terrified.

He held the cloth on her head and looked up to heaven. "God, I don't deserve to ask you anything. I haven't stepped foot in a church in years, but I swear if you let Caroline live, I'll go talk with Preacher Smith and try to get my life straight again." He squeezed his eyes. "Please help my friend. I love her. Please let her live."

Never had he been so scared. What he felt now was close to what he felt when he watched his stepfather shoot his stepmother. As a child he had been terrified for his life. Now he prayed for Caroline's. She had such a wonderful life ahead of her. She deserved to live.

Keeping her cool to help break the fever was all he knew how to do, but he did need to warm the room. He left the cloth on her forehead and headed to the fireplace. After getting a fire going, he went back into the back room to check on her. He talked softly to her and told her how wonderful her life was going to be. "You might be marrying Samuel, but I'll always be here for you. You're not getting out of my life that easy, but you need to wake up, Caroline. Please wake up."

For the next few hours he sponged her, hoping she'd wake up, but it was early morning before he felt her fever had lowered some. He didn't want to leave her, but he had to go back to the office to let his relief in.

"Caroline, I have to go, but I'll be back as soon as I can. Don't get up if you wake up." He knew she couldn't hear him, but it made him feel better. Once more he passed a cold cloth on her forehead, then bent down and kissed her on her warm lips. He wanted to pull her in his arms and hold her close and never let anything happen to her, but he knew he shouldn't. It was Samuel's job to keep her safe now, not his.

He probably should have gone straight to the Brown's house to get Samuel or Mrs. Brown to come help during the night, but it never crossed his mind. Now that the sun was coming up, he'd think about going for them since Emma wasn't in town.

Reluctantly, he got up to leave. Not having a key to get back in, he'd have to leave the back door open. He looked at her once more, then hurried out.

By the time he got near the jail, he saw the other deputy sitting on the bench on the sidewalk. He stood up with a frown on his face. "Do you know how cold it is out here? I'm freezing. Where've you been?"

"I'm sorry. I had a little emergency I had to take care of." He unlocked the door. "I have to go to the Browns' house. Do you need anything?"

"The Browns? Are you crazy? They don't care a lot for you, I'm told."

"They'll have to forget about me. Caroline is sick and needs help."

"Oh, no. What can I do?"

"Since I'm not here, you need to stay here, but if Vic comes in, tell him to get word to Dr. Fletcher at the ranch. He might ask you to ride out there. I'd like Vic to go to Douglas's office to check on Caroline until I get back. The back door is unlocked."

Matthew ran out of the office and down the street toward the nicer, richer part of town. Going to the Brown's house was the last thing he wanted to do, but as her fiancé, Samuel needed to know about Caroline. He was doing the right thing.

The lights in the front of the Brown's house were not on, but one shone through a back window so he headed to what he assumed was the kitchen. He climbed the back steps and knocked on the door. He heard footsteps then a lady's voice.

"Who is it?"

"I'm Deputy Jennings. I need to see Samuel."

The lady unlatched the door and opened it slightly.

Matthew pulled off his hat. "Ma'am, Samuel's fiancé is sick and he needs to know."

Finally, she opened the door. "Come in, Sir. I think I

heard someone stirring upstairs. I'll go up." She started to leave, then turned. "Coffee is ready if you'd like a cup."

"No, ma'am, but thank you."

The middle aged lady left him standing by the door. Her uniform was impeccably starched and pressed.

Matthew looked around at the large, well-equipped kitchen. The stove sat on the back wall with ample counter space on each side of it. A small icebox was nestled near it. A white table and four chairs sat in the middle of the room. Everything was fresh and modern. In the far corner a huge fireplace with a raging fire welcomed him. He walked to it and warmed his hands. He could see Caroline's home looking like this. He would never have to worry about her comfort as long as she was married to Samuel.

The lady walked back in. "Mr. Samuel will be down shortly."

"Thank you."

"Are you sure you don't want any coffee?"

"I'm fine thank you," he said, even though he needed a cup. No way would he enjoy it being in the Brown's kitchen.

Hurried footsteps told him someone was coming down the steps. He straightened up when Samuel walked in. Matthew could tell he'd just gotten out of bed. His shirt was wrinkled not tucked in his trousers. His hair wasn't combed

"What are you doing here at this time of the morning?"

Nice greeting.

Matthew wanted to throw out an answer that matched Samuel's harshness, but he didn't. He was here because of Caroline.

"It is early, and I'm sorry, but Caroline is burning up with fever. Dr. Fletcher is not in town, and I thought you needed to know."

"You've got that wrong, Deputy. I'm sorry she's sick, but she and I are no longer engaged."

Samuel's words shocked Matthew. He said nothing as Samuel grabbed the back of one of the kitchen chairs and stared at him.

"Miss Fletcher turned on my family, but I'm sure you know that. You and that inspector were talking to her yesterday morning."

"Yes, we were, but this has nothing to do with your situation at the bank. Caroline is sick. Very sick. I thought you'd want to help her."

"You'll have to find someone else to worry over her. I'm sure you won't have any trouble doing that."

His words stuck deep. What Samuel said was right. He'd always worry about Caroline, but Samuel wouldn't understand the bond the two of them had. "I had no idea you two were no longer engaged. I found her when I was doing my rounds last night. She has not spoken. Her fever is really high." He put his hat back on his head. "I'm sorry to have bothered you."

"And how is it that you found her last night? Was she outside or were you inside of the office where she's staying?"

"No, Samuel. As I said, I passed the office on my rounds and saw her lantern was still on. I wasn't even sure anyone was staying there. When I checked the door, it was open. She was in the bed unconscious, burning up with fever."

"So you say."

"Yes, that's what I say." He reeled in his anger and what he wanted to say, turned and grabbed the doorknob. "I'm sorry it didn't work out for the two of you." At that he yanked the door open and stomped out.

For a second it was hard for him to move down the steps or to breathe. The man who was supposed to love Caroline didn't even offer to help her. Samuel didn't deserve her. He mumbled a few remarks under his breath, pulled his coat tighter and headed back to Douglas's office. By the time her opened the back door, he had calmed down a little.

Victor sat by Caroline's bed. "I think she's trying to come around. I've kept the cold cloths on her head."

Matthew walked by the bed. Caroline's face was still pale. "Has she moved?"

"She moved her head earlier, but didn't say anything. I sent my deputy out to the Fletcher Ranch to get Emma."

"Hope she gets here soon. She scared me to death last night." Matthew reached down and took her hand. "Caroline, can you hear us?"

She made no response.

"I'm worried about her, Victor. She's been like this since I got here about midnight."

"I'm worried, too." He looked up. "Is Samuel coming?"

"Oh, no. He just told me they are no longer engaged. He said Caroline turned on his family. I guess he found out she told us what she'd heard."

"He might not be engaged to her, but he should be worried about her if he loved her."

"Yeah, well, he said I'd have to find someone else to worry over her."

Victor shook his head. "That's pitiful." He looked at his niece. "I wish we knew something else to do for her."

"We can pray. That's all I know how to do."

CHAPTER SEVENTEEN

Caroline didn't want to open her eyes. Her head throbbed and every part of her body ached.

She heard talking and wanted to see who was with her, but the eyes wouldn't open.

She vaguely remembered being with Samuel last night at the office. She groaned. *Did he break up with me? Did I dream that?*

Was that Samuel who sat by me all last night? Did he kiss me? If he kissed me maybe he didn't break up with me.

Her body shivered. She was freezing. She pulled the covers closer to her neck. *Was that Matthew here last night instead of Samuel?*

Her thoughts were jumbled.

"Caroline, are you awake? This is your Uncle Vic. Open your eyes, love. We're so worried about you."

"Uncle Vic." *Did I actually say the words or did I think them?* Cobwebs filled her head.

"Caroline, wake up. Matthew and I are here at Douglas's office with you. Matthew has been here since he found you last night."

She felt someone put another blanket on her and tuck it around her tightly. *Glorious warmth.*

"Caroline, this is Matthew. I'm going to raise your head. You need to sip some water."

His big hand slipped under her head and lifted her.

She opened her eyes just enough to see him lean over her.

"Try to drink some of the water." He placed a cup to her lips.

She let the cool water flow over her parched lips and into her dry mouth. She moaned.

"That's it. You need to take a couple more swallows then we'll let you go back to sleep."

Again she opened her eyes. "Thank you, Matthew."

He smiled. "You're welcomed. Now rest."

She tried to nod, but felt blessed sleep take over.

~

"I think she'll be okay, but I wish Dr. Fletcher were here." Victor stood up near Matthew.

"I wish she'd be here, too. I'd feel a lot better." Matthew bit his lip.

Victor pulled his gaze away from his niece and looked at Matthew. "Can you stay here a little while longer? If you can't, I can find one of the ladies in town to come until Dr. Fletcher comes in."

Matthew looked down at Caroline. He didn't want to leave her. "I'm fine. I can stay, that is, if your other deputies can work the jail with you."

"We're fine over there. My niece is my main concern right now. I have a feeling the entire Fletcher clan will be here as soon as they hear what my deputy has to tell them."

"Yep, knowing Mr. Fletcher, he's already riding toward town."

Vic hit Matthew lightly on the back.

Matthew grimaced.

"Oh no, did I hit your wounded arm?"

"No, I guess I'm a little careful to keep it away from everything. It's doing fine."

"Good." Victor looked at Caroline once more, then back at Matthew. "I'm so glad you found her last night. I don't know if that fever would've gone down on its own."

"I am, too. I wanted to do more for her, but the only thing I knew to do was to try to lower the fever."

"And that may have saved her. We've had several people die in town from this flu. It's nothing to mess with."

Matthew watched Vic touch Caroline once more on the arm, then lean over and kiss her on the forehead. "Take care of my niece, Matthew."

He nodded as Vic walked toward the door. Matthew pulled up a chair and sat next to Caroline.

He'd sit here forever if she needed him.

~

The slamming of the front door woke Matthew. He still sat next to Caroline, but must've have fallen asleep. He stood up with his hand on his gun,

Lucas Fletcher ran through the door into the back room. "It's me, Matthew."

Matthew pulled his hand away from his gun and let out a breath he'd been holding. "Glad you're here, Mr. Fletcher. I didn't realize we'd left the front door open."

"It wasn't. I made Douglas give me a key when I realized Caroline would be here alone sometimes." Lucas ran to the bedside and knelt down by his daughter. "Caroline, baby. I came as soon as I heard." He looked up at Matthew. "Thank you for staying with her and helping her."

Matthew put his hand on Lucas's shoulder. "She woke up a little bit ago. Her fever seems lower. I think she's going to be okay."

Lucas nodded. "Emma and Douglas are on their way in the buggy. Emma will know what to do."

"I wish Emma could've been here last night. I would've felt better. I have to tell you I was scared to death for her."

Lucas stood up and hugged Matthew. "I was so scared I could hardly breathe while I rode here."

"I know exactly what you're saying. I felt like that all night. Caroline needed her father here with her, but I didn't want to leave her."

"You did the right thing. That fever needed to come down." He frowned. "Where's Samuel? Does he know? He should be here."

"He knows, but. . ." Matthew hesitated, not sure how much to tell him, "he told me to find someone else to worry about her. It seems they had words last night."

"What?"

"I went to the Brown's this morning to get him." Matthew stopped and rubbed his hand across his chin. "He told me they broke up and insinuated that I was with her last night before she got sick."

"I'm totally confused. They broke up? Did Samuel say what happened?"

Again, Matthew hesitated. He couldn't lie to the man who had saved his life. "I'm not sure I should be the one to tell you."

Lucas lifted both hands in the air. "What happened, Matthew? Caroline is in no condition to tell me, but I can tell you I knew something was wrong. For the last week or so she has not been herself. She's been worried about something. Please, tell me."

Matthew blew out a big breath and started explaining what Caroline heard in the bank.

Lucas shook his head. "Why didn't she come to me? I try real hard to let her run her own life without me being involved, but I should've pried it out of her."

"She knew you'd be really upset. She came to me only because I'm in law enforcement. She needed advice. I got her permission to talk to an attorney in town to find out what to do, then I went to Victor."

"You and Victor both knew and didn't tell me?"

"Yes, sir, but until an auditor found reason to believe that something was amiss at the bank, we felt no one else should know."

"But Samuel found out she's the one who got the auditor involved."

"Yes. The auditor has been at the bank for two days." He went on to tell him about the two men who saw her with the auditor and him on the porch of the boarding house.

"I'm sure Samuel wasn't too pleased with that."

"No, sir. He wasn't. I'm sure he misinterpreted the situation. She loved Samuel and would never do anything to make him think she was being unfaithful."

Lucas blew out a big breath. "They could have a mess at the bank." He rubbed Caroline's forehead then looked back at Matthew. "We're so thankful for what you did for her, but how in the world did you know she was sick?"

Matthew told him about being on rounds and seeing the light on and door unlocked.

"Glad you were concerned enough about her to check the back door."

"I'm glad you approve of my being with her all night. I would've never forgiven myself had something happened and caused that lantern to start a fire, but Samuel didn't see it that way."

"That jerk. I never thought he was right for her."

He looked as if he was about to say more, but the front door flew open and Emma and Douglas stormed into the back room. Immediately Emma ran to Caroline's bedside. Douglas stepped next to Matthew and Lucas.

"I've never been happier to see anyone." Matthew grabbed Douglas's hand. "Thank you for getting Emma here so fast."

"Caroline is our girl. I could've kicked myself for going to the ranch last night. We should've been here with her."

Matthew squeezed Douglas's hand then let it go. "No one knew she'd get sick, and your kids need you home. I'm thankful we have Emma to take care of her now. I can breathe again."

Douglas looked around. "Where's Samuel?"

Matthew and Lucas looked at each other, but Lucas spoke first.

"I think our Caroline won't be taking on the Brown name."

Emma, who was kneeling next to the bed, looked up. "I'm not surprised. Those two didn't have anything in common. I don't think she would've been happy."

"Emma and I talked about it quite a bit," said Douglas. "I know she had all those plans for that spring wedding, but she won't be disappointed in the end." He looked at Matthew and smiled.

Matthew knew what Douglas insinuated. He cleared his throat. "I need to get back to the jail. I haven't been back since I left on my rounds last night." He found his hat and stuck it on his head. "Please let me know how she does."

Matthew turned and hurried out of Douglas's office. He wasn't sure how he felt about the turn of events with Caroline and Samuel. He loved Caroline, always had, but no way would he try to win her over until he knew he had something to offer her.

~

For the next week life spun nearly out of control for Matthew. He followed Caroline's progress through Vic and Douglas, but he didn't go to the office to see her. Her engagement had been broken, and he didn't want to invade her privacy. She needed time to get well and to move on with her life without Samuel. She had a lot to think about.

Gossip buzzed around town. The Brown-Fletcher wedding would've been the biggest event in Independence for the past few years, and its citizens whispered about what could've happened to break up the engagement. As Matthew listened to some of the gossip without commenting, he decided some of the people were more disappointed that the festivities were now canceled rather than being concerned about Caroline.

Some of them asked point blank whether he and Caroline would now get married. Finally, he avoided anyone who looked as if they wanted to stop and talk.

Five days after he'd found her sick, he sat behind the jailhouse desk. Someone tapped on the door, then opened it.

Caroline held onto the door and looked inside. "May I come in?"

Matthew's breath caught in his throat. He pushed his chair back and stood. "Yes. Please."

She stepped in and looked around. "Uncle Vic isn't here?"

"No, did you need him? I can go find him."

"No, I came in here to see you."

Wan and strained, her face couldn't hide the fact that she had been near death. His heart went out to her. It was all he could not to go to her. He swallowed.

"Then come in and sit." He walked around his desk and pulled out a chair for her. He touched her arm to help her. "Can I get you some water?"

She looked up and smiled. "No, I'm fine." She took several deep breaths. "Emma told me you found me the other night and stayed with me all night trying to get the fever down. She said you might've saved my life. I wanted to thank you in person."

Matthew stepped away from her and propped one hip on the desk. "You don't have to thank me. You know I would never leave my old friend alone and sick."

She looked down at the door. "I really appreciate what you did. I kind of remember you being there, I think."

"You were pretty much out of it, Caroline. You had us all worried."

He stood up, not able to say more. She looked sad.

"Douglas is taking me to the ranch. Father wants me to be home. I'm sure all that good cooking that Bonita will serve me will get me back on my feet."

"I'm sure it will. I'm glad to see you are up and able to travel."

She started to stand, but swayed. He grabbed her with both hands and without thinking, pulled her thin body to him.

He closed his eyes and held her tight.

She placed her head against his chest and for several minutes he savored her warmth. She didn't move and said nothing.

Finally, she pulled away. "Douglas is waiting in the carriage. I told him I wouldn't be but a second."

He didn't want her to leave. "Of course," he said. "Like I said, I'm glad you're at least able to get out of bed. Being at the ranch will help you."

She nodded and looked at the floor. "I heard you went to see Samuel."

Matthew straightened up and took a step back. "I did. I didn't know you two had broken off the engagement. I went to the Brown house at daylight when I felt I could leave you for a few minutes. I thought he should know."

"I also hear he never came to check on me."

She raised her gaze to him.

His heart broke for her. "Right. He didn't think it was his place anymore."

"No, I don't guess it was."

"Caroline, the man has a lot on his plate with the mess at the bank. I'm sure he will come around and realize what a horrible mistake he made by letting you go." He didn't believe any of what he'd said, but he couldn't stand to see her so sad.

"I think it was for the best." She pulled in a ragged breath. "I really have to go."

Matthew helped her through the door, not wanting her to leave, but knowing he needed to let her have her space.

At the carriage Douglas jumped out and helped her into the front bench.

"Take care of her, Douglas."

"You know I will."

Matthew watched as the carriage eased down the main street. Now that she and Samuel were no longer engaged—at least for the moment—he wondered if she'd come back to town. She had a good life at the ranch. She certainly didn't have to work at the vet office.

When the carriage disappeared, he went back inside the jail. Caroline had a lot to think about, but so did he. He looked down at the paperwork on his desk. Today was the last day to qualify for the position at the prison he now desperately wanted. Scooping up the handwritten papers, he headed out the door once again.

He nodded to several men on the sidewalk, tipped his hat to three women as he passed them, but was glad when he saw the courthouse ahead of him. He had no desire to talk with anyone today.

He entered the courthouse and made his way down the hall to the appropriate room to present his application for the election. He stopped outside the door and swiped his hand across his chin.

What am I thinking? I can't win an election. He looked up to the ceiling. *God, how am I to know if I'm doing the right thing?*

He was just about to turn around to leave when a man opened the door and came face to face with him.

"Matthew Jennings, it's about time you got down here. We were all worried you had decided not to throw your name in for the position." The man smiled big. "Come on it. I'll take your paperwork and make this official. I can't wait to tell the rest of the town that you haven't changed your mind."

Matthew followed him into the room and went to the marble counter. The man walked around the counter, then hurried back to face him. "Let me see what you've come up with?"

Without saying a word, Matthew handed him his two pieces of paper.

The man skimmed over it and scratched his head.

Sweat trickled down Matthew's back.

"I think this will do. No one else has turned in paperwork, so if it stays that way until the office closes at five, we'll have us a new County Deputy Marshall." The man stuck out his hand and grabbed Matthew's. "Proud of you for doing this."

"Thank you, sir." He gave him his best attempt at a smile, then left the room.

He wasn't sure if he was thrilled he'd officially entered the race, if there was to be one, or if he had taken on something he'd regret later.

He didn't have much time to think about his feelings. As he was leaving the courthouse, George Burge walked through the doors.

"Well, look who it is. I heard you might try your luck for the position at the new prison." George laughed. "Good luck with that."

Matthew looked down at what was in his hands. "Are those your qualifying papers? Are you trying your luck as well?"

George laughed again. "There's no luck involved, Deputy Jennings. I've lived here all my life. I have the ranchers all over the outskirts of town who are going to vote me in. I know you don't even have a Jennings family to back you."

Matthew stiffened. "You're right, George. I lost my blood kin, but what I have is as good or better than any family around here." He tipped his hat. "Have a good day."

His blood boiled. All of a sudden, he knew he'd done the right thing today.

Thank you, God. You couldn't have sent a better person to make me realize I made a good decision.

CHAPTER EIGHTEEN

Sunshine flooded Caroline's bedroom. She lay with her head propped up on a pillow wishing she could be out in the corrals working with the horses or even helping out in the kitchen, anything but lying in the bed wasting her days. Never in her adult life had she been confined to the bed, and it wasn't what she wanted to do.

Since Douglas had driven her home in the family carriage three days ago, the family and Bonita and Carmella pampered her with love and food but refused to let her get out of bed.

Today she was changing that scenario. Dealing with sick animals on the ranch, she knew if they stayed down too long, they lost their energy and eventually couldn't get up. She wouldn't end up like one of them.

Carefully, she sat up and let her legs dangle on the side of the bed. She waited for the dizziness to hit her. It didn't.

"Perfect." She slid off the bed and let her feet slide into her morning slippers then carefully held onto the bedpost and stood. With a smile on her face, she let go of the post and knew she'd be okay.

Going about her morning routine took longer than usual. Several times she had to sit in her rocker to regain her strength, but eventually she headed to the door. As she opened it, the aroma of Bonita's breakfast wafted around her. Her stomach growled. She held onto the railing, made her way down the hallway, then got to the top of the stairs. With a big exhale of breath, she held on tightly and took one step at a time until she got to the bottom of the staircase. She stood for a couple of seconds, then headed toward the dining room where she heard the family talking.

She stepped into the dining room. "Good morning."

Everyone turned to her.

Lucas jumped up. "Caroline, should you be up?"

"I'm fine, Father. I had to get out that bed."

Abigail walked over to her. "Come on in and sit down. I agree with you. It was time for you to get out of the bed."

Lucas pulled out a chair near him, and Abigail helped her walk toward it.

"I'm starving. I can't wait to see what Bonita has cooked."

"I asked for flapjacks," said William," but whatever they make, it'll be yummy."

"You're exactly right." Caroline smiled at her little stepbrother, then looked at little Emma who sat quietly near Lucas.

The swinging door flew open as Bonita pushed her way into the room carrying two plates filled with eggs and ham. Carmella followed her carrying a platter of flapjacks.

"She made them!" shouted William.

Everyone smiled at his excitement.

Abigail looked at her son. "Tell them thank you for taking the extra time making your favorite breakfast."

"Thank you, Miss Bonita. I can't wait to eat them."

"You are more than welcome, young William."

When Bonita had gone back into the kitchen, and everyone was concentrating on the plates in front of them, Caroline took a bite, then leaned back in her upholstered chair. This was her family, her home, her way of life, and in a way she was glad she would not have to move into that house that Samuel was having built for her. It would have been the grandest house in Independence, but it would've lacked the character and love and the memories that filled this home that her great, great grandfather had built.

"You okay?" Lucas raised an eyebrow and smiled at his daughter.

"Yes, Father. I'm fine. I'm so glad to be back at the ranch. Just being here will help me get back on my feet."

"That's what we're hoping. This is where you belong."

"You're right. I loved being in town and working with Douglas, but I missed this ranch."

Abigail spoke up. "And we missed you."

"Thank you, Abigail. I really missed all of you. After breakfast, I'd love to go to the barn."

Lucas and Abigail looked at each other.

"I'll be glad to walk with you," Abigail said.

Caroline settled back in her chair, ate a little of her breakfast, and enjoyed being home.

After breakfast, Abigail helped her back to her room.

"I do want to go to the barn, but I think I'd like to lie here for a few minutes before I get dressed."

"I have to get the children settled. I'll be back afterwards and will help you dress."

Caroline stretched out on the bed and didn't fight the urge to go back to sleep. She was home and on her way to recuperating.

When she opened her eyes she knew she'd slept longer than she anticipated. The sun was high over the ranch house.

A tap on the door made her sit up. "Come in."

Bonita stepped in carrying a tray of fruit, sliced meat, and a bowl of veggies. "We thought you might like a small meal before going back down."

Caroline laughed as Bonita pulled up a bedside table and placed the tray on it.

"I think I just got up from breakfast."

"That was several hours ago. You can stay in your room for as long as you want. Rest is good for you."

"Thank you, Bonita. I guess I missed my barn outing."

"Those animals aren't going anywhere. They'll be some place near when you decide to walk out there. You rest." Bonita waved and headed to the door, but turned around before opening it. "You make sure you bundle up. It's cold out there."

Caroline nodded, then sat on the side of the bed and reached for the sliced meat. "How is it possible to be hungry after that big breakfast?" But she was hungry, and she ate almost everything on the plate.

By mid-afternoon Caroline felt her energy had returned. She dressed and headed to the barn alone. The scent of the horses, hay and feed energized her. Even working with the animals in Douglas's office didn't give her the satisfaction of being around these animals. One by one she went to each stall, filled the troughs and talked with each horse.

Finally, the lifting and walking wore her out. She sat on the hay to rest before heading back in. Leaning her head against one of the bales, she closed her eyes. *Thank you, God, for letting me live through the flu and being back home with my family.*

After a while she decided to go back in the house before the family sent a search party after her. She giggled as she stood up.

The barn door opened. The silhouette of a man filled the opening.

"Mason, is that you?" She squinted to see who it was.

"No, Caroline. It's Matthew." He hesitated. "I didn't know you were in here."

"Matthew? I'm surprised to see you here. What are you doing at the ranch?" Her heart skipped a beat.

"I needed to talk with your father. Carmella told me to look in here, but obviously he's not here. I'll leave so you can do whatever it is you were doing."

"No, Father is not in here, but please don't leave. I wasn't busy. I wanted to spend some time with the horses, that's all."

He pulled off his hat but didn't move. "Are you well?"

"I'm on my way." She smiled. "My family has pampered me since Douglas brought me home."

"I'm glad to hear that. I, we, were all worried."

She took a few steps towards him, hoping he wouldn't leave. "I want to thank you again for taking care of me that night. It's all a blur."

"You were really sick. I can understand why you don't remember much."

"I do remember you being with me. I felt safe."

Matthew still hadn't moved. "I couldn't leave you alone."

She nodded. Why did this feel so awkward? This was her old friend. Her companion for years here at the ranch, but today nothing seemed easy. "Please, come sit with me."

Even in the dim light of the barn she could see the muscles in his jaw twitch. Did he feel as awkward as she did? Did he not want to talk with her?

Finally he stepped towards her. "Do you know where you father is?"

"No, but I'll walk around the house with you if you'd like to look."

"Yes, that would be nice."

Her heart beat with joy. She took a deep breath and walked toward him. "I heard you had put you name into the race for the county deputy position."

"I did. That's why I need to see your father."

"Then let's go see if we can find him."

She took his hand, but he didn't move. Instead, he pulled her to his body and gave her a big hug. The big breath he let out warmed her neck.

"I've missed you, Caroline." He stepped away. "I hope we can spend a little time together again now that you're on the way to recovery."

"And now that Samuel isn't in the picture anymore."

He smiled a crooked smile. "Yeah, that too. I guess I

ought to say I'm sorry for your breakup, but I'd be lying. I was happy you had someone to give you all the things you deserved in this life."

She dropped his hand. "What do you mean, 'what I deserved'?"

"I was going to say he'd give you all the material things that you're used to—that big house, nice carriages, servants to help with the house and the children."

"Stop it, Matthew. Do you think that's what I want?"

"It might not be what you consciously want, but it's what you're used to."

"Maybe used to, but not what I dream of having or need. Happiness comes in many forms and that is only one of the ways that people find happiness."

"And he would've been able to give you that part."

Caroline's blood boiled. "So you think I'm so shallow I have to have beautiful and expensive things around me to find happiness."

"You're not shallow, Caroline. You simply never had to want for anything growing up,"

"I can't believe you just said that. Did you think I didn't want to have my mother with me? Every waking moment I missed her and wanted her and there was nothing anyone could do to give that to me." She turned her back to Matthew. "Don't you ever say I grew up with all I ever needed."

She felt him walk up to her. He placed both hands on her shoulders. "You're right. That's a want and a hurt no one can help."

She squeezed her eyes and spun around. "I'm so sorry. You, too, went through that. Maybe that's why we were so close to each other when we were young. We understood the hurt we were each going through." She placed both hands on his cheeks. "Except you didn't have family to help you through your hurt as I did. Maybe I am shallow."

He pulled her to him.

She melted against his strong chest.

"You're not shallow," he whispered. "I was happy Samuel would have given you beautiful things."

"Maybe he would've." She put her hands on her hips. "Is that why you didn't fight for me?"

"What do you mean?"

"Fight for me. Try to win me back when you came home? You acted as if you were in my way."

"Maybe I was."

"That's ridiculous. Had you still had feelings for me you would've tried to win me away from Samuel."

"I never quit having feelings for you, Caroline. Never." He pulled her close, lifted her chin with his finger and kissed her softly.

She closed her eyes and relished the feel of his lips on hers, then she surprised herself. She threw her arms around his neck and kissed him back. For the first time in a very long time she felt as if she was where she was supposed to be. Never had she kissed Samuel in this way, and never had he kissed her with the passion that Matthew showed.

She didn't want the kiss to stop, but he pulled back.

"What's wrong?"

"Nothing's wrong, but the timing. You need time to get your life straight without Samuel in the picture. You can't go from being engaged to kissing me without having time. The next time I pull you in my arms, I want to make sure you know it's me."

"There you go again thinking you know what's best for me."

He pulled her close, but not touching, then kissed her forehead. "We both have a lot to think about with our lives. I'm running for this position, and you need to decide what to do now that your life with Samuel isn't in the picture, or at least for the moment."

"This moment and always. Samuel is out of my life."

"I'm not so sure about that. I guess in the back of my mind I see you two getting back together."

"No, I don't want to be with Samuel. I saw a side of him I don't like. I don't want that man or his family to be the family of my children."

"There are sides of me you might not like either. We're all not perfect, Caroline."

"I know." She turned and walked to Lady's stall and rubbed her nose. "I've known you most of my life. I think I've seen most of your sides." She turned to face him. "I've seen your good and your bad."

"Not all of them. I'm a lawman. Except for working on a ranch for someone else, it's all I know how to do."

"There's nothing wrong with that."

"I didn't say anything was wrong with it. There's a lot of good in the law life I've chosen, but it's dangerous and sometimes to keep others safe, we have to do things that others might not approve of."

"I know. Leaving Independence and going away to school taught me a lot of things about life. I'm not the same girl you knew from our time back here at the ranch."

He bit his lip. "Then you'll understand I need time and so do you. You can't quit loving someone overnight, someone you were going to marry."

"Maybe I didn't love him enough."

"Then you have more to think about than I thought you did." Matthew put the hat on his head. "I have to go."

"But you'll come back soon so we can talk."

He nodded. "I'll be back, but right now I have to find your father." Matthew walked to the barn door, but as he opened it, he stopped.

On the other side of the door, Samuel stood with a frown on his face.

~

Caroline's hand went to her chest. "Samuel? How long have you been standing at the barn door?"

"If you'd like to know if I heard what this man and my fiancée talked about and whether I saw the two of you kissing, yes, I saw and heard it all."

Matthew closed the barn door and turned to Samuel. "Then you'll know your former, and I emphasize former, fiancée is trying to move on since you dumped her."

"I didn't dump her. I was upset she turned on my family."

Matthew inhaled a big breath to calm his nerves and not say something to inflame the situation. "Caroline did not turn on your family. She didn't want to say anything to anyone, but the lady has a conscience. She couldn't live with herself if she'd have kept what she heard to herself."

"So you say." Samuel looked over Matthew's shoulder. "I'd like to talk with Caroline. Alone."

Matthew looked at Caroline. "Are you okay with that?"

"I'm okay, Matthew. Samuel is in my father's barn. He wouldn't do anything stupid."

"Maybe," Matthew said under his breath. He turned back to Samuel. "I won't be far."

"The big deputy is going to protect my woman?"

"Don't push me, Samuel. If you have something to say to her, go right ahead, but don't take too long. Mr. Fletcher is probably on his way here, and I'm not sure he wants you on his property."

"We'll see about that."

Matthew looked at Caroline.

She nodded and mouthed. "I'm okay. Thank you."

Matthew pushed past Samuel and left the barn. Once outside, he squeezed his eyes and wanted to hit something, but he saw Lucas Fletcher walking toward the house. He waved his arms to get his attention and waited to see if he'd walk toward the barn.

He did. Feeling better, Matthew walked toward the fence to meet him, not wanting to go too far away from Caroline and Samuel.

"Matthew," Lucas said as he got near, "one of my new men said he'd seen two men come this way. I thought I'd better see who it was." He looked around toward the barn door. "Is someone else with you?"

"There's someone else but he's not with me. Samuel is with your daughter."

"That no good snake. Are they in the barn alone?"

"Yes, I didn't want to leave, but she said she'd be okay. I wasn't going far."

"Thank you. Did you need to see me? I want to go in to give that man a piece of my mind."

Matthew chuckled. "We're having a town meeting to let the voters see who is running for the position at the new prison. I wanted to make sure you knew and hoped you'd be there."

"You tell me when and I'll be there. I wouldn't miss it. I plan to take as many men from here to vote on Wednesday. That's when I heard the election would take place."

"You heard right. We're having that meeting on Tuesday night."

"I'll be there and then plan to sleep at Douglas's office. I hate to leave Abigail and mother alone but this is important.

"Thank you, sir."

"Now, I think I have business in the barn. You want to join me?"

"No, I think you need to do this alone, but I'll hang around until I see Samuel leave."

Lucas nodded, then spun around and headed to the door.

Matthew had told Lucas he didn't want to go inside, but he'd give anything to hear their conversation. He'd believed Caroline when she said she didn't want to be with Samuel, but saying it when he wasn't around and now being with him face to face were two different things. She'd said he needed to fight for her, and maybe he should, but she knew how he felt about her. It was time for her to find out how she really felt about Samuel.

He walked around the corral several times, then hopped up on the fence to wait. He should probably leave, but he needed to make sure Caroline was okay. If he had the opportunity to talk with her alone, he needed to hear her say she wanted to leave Samuel for good.

He didn't have to wait long. The barn door flew open and Samuel stomped out. He turned to go toward his carriage, but when he saw Matthew, he turned toward him.

As he got within a few steps of him, he spoke loud. "You can have her, Mr. Jennings. We'll see how she likes living on a deputy's salary."

"She's not yours to give, Samuel. Caroline has a mind of her own. If she wants to be with me, the salary won't matter. If she decides material things are what she needs instead of real love then she might go back to you, but I can tell you if she decides she wants me, she'll have my truest love always."

"You can't live on love, sir, but if you two want to try, go for it." He spun around, kicking dirt, and headed through the corral.

Matthew smiled. His Caroline had come through and done what he wanted her to do, but she needed to be sure. He jumped down from the railing. He wanted to hold her and kiss her until she realized she loved him as much as he loved her, but it wouldn't happen today.

She needed to make up her mind alone.

He'd give her time.

For her, he'd wait forever.

CHAPTER NINETEEN

The town hall overflowed with men from within the city limits that Matthew recognized and quite a few strangers from heaven-knows-where. He knew some of the men who lived near Fletcher Ranch, but so many he did not know. He wondered why they were here. Who had encouraged them to come in to vote tomorrow? Could the Browns hate him so much that they found someone to run against him? There was no way he could prove it, but he didn't believe in coincidence.

George Burge could've brought in cowhands and troublemakers from all over to vote for him. Matthew had to wonder if they were compensated for their trip into town.

"Big turn out."

Matthew recognized Lucas's voice before he turned. "Yep. I wonder where they all came from."

"I can tell you right now that a lot of them are not from around here. George Burge has pulled from everywhere to get a vote."

"And it might work."

"Don't count on it. Independence is a big city. People will come out to vote tomorrow. We'll get the word out."

"Can I have your attention?" The man behind the podium banged the gavel several times. When it was reasonably quiet, he continued. "I'm William Hill, I'm your city mayor for those who are not from around here." He eyed several of the newcomers.

A couple of the men grinned.

"You're here tonight to meet our two candidates who want to run our new prison. I am supposed to be an unbiased mediator so I won't do anything but introduce them to you, and we'll let them tell you who they are." He introduced George Burge first.

Several guys stood up, stomped their feet and yelled their approval.

"This could get ugly," Matthew said as he took a seat to hear what this man was going to say.

George walked to the podium. He looked around and swallowed.

"I don't think public speaking is his strong suit," Lucas whispered.

"It's not mine either."

George coughed then swallowed. "My name is George Burge, and I want your vote so I can run that new prison for you, run it the way it should be run. I've been living around the Independence area since I was a kid. My family is local. I have relatives up and down the river, and I can tell you this, someone running that new facility needs to be someone who is local and who has ties to the community. That person would be me."

Again, the men in the back of the room stomped their feet and yelled.

"As I was saying, I'm from here. My family is here, unlike my opponent who doesn't have family here. In fact he has no family."

Matthew's blood boiled. He bit his lip to keep from saying anything.

Lucas touched his arm. "You'll get your turn."

"You may not know this but Matthew Jennings was picked up as a kid trying to steal from the mercantile. What kind of warden would that make him?"

Again, the men in the back clapped and cheered.

George smiled. He went on to say how he knew everyone in the county, had lived there all his life, and worked hard for what he had.

Matthew looked around. Even the men he knew were nodding.

Lucas leaned near to Matthew. "Don't let it get to you, Matthew. The man is a jerk and those who know him recognize him for what he is."

"But not everyone knows him, even though that's what he says."

Finally, the mayor walked up to him. "Thank you, Mr. Burge. You can close your remarks so we can get on with the rest of the meeting."

Matthew took a deep breath. He had never spoken in front of a group, and after Joe's remarks, he wasn't sure what he'd say.

When his name was called, he took a deep breath and stood up. Several men clapped as he walked to the podium. He took a second to catch his breath.

"Good evening. My name is Matthew Jennings and like Mr. Burge, I want to run the new prison for you." He took another deep breath and relaxed a little.

He started by giving his qualifications as a lawman starting with his time in Jefferson City and ending with his present position in Independence.

He stopped and looked around the room, then started again. "Everything that Mr. Burge said about me is true. I do not have blood family here." He went on to explain about the fire and how Charlie Wright took him in.

"The home life there was anything but ideal, though Mrs. Wright was a loving woman and tried to make my life easy. Mr. Wright was just the opposite. He reminded me every day that he had saved me and that I owed him." He stopped for a second hoping his voice wasn't quivering, then he continued.

"He treated his wife horribly and one day it came to a

head. They were in one of their horrible arguments, but this time it turned really ugly. He pulled out a gun and shot her. I was nine years old. I saw what happened and ran out the door. Mr. Wright tried to catch me, even took a few shots at me, but I got away. I was terrified. I hid in the woods for two days. On the third day I had to find food so I went to town and ate out of the slop from the local restaurant. I ended up getting sick. I went into the mercantile and tried to steal two pieces of fruit, but the owner caught me. He took me to the sheriff's office where Lucas Fletcher happened to be. Mr. Fletcher took me home and the rest is history. The man treated me like his own son. The entire family accepted me."

He took another huge breath. "As Mr. Burge said, I have no relatives alive, but what I had at the Fletcher Ranch was an answer to my prayers. The Fletchers may not be my real family, but they're family. I stayed with them until I needed to go to Jefferson City when my stepfather got out of prison. He was sick. I guess I was trying to find forgiveness in my heart by helping him."

"That's why I left Independence, but I came back. This is my home and I intend to stay here as long as possible. I want that position at the new prison and if you have it in your heart to vote for me, I'd appreciate it. I'll do everything in my power to make you proud of me and that prison."

The room exploded in applause. Several men stood up and shook his hand as he headed toward his seat. By the time he got to Lucas, his heart beat rapidly and his face broke out in a smile.

Lucas stood up and patted him on his back. When guest speakers were called from the audience, Lucas went up. "You men know me and know I don't like to speak in public, but tonight is different. I want to be up here because I think Matthew Jennings is the man for the job. He has my vote and I hope he has yours." He reiterated the story of Matthew's early years. When he finished, the audience applauded once more.

By the end of the evening, Matthew felt good about what had taken place. After shaking hands with most of the men there, he was one of the last people to leave. As he walked out the door, he stopped.

Caroline stood outside next to the wall by the door.

~

"Congratulations, Mr. Jennings. You did a great job." Caroline stepped into the light and smiled big. Her excitement for Matthew made her chest tickle.

Matthew smiled big as well. "I can't believe you're out here. You heard?"

"I cracked the door and watched and listened. It infuriates me that women aren't allowed into town meetings, but I made sure I was here to see you."

"Does your dad know you're here?"

"He does now. I had Mason drive me into town. I saw Father when he came out. He wasn't too happy I was here, but I told him I'd be at Douglas's office as soon as I saw you. I'll stay there tonight with him. That seemed to ease his mind."

"I'm glad you were here. I wish I had known before I went up to the front to speak. Just knowing that would've given me a little encouragement, and I needed it."

"I don't know. You looked pretty confident as you marched up there. I was proud of you."

The door opened and the last few men walked out. Each one shook Matthew's hand and congratulated him.

"We'll do everything in our power to get men out tomorrow to vote for you," one of them said.

"Thank you, sir. I appreciate that."

He watched them walk away. "There're some good men in this town."

"Not counting Mr. Burge and his loud-mouthed cronies."

Matthew laughed. "Yeah, you're right. Can I walk you home?"

"You'd better. Father will never forgive me if I walked to Douglas's alone." She grabbed his hand. "I've been waiting all night to do this and be by you."

Matthew squeezed her hand. "Same here." He turned to face her. "If we weren't on the main road, I'd give you a kiss."

"And I would love that." She smiled and this time she squeezed his hand.

His face broke into a huge smile. "Come on. Let's get you to Douglas's office. I have a big day tomorrow."

She snuggled next to him. "Yes, you do, and I'll be in town as well so I can help you do whatever needs to be done."

He put his arm around her shoulders.

They walked along the sidewalk slowly. Several men passed them and nodded.

Caroline looked up. "I guess it will be all over town that you had your arm around me tonight."

"Let them talk. I've heard all kinds of comments about us since Samuel called off the wedding." He looked down at her with serious eyes. "Speaking of which, what happened after I left the barn the other day?"

"Samuel was a total jerk. He acted as if I ruined everything. Not once did he say his family was at fault with the bank, but he did say his father and mother were not happy to be the laughing stock of the town because the wedding was off."

"What's he going to do with the house he's building?"

"I'm not sure. I didn't ask because I'm afraid it will be a sore spot if the bank is held responsible for the money Richard has taken. I'm afraid the family will lose everything."

"I hope not. I want Richard to be held accountable, but not Samuel or his mother if they had no knowledge of what he was doing." He pulled her tighter. "I have to say I'm glad all this happened before you married into the Brown family."

"I am, too."

They turned the corner and headed toward Douglas's office. Lucas was sitting on the front porch.

Matthew laughed. "Your father is waiting for us. I don't think he trusts me."

"I don't know that he'd trust any man with me. You know how protective he is of me. You'd think I were still fifteen."

"In a way I wish we both were still fifteen."

Caroline stopped and turned to him. "Would you do things differently?"

"Yeah, I think I would have. Maybe I wouldn't have gone to Jefferson City, but then I'd have always wondered about my true feelings for that man."

She turned back around and started walking again. "And I might not have gone off to finishing school. I think Father sent me there to get over you leaving me."

"Ouch. That hurts. I didn't leave Independence because of you."

"But you didn't stay either."

He nodded. "I know. I still have a lot to sort out in this brain of mine."

"And in your heart."

He turned and placed a finger on her lips. "Yes, and in my heart. After this election, we need to talk."

"Yes, we do."

"Glad you walked my daughter home." Lucas's voice pulled Caroline's attention from Matthew.

Lucas walked to the edge of the porch.

"Yes, sir. I would never have allowed her to walk home at night alone."

Caroline walked up the steps and stood by Lucas. She turned to Matthew and smiled. "I'll see you tomorrow to help where ever I can."

"Thank you, Caroline." He looked at Lucas. "If you don't have room here for both of you to be sleep comfortably, my room is available. I can sleep at the jail."

"I think we'll be okay, but thanks. Good luck tomorrow. I think you have a wonderful chance to pull this off."

"Let's hope."

Caroline leaned into her father's arm he put around her shoulder as she watched Matthew walk away.

"He's a good man, Caroline."

"Yes, I know that, but I have a feeling he's not so sure about himself. I hope he gets this position at the prison. I think he really wants it."

"And what about you? Do you want him to be the new Deputy Marshal?"

"Of course, I do. He would do a wonderful job."

"We all know that. What I was asking was how you feel about him being in town permanently now that you and Samuel are no longer engaged."

Caroline looked down at the floor and smiled. "I'm happy he'll be here. I've always wanted him close by."

"Good. That's what I was hoping you'd say."

"But please don't get ahead of the situation. We might be back in town together, but I'm not sure he wants to be part of my life at least for right now. He has a lot to work out before he can share a life with anyone else."

"Can you give him time to do that?"

"You know I can. Since he's gotten back to town I realize how much he means to me. As you said, he's a good man. I hope he can figure that out for himself."

Caroline watched Matthew turn the corner. When Matthew was out of sight, she turned back to her father. "I love him, Father. I always have."

"Then don't give up on him. Love always finds a way."

CHAPTER TWENTY

Matthew leaned against a post on the front of the mercantile and watched men flow into the town hall where the voting was taking place. Several men saw him as they came out and walked across the road reassuring him they had voted for him.

He thanked each one.

Finally he walked across the road and headed inside the hall so he could cast his ballot. He pulled off his hat and walked up to the table.

"Hello, Mr. Jennings. Here's a ballot and a pencil for you. You can vote over there at that table, but we know who you'll be voting for."

He took the paper ballot and pencil. "Thank you. I don't need to go over there." He looked at the two names and put a mark by his name. Seeing his name on the ballot was surreal. Blowing out a big breath, he folded the paper and placed it in the box.

"You can come back this afternoon about four. That's when the sheriff will be here and we'll open the box. You and Mr. Burge are allowed to watch us count."

"I might do that." He put his hat on his head and walked out.

Several men passed him going in. Most smiled or patted him on the back.

Matthew headed for the jail. He needed to do something

to keep his mind off the ballots and what he'd do if he didn't win.

Would he stay in Independence and work for George Burge? He didn't think he could stand working for someone with no law experience especially for a man with his attitude. It would be a huge decision to make. Matthew wanted to be with Caroline, but if he lost, what could he offer her?

Even if he won, would the salary of the Deputy Marshall be a suitable job to offer Caroline the kind of life he felt she deserved?

He had a lot to think about.

When he got almost to the jail, he saw Preacher Smith coming out of the office. Several times a week, the preacher came to the jail to talk with the prisoners. Today the cells were empty so Matthew was sure Preacher Smith spent his time visiting with the deputies or Victor.

"Matthew? How are you doing on this beautiful, but cold election day?" Preacher Smith walked up to him and stretched out his hand.

Matthew shook it. "I'm doing great. How about you?"

"My day has gone great. I started it by voting and, of course, I cast my vote for the man best suited for the job."

Matthew laughed. "I hope that man was me."

"You know it was."

"Sir, are you heading back to the church?"

"I am. Is there something you need?'

Matthew shuffled his feet. "I don't know. I don't want to take up your time."

"My time is yours, Deputy Jennings. Follow me and we can have a cup of tea or coffee and talk."

Matthew turned to follow, wondering why he had said anything. He needed to talk with the preacher, but he didn't want to talk today, not on Election Day.

He walked alongside the preacher and listened to him chatter about different people in the congregation. "That Mrs. Curry brought the best apple cobbler last Sunday. I'm surprised I don't weight three hundred pounds with all these good cooks."

"Yes, sir, especially with the way your wife cooks." He stopped walking. "I think I should go back to the jailhouse and help Victor. We can talk another time."

"Matthew, I just left the jail and I can tell you Victor doesn't need you right now. I think what you need is to follow me and we can have us a little chat."

Matthew didn't move.

Preacher Smith put his hand on Matthew's shoulder. "I would feel honored if you'd follow me to the church or anywhere and talked with me. If you win this election—and I think you will—you need to go into that job with little else on your mind. Maybe a chat is just what you need to wipe the slate clean."

Matthew took a deep breath and nodded. "You're probably right."

"I think Molly is still at the restaurant. We can go to the house and brew us something to drink."

Matthew followed him. By the time they entered the preacher's house, he felt more at ease. He wasn't even sure what he would say to this man, but he knew he needed to get a lot off his chest.

Preacher Smith opened the front door to the modest one bedroom house next to the church. "Come on in. What would you like? A cup of coffee or tea?"

"I think I'd like tea. I haven't had a cup in ages."

"That's exactly what I want." Preacher Smith put on a pot of water on the wood stove, grabbed two cups from the cupboard, and placed a cloth over each. After he positioned a spoon of tea on each, he sat down and faced Matthew. "Now tell me what's on your mind."

Matthew squirmed. Talking about his inability to do something was not in his nature.

The preacher sat quietly.

Matthew nodded. "You're right I do have a lot on my

mind. I've had a lot to think about for years." He took a deep breath and started by reiterating how his stepfather killed the only mother he'd known.

"I hated that man for all these years. I wanted him to die a horrible death for what he did to his wife. She was such a wonderful lady, someone who tried hard to make my life comfortable." He stopped. "Admitting that is not exactly what you thought you'd hear today, was it?"

Preacher Smith smiled. "Those feelings aren't as foreign as you might think, especially to someone who has experienced what you went through. No child should go through losing his parents and then watching his stepmother killed. That's traumatic for anyone. Our God is a loving and understanding god. I'm sure he understands what you went through and how you felt."

Matthew stared out the small kitchen window. "I knew those harsh feelings were doing nothing but hurting me. All the years he was in prison, I tried to forgive him, but it didn't work. It was eating at me. Four years ago he was released from prison because he was dying. I went up to Jefferson City because I knew I had to try to forgive him. I left the woman I loved to try to find the forgiveness and the peace I needed. Later, I realized I was being selfish."

Preacher Smith sat quietly, but tilted his head. "Selfish?"

Matthew took a jagged breath. "I guess I was only thinking about me. The only thing I accomplished by going up there was to start working in the prison system. I liked working with the prisoners. I watched and listened to them. They all had hard lives."

"But unlike you, they turned to crime. You didn't."

"No, I didn't but I can attribute that to being raised by the Fletchers. He showed me what was right and what a decent family looked like. He took me to church with the family. While I was in the Wright's house, Mrs. Wright taught me some hymns and gave me a small Bible that I still have, but her husband never would allow us to go to church."

"The Fletcher family is a great influence on anyone. You were lucky to have been taken in by them." Preacher Smith stood up. "Our water is boiling." He walked over to the stove and slowly poured the water over the tea. When he finished, he carried two cups to the table, then turned and brought over a tin of honey and sat back down.

"Thank you, sir." Matthew spooned honey into his cup and took a sip.

"There's nothing like a good cup of tea to sooth the mind." Preacher Smith sat up straight. "So you went to Jefferson City to find forgiveness, and it didn't happen."

Matthew nodded. "I tried. I watched Charlie Wright die a slow death. I kept thinking he'd say he was sorry for killing his wife, but he never did. One day I heard him mumble something that sounded like, 'She got what she deserved.'" He pulled in a ragged breath. "I made him comfortable, but I never forgave him for killing the only mother I ever remembered."

"And you think God will not forgive you for those feelings."

Matthew nodded, but didn't look directly at the preacher.

"I'm not God, and I don't profess to know what he does, but I can tell you I think he understands your feelings. You tried, Matthew. It's not like you haven't. I think you need to push those feelings aside and move on with your life. You have a wonderful future here in Independence. I don't know a man around here who wouldn't feel the way you do."

Matthew downed the rest of the tea. "So do you think I might wake up one day and realize I forgive him?"

"I don't know about that, but what I do know is that letting go isn't easy. We hold onto things. We're all human, but we have to trust in the Lord. He wants something better for us than hanging onto our anger. God is in control. We're not, but we are in control of how we handle our situations.

We have to give ourselves over to God. We have to let ourselves go toward him. I've seen you walk past the church on Sundays and look. That's a start. Now you have to come in and join us and let yourself be open to what God has for you."

Matthew sat a long time not saying anything.

"Matthew, you're one of the finest men in this town. You need to forgive yourself and move on with God's help." The preacher stood up.

Matthew did the same. "Thank you. I should have stopped in a long time ago."

"Probably, but sometimes we have to find the right time. Today was that time for you. I hope by this afternoon we'll find out you won the election. You have a lot to offer this town."

"We'll see."

"If you think you're ready, I'd love to see you in church on Sunday. We'll all celebrate your victory with you."

He chuckled. "I hope there is something to celebrate."

The handshake that Matthew gave the preacher was hard and sincere. "Thank you for listening."

Preacher Smith smiled. "Now before you go I have something to ask you. What are you going to do about Caroline Fletcher?"

Matthew shook his head. "That's a question I'd like an answer to myself."

"Why not make the first move and ask her to go to church with you on Sunday?"

"Might be a good start. Thanks."

He walked out of Preacher Smith's house feeling better than he had in years. He still had a lot to think about, but he'd start by opening his Bible and reading some of what the preacher had told him.

The north wind had picked up as he walked down the street toward the town hall. He hoped the cold weather wouldn't keep away those voters who were in favor of his running the new prison.

As he turned the corner, he smiled. Wagons were lined up in front of the hall with people coming and going. The wind didn't keep them away.

"Let's hope they're on my side."

~

Caroline walked around the crowded town hall talking to people standing in line. No one expected so many people to show up today, but even near to closing time people were still coming in. Some she recognized as families who had lived here all their lives, but some she had never seen. Those she assumed were some of Mr. Burge's friends.

"How are you doing, Caroline?"

She turned at the sound of a familiar face. "I'm doing fine, Mr. Harvey. Thanks for coming out today to vote."

"I wouldn't have missed it. I was one of the first ones here this morning. I just came back in to see how things are going." He looked around and frowned. "I don't know some of these men."

"I think they must've come in for Mr. Burge."

"There're a lot of them. I don't like the looks of that. Has it been like this all day?"

"I haven't been here all day, but this afternoon more people came in that we have never seen before than earlier."

"I don't like it." Mr. Harvey put his hands on his hips. "I'll bet some of them don't even live around here. I think Burge brought them in from other towns."

"That doesn't seem fair, does it?"

"Definitely not, but this guy isn't a fair player. I'm not even sure why he's running or who put him up to it, but we'll keep our fingers crossed he doesn't pull in enough votes to win."

Caroline wondered if the Browns had anything to do with Burge entering the race. None of the Browns liked Matthew and would probably love to see him lose. She pushed those thoughts aside and looked up at Mr. Harvey.

"Thank you for being on Matthew's side."

"Of course, I'm on his side. He's the man for this job." He looked around. "Have the Browns from the bank come in?" When he realized whom he had asked, he held his hand up. "I'm sorry, Caroline. I'm sorry about you and Samuel. I was just wondering if they would come in to vote since the bank is in so much trouble. If I were them, I'd go hide my face."

She wondered if this man had read her mind about the Browns. "We are all hoping the auditor doesn't find anything that would bring charges against them, but to answer your question, I haven't seen any of the Browns today."

"Speak of the devil." Mr. Harvey looked toward the door, then turned. "Mr. Brown and Richard just walked in."

She groaned to herself. Samuel wasn't with his father and brother. The last thing she needed today was to confront Samuel in front of all these people. When he didn't follow the guys in, she breathed a sigh of relief.

Mr. Brown and Richard walked toward the table where they would vote. She didn't want to talk with them so she turned and walked toward the door, but before she reached it, George Burge stepped in front of her.

Victor had his deputies stationed around the room and outside the hall in case Mr. Burge had his men created a disturbance. So far nothing had happened, and she hoped George wasn't about to cause a scene now. She wondered if Matthew had stayed away to keep the election peaceful.

"Looks like your guy is scared to face the voters today." George Burge smiled a quirky smile and leaned much too close to her.

She stepped back. "I don't think so, Mr. Burge. He's planning to be here soon. Now if you'll excuse me."

"I guess you're off to find your future Mr. Brown."

She had no idea why he said that but she pushed her way around him, then looked back at him. "No, Mr. Burge, I have no desire to see Samuel Brown."

"Aah, do I detect a little problem in that relationship?"

"Excuse me, sir. I have to be someplace."

He chuckled as she walked around him. She wanted to respond to his nosey question, but she, too, didn't want to create a problem while the voting was going on.

She spoke to a few men on her way to the front, and as she opened the front door, Samuel stepped in front of her.

Startled, she took a moment to compose herself. "Samuel, come in. I was just leaving." She tried to step around him, but he grabbed her arm.

"Stop, Caroline."

She tried to pull away but he wouldn't let her arm go. "Samuel, please let me go."

"Oh, I'll let you go, but we have stuff to discuss."

"We have nothing to talk about, especially in here so please let go of me."

"Oh, I think we do."

Once more she tried to get away from him, but he held her tighter.

"We have a lot to talk about. You stop and talk to me."

"Please, Samuel, let me go."

One of the deputies by the door stepped near to her. "Miss Fletcher, is everything okay?"

"I think so, but I'm not so sure." She faced Samuel.

"Mr. Brown, I don't think the young lady has time to talk with you."

Samuel's face turned red. "You have no idea who you're talking to. Now get out of my way."

The deputy put his hand on his gun, but Samuel grabbed Caroline and pulled a knife out from under his coat. He held it close to her neck.

Everyone around her let out a collective gasp.

The deputy held up his hand. "We're okay. You don't have to do anything drastic today."

Samuel pulled Caroline close to him and dragged her away from the door.

With his arm wrapped around her stomach, she had trouble breathing. He shoved her toward the wall.

"You come with me, and you won't get hurt."

With his face close to hers, she could smell liquor on his breath. Nothing about this moment seemed real. Samuel wasn't a violent man and he never drank that she knew of, but today things were different. He scared her today even more than he had at Douglas's office.

By this time Victor and two of his deputies shoved their way through the crowd.

"Samuel, you need to let that young lady go." Victor stepped out in the clearing and put his hand on his gun."

"I don't have to do anything you tell me to do." His words were mumbled.

Samuel's father walked up to Victor. "Leave my boy alone. He's been through enough this week. He just wants to talk to Caroline."

"Then he needs to let her go and do it peacefully. He's hurting her."

"Serves her right." His words were whispered, but they could be heard.

"Samuel, if you don't want me to use this weapon, you need to take your hands off Caroline."

"Over my dead body. I'm not letting her go. Get out of my way."

He looked around at the deputy at the front door, but the man refused to move or to take his hand off his knife. He tightened his arm around Caroline.

She whimpered when the knife pressed against her throat. She could feel his body tense and his breathing get harsher.

He shoved her against the wall, looked around, then yanked her back against him and pushed her toward the back of the room.

Caroline pulled in a huge breath. "Samuel, I don't know what you want from me, but we can talk in here if you want."

"Shut up. I don't want to hear your voice."

He moved the knife to her back, then wrapped his other hand across her throat, choking her. She tried to yank away, but he pulled tighter.

She closed her eyes and said a silent prayer. *Dear God, help me, please. Don't let anyone get hurt.*

CHAPTER TWENTY-ONE

Matthew headed for the town hall, but slowed down before crossing the street. Something wasn't right.

Several men stood in front of the hall looking through the window. One of the men saw him and motioned for him to come.

Matthew hurried across and jumped up on the wooden walkway. "What's going on?"

"You can't see them from here," the guy said, "but Samuel Brown has Caroline with a knife to her throat."

"What?" His heart raced. He leaned close to the dirty pane. "Where are they?"

"The last I saw them he was pushing her toward the back."

Matthew nodded. Words wouldn't come. Quickly he analyzed the situation. He could sneak into the front door, but if Samuel saw him, he might get nervous and do something to Caroline.

His law enforcement instincts kicked in. He turned and ran down the sidewalk and headed down a small ally. The man's words spun around in his head. Why would Samuel put a knife to Caroline? Just the thought nearly strangled him.

As he got near the back of the town hall, he inched his way along in the shadows next to the wall. He wasn't sure what his plan was, but he had to do something. His Caroline was in danger.

When he got to back door, he stopped and listened. Muffled talking reached his ear, but he couldn't make out who was talking. He knew Victor could still be inside and if he wasn't, one of his other deputies would be, but they had few choices if Caroline was in danger.

He grabbed the handle of the door and pulled a little. It moved. It wasn't locked. *Thank you, God.*

He eased it opened and looked in. The hall was packed but all the men faced Samuel next to the side wall. He held a knife to Caroline's back. Victor stood in front of the crowd but he didn't have his gun drawn. *Good move, Vic. Let the man think he's in charge.*

He was just about to slip into the room when Samuel pushed Caroline toward the door. Matthew stepped away from the door, melted against the wall, pulled his weapon out of its holster, and waited.

Something caught his eye. He looked toward the ally where he'd just come. One of Vic's deputies slipped against the outside wall and headed his way.

He nodded in his direction.

The door flew open. Samuel backed out, still holding Caroline against him. He moved the knife from her back to her throat. He still faced the room.

Matthew waited for the right moment. If he grabbed Samuel, he'd have to be sure to get his hands on the knife. If the man was nervous, as he surely was, he could easily cut her delicate skin.

"Stay away." Samuel yelled into the room. "Stay away or I'll slit her throat."

He stepped backwards out the door and put one foot on the ground.

Matthew prayed for Caroline's safety. He took the opportunity to pounce. In one big motion, he threw his body against Samuel's and grabbed the knife, but the man didn't let go of the weapon.

Matthew's attack startled Samuel, but he held his ground. Matthew wouldn't let go of the knife, but he forced Samuel's arm away from Caroline. She pushed away.

Matthew didn't take his eyes off Samuel, but saw Caroline out of the corner of his eye. She collapsed against the wall. If he could subdue Samuel, he knew Caroline would be okay. Samuel still held the knife. Matthew yanked both of them away from Caroline. He didn't want Caroline to get injured if they fell toward her.

When he had Samuel facing away from Caroline, he threw the man against the wall. Samuel slid down to the ground. At the same time the other deputy reached Matthew. He stooped down and helped Matthew hold Samuel down. Samuel yanked his body from side to side. The knife flew out of his hand.

"Stop it, Samuel, or we'll hurt you."

Finally, he felt the man give up. Samuel's body fell limp against the ground. The other deputy pulled out his hand cuffs. Matthew flipped him over and pulled his arms around to his back.

The back door flew open and Victor and a hoard of men pushed through.

Matthew knew they had the situation under control. "Take him," he said to the deputy.

He needed to get to Caroline.

~

Caroline slumped against the wall. She coughed trying to catch her breath. She rubbed her hand against her throat as she watched Matthew and the other deputy subdue Samuel.

What had happened? What had made Samuel snap? As soon as those questions came into her mind, she knew the answers. Obviously, the bank situation was not going well for the family.

Matthew stood up, faced her and within two steps had her in his arms. Tears flooded her eyes as she melted against him.

"Are you okay?" He placed a hand on the side of her face. "I was scared to death for you."

"I was terrified."

He brushed a tear from her cheek. His rough fingers felt heavenly. She wanted to be alone with Matthew. She needed him to hold her while she figured out what had just happened, but Victor walked their way. He put his arms around both Matthew and Caroline.

"Good job, Matthew. Are you okay, Caroline?"

"I am now. Thank you for all you and your deputies did."

Matthew let her go.

She stepped back, but kept her hand on Matthew's arm. She didn't want to be away from him.

"I'm glad I got here when I did," Matthew said, "but you had the situation pretty much under control when I looked through the window."

Victor chuckled. "I wish I would've felt that way. Just knowing Caroline was in danger, I felt helpless."

"Thank you, Uncle Victor. I think you did great." She looked at Samuel, who was being dragged away by the other deputy. "I can't believe Samuel acted like that. That was so unlike him."

Matthew looked at her. "Men do strange, unexpected things when they're backed in a corner. I think Samuel felt he had lost all his options with the bank mess and your involvement. Unlike his brother Richard, he's basically a good man. I have a feeling he didn't know how to handle what he was facing."

"I could smell liquor on his breath," she said. "That's so unlike him."

"As I said, men do unexpected things when they don't know what else to do."

Victor took her hand. "It's over now. The entire Brown family is in trouble, but I don't think you have anything to worry about with Samuel in jail for what he just did. Richard and Mr. Brown will be joining him shortly."

Matthew and Victor watched as Samuel and the deputy disappeared around the corner.

Several men at the door clapped.

"Good job, you two," one of them said.

A roar of applause and shots went up.

Victor walked to the men at the door. "Let's get back to this election. I hope someone has been with the ballot box."

Several men quickly turned and pushed their way through the crowd.

"I don't think anyone had time to do anything," Victor said, "but I wouldn't put it past Mr. Brown and Richard or George Burge to try to stuff the ballot box."

Matthew turned to Caroline. "You okay to go back in or do you need to go to the vet office to rest?"

"I want to go back in. I wouldn't miss the counting of the ballots." She squeezed his hand. "I want to be there when they announce your name as the new Deputy Marshall."

"Let's hope we got enough people in here to vote for me. I'm not so sure with all the new faces I saw today." He took a deep breath. "Let's go in and see if someone stayed at the ballot box."

She didn't move.

"What's wrong?"

"Nothing. I just want to be with you a few more minutes. I was so scared when he had that knife against my throat. The only thing I wanted was to see you come storming through that door."

"How about sneaking through the back door?"

She laughed. "That worked. I simply needed to know you were here. Thank you."

"Caroline, you were in danger. Nothing could've stopped me from getting to you."

He looked as if he would say something more but didn't. Instead, he kissed her on the forehead.

She looked toward the door. They were alone. She reached up and kissed him on the lips. When he kissed her back, she threw her arms around his neck and kissed him harder. She loved this man and never wanted to be away from him.

He pulled away with a smile on your face. "We need to go in."

She put her hands on her hips. "You're always way too sensible."

Matthew laughed. "At the moment I don't want to be, but I guess one of us needs to be."

~

At four o'clock the town hall was packed again with both men and women. Matthew talked with most of them, but what he wanted to do was to get Caroline away from the crowd. He needed to be with her, hold her, and kiss her. He loved her, but he knew how important the results of this election would be for him, so he stayed. If he wanted to offer Caroline a future with him, winning this election was the first step.

But would it be enough? That question never went away.

"Matthew, you ready for this?" Victor walked up to him.

"Yes, let's get it over with."

"Let's do it." Victor patted him on his back and headed toward the ballot box where his deputies stood.

Victor turned to the crowd. "I know everyone wants to be able to see, but that will be impossible. I want Mr. Burge and Mr. Jennings to come forward to be able to see. They can call three people to be observers with them."

"Here goes," Matthew said to himself. He looked around.

Lucas walked towards him. "Mind if I watch with you?"

"Can't think of anyone else I'd want by my side, except maybe that daughter of yours."

Lucas looked around. "She's not far. I'll get her."

Matthew walked through the crowd. He was glad to see women were present. He shook hands with as many men and women as possible as he headed to the table.

Victor stood behind the ballot table and waited until everyone was in place.

George Burge walked up alongside of Matthew.

Matthew turned and stuck out his hand. "Here goes. I hope we can be friends after all this is over. This city needs two good men helping with crime."

George frowned, probably trying to figure out how to respond to Matthew's kind comments. He didn't answer.

Matthew had his doubts that they'd ever be friends after this race was over, but he didn't need to make enemies whether he won or lost. He offered his hand to George.

George took it, shook it limply, then pulled his back.

Victor got the attention of the room once more. "Just to let you know, we had someone by this box the entire time we had the disturbance earlier. The ballots were safe, even though I'm told several people who we will not call by name, wanted to take the opportunity to vote another time. Luckily, the deputy at the box recognized them as someone who had already voted and put an end to it." He looked around. His gaze stopped at Matthew. "Are we ready?"

Matthew turned to see Lucas and Caroline come toward him. He nodded toward Victor.

His heart melted. His life was falling into place. A victory would help him decide what his future would hold here in Independence with Caroline.

He looked at Caroline coming toward him with a smile on her face and prayed his future would actually include her.

CHAPTER TWENTY-TWO

Matthew stood next to the ballot table with Caroline on one side and Lucas on the other. George Burge and his observers lined the other end of the table. Men and women hovered at their backs trying to see the ballots as they were counted. As each ballot was unfolded, the mayor held up the paper for a second after it was read so everyone could see it.

"This is too close," Lucas whispered.

Matthew watched the man swallow. Only a few ballots lay in the box uncounted and the tally at the moment was one hundred and two for Matthew and one hundred even for Joe.

Sweat rolled down Matthew's back. He wasn't sure it was from the men breathing down his neck behind him or from nerves.

Caroline grabbed his hand and held it tightly.

Her smile eased his mind.

Victor wiped his forehead. Was he as nervous as the rest of them?

The mayor reached into the box and pulled out another folded paper. "This one scores one for . . ." he took his time with each ballot. "This one scores one for George Burge."

As with each name called, half the room cheered. The other half groaned.

"You're still ahead," Caroline whispered next to his ear.

"I know. It only takes one to win, but we have only two

or three left."

Again, she squeezed his hand.

"Thanks for being here." He squeezed hers back.

"And the next one scores one for. . ."

"Come on," someone in the back shouted. "Don't drag this out."

"Okay, this one scores another one for George Burge."

Matthew swallowed. The possibility of George winning this election was real.

"And the next ballot is for, and I won't make you wait, is for George Burge."

"This is awful," Caroline whispered. "He can't possibly run that prison."

"But he might." Matthew looked deep into her eyes. "There are two ballots left and we're tied."

"Hurry up." One of the men called from the back. "This is torture."

"Okay. Okay." He grabbed another piece of paper and unfolded it. "This one is for Matthew."

"Yes!" Caroline shrieked.

Matthew grabbed her hand. "If that last one is for George, I don't know if I can go through another election."

"Yes, you can because we'll do it together. You've come too far to pull out now."

Matthew rubbed his hand across his chin. His forehead beaded with sweat as the mayor reached in for the last ballot.

"This is the last one. We'll either have a tie and another race or we'll have a winner." He took a deep breath and opened the folded paper. His face broke out in a smile. "We have a new County Deputy Marshall for Independence." The room exploded in cheers

Knowing the vote was for him, Matthew closed his eyes. *Thank you, God.*

The mayor held up the paper. "This vote is for Matthew Jennings. Congratulations, Matthew." His voice was drowned out by cheers, shouts, and clapping.

Caroline threw her arms around Matthew's neck. He pulled her to him and kissed her on the lips, not caring who was in the room. His eyes moistened with unexpected tears. He hadn't cried since he'd hidden in the woods alone and scared after seeing his stepmother shot, but these tears were different. They were tears of joy.

He brushed them away before letting Caroline have a chance to see them. He kissed her again. He never wanted her out of his arms.

But the moment with Caroline didn't last long. Men surrounded both of them patting them on their backs. Matthew shook hands with as many men as possible, still holding onto Caroline, but he knew the right thing to do was to go shake the hand of George Burge.

He pulled away, smiling, and shaking hands. He looked down at Caroline. "I have to see George before he leaves the hall."

"Yes, you need to." She pulled her hand away. "You go. I'll stay here."

He maneuvered his way through the crowd and got to the front of the room right as George got to the door.

"George, wait up."

George looked over his shoulder, his face solemn.

Matthew stuck out his hand. "It was close. You put up a great race." He waited for George to shake his hand, but the man just stood staring at him.

Finally Matthew pulled his hand back. "Look, George, we've never been friends, but that doesn't mean we can't be cordial to one another. This is a small town."

George blinked. "Yeah. Right." He turned around and left the hall.

Matthew watched his opponent leave the room followed by several of his friends. At least he hadn't tried to cause any trouble. Samuel had done enough of that.

"Speech. Speech." From behind Matthew the room exploded in a roar. "Matthew, come on up. Speech. Speech."

He shook his head. He hated speeches, but now that he'd won, he'd better at least thank those who had stayed to support him.

Caroline walked up to him and took his hand. "You ready for this? Everyone is waiting and happy for you."

"You know I don't like public speaking, but I guess I'd better learn to like it."

"Yes, you do. Being in charge of the prison will require you to talk to a lot of people." She smiled. Her eyes glistened. "I'm so happy for you, Matthew."

He squeezed her hand. "Come with me. Having you here makes me want to try to do anything."

"Then let's go."

She led the way through the crowd, but stood back as Matthew stepped up on the small platform in front of the room.

When he held up his hands, everyone clapped. He waited for the noise to stop. "Thank you. Thank you from the bottom of my heart. Never in my wildest dream did I ever imagine I'd see my name on a ballot and actually win an election." He waved his hand in front of his body. "You are the reason for this. Thank you." Another roar went up.

He took a deep breath and continued, and the more he talked, the more confident he became. He thanked Victor for all he'd done in Independence.

Victor turned to the crowd and waved his hands. "I've loved my job and will help Matthew as much as I can, but I have to tell you, I'm ready to be home with Bettye." He pulled her to his side and kissed the top of her head.

Cheers erupted.

"Victor has been my mentor, my confident, and like family to me since I met him years ago when the Fletchers took me in." He looked at Lucas. "And speaking of the Fletchers, I wouldn't be here today had it not been for Lucas Fletcher and his family. I thank you for the bottom of my heart."

Matthew swallowed and got control of his emotions, then he talked about the new facility and what he wanted to do for the community.

Looking around, he smiled. These were his neighbors and his friends, and then there was Caroline. He swallowed.

For the first time in his life he felt as if he were home.

~

Caroline stood with her hands clasped in front of her body. She was so proud of her childhood friend. He stood in front of the room looking confident. Tall and dark complexioned with thick black wavy hair, she thought how dashing a figure he presented.

Would his children have that beautiful hair and skin?

She looked around. Did anyone know her thoughts? Why would she think that?

As soon as that thought popped into her head, she knew why. She loved him with her whole heart and wanted him to recognize how she felt about him. Would there ever be a time he would be willing to open his heart to her?

She knew he loved her. He'd told her so, but would he ever let her into his life again? Something always made him back away. Maybe it was her turn to make a move.

Everyone started clapping. She realized he'd finished his acceptance speech and headed toward her. Her heart pounded.

After getting through the crowd and being hugged and hit on the back by one man after another, he finally got to her.

"Good job, Matthew. You've become quite a speaker."

"I stumbled through another one, but I am starting to feel a little better getting up to speak."

Lucas walked up to them. "Caroline, I'm riding back to the ranch. Are you coming with me?"

She looked at Matthew then back at Lucas. "I'd like to stay in town. Douglas rode back to the ranch right after he voted today, but he said I could stay at the office as always."

Lucas looked at Matthew, but Matthew spoke up first.

"Sir, I'll make sure she gets to the office safely tonight, and I'll have our deputies go by there when they make their rounds."

Lucas nodded.

"Father, remember our talk about me not being a child." She took his hand. "Thank you for worrying, but I swear I'm okay."

"I know you are." He let out a big breath, then leaned down and kissed Caroline on her forehead. "When do you think you'll be back at the ranch?"

"I'm really not sure." She looked at Matthew, then back at Lucas. "If Douglas needs me I might stay a couple days unless you need me to do something at the ranch."

"No, we have everything under control. Help my brother if he needs you."

"Sir, when she's ready, I'll ride out to the ranch with her."

"Thank you. I appreciate it." He put his arms around his daughter once, hugged her, then turned and left them.

Several men passed and congratulated Matthew, then Victor came up.

"You did it. Bettye is counting the minutes until I'll be giving up this badge."

"When will the judge be coming through to swear me in?"

"I heard next week so you'd better get ready. You'll have my desk all to yourself before you know it."

"I'm ready, Victor."

"I know you are." He patted him on the back, kissed his niece, then left.

"Aunt Bettye will be glad to have him home. I heard her tell Abigail how she has really been worried about him."

"He's ready to be home. He's tired of this job and the responsibilities" He thanked several other men leaving the town hall, then took Caroline's hand. "I'm starving. Would you like to go to Molly's and eat with me?"

Caroline felt her face break out in a smile. "I thought you'd never ask."

CHAPTER TWENTY-THREE

Matthew walked through the empty halls of the new prison. Even though hammering still sounded throughout the building, he knew it would be ready soon. Prisoners from the surrounding areas would be filling these cells.

Thank you, God, for letting me have this opportunity. Now, I need you to show me how to do this job the right way.

He stuck his head into one of the empty cells, knowing he could've been in one of these had Lucas Fletcher not taken him into his family. He would be grateful forever for what the Fletchers did for him.

The last time he had visited the facility the doors to the cells had not been installed. Today he examined the two doors on each cell. One door consisted of solid iron; the other of grated iron. He stepped into the first cell and walked to the window also covered in grated iron and hated the fact these windows would not keep the cold air out in winter. Even today the cell block was frigid. One day he hoped more suitable accommodations could be added.

Confident the cell would hold any type of prisoner intact, he walked into the hall.

"Mr. Jennings, can I have a moment of your time?"

Matthew turned around to find Emma's brother. "Edward, it's so nice to see you." He stuck out his hand.

Both men shook.

"Before you tell me what you want, tell me how you've been. I haven't seen much of you since you and Douglas had your little, what should I call it, encounter?"

"That's a nice ways of saying we shot each other."

Matthew laughed.

"I've been trying to find decent work. I tried the ranches, but I have to tell you I'm not a ranch hand. I can do the work, but I really don't like it. I think I'd rather work with men than animals."

"But you've stayed out of trouble, right?"

"Yes, sir. Walking the straight and narrow. That's why I'm here. I'm wondering if there's anything here at the new jail that I might be able to do. I'd even consider starting as a janitor."

"Believe it or not, I've been thinking about you and several other men in town who I'd like to have with me here."

"Really? You remembered me?"

"Of course I remember you. Emma is part of the Fletcher family. We love her and you're her brother. How bad could you be?" He laughed.

Edward laughed as well. "I kind of got off track there for awhile, but I'm a better person than what you saw earlier."

"I know you are."

Edward shuffled his feet and rubbed a hand across his chin.

Matthew knew the man was nervous, but he let him figure out what he needed to say. He'd been in situations like this many times, and he knew Edward would come around and find the courage to say what needed to be said.

"I have no experience in law enforcement, except for being in a cell, but I'd like to learn." He coughed. "But if it means starting by cleaning cells, I'll do that."

"That's good to know, but I don't need a janitor. I need guards. The only requirements we have for our guards is having the willingness to work, handling yourself in a mature, sensible way around the prisoners, and keeping your nose clean."

"Yes, sir. I realize I have to prove myself."

"And I think you can. If you want to be part of this prison, I'd love to give you a chance. I can't officially hire you today because I'm not official until the judge comes through next week, but you can be confident that if you come by next week, I'll get you started doing something around the other jailhouse until we move into this facility."

Edward grabbed his hand. "Thank you so much. I swear you won't be sorry for hiring me."

Matthew felt good about the man. He and Emma came from the same stock and she was a wonderful person. Edward would come around. He felt sure. As he'd told Edward, he wanted to talk with a couple other men about positions. The first would be Joe, presently the town drunk, but he knew with a little responsibility, the man could once again be an upstanding man in the community.

After Edward left, he walked through the silent halls, opening doors to cells and checking out rooms that would be used for storage.

"Hello, Mr. Jennings." One of the workers turned around and greeted him. "Congratulations on the win. We're excited you will take over this facility."

"Thank you. I appreciate your saying that."

"The rooms that will be your living quarters are ready. You can start carrying your things in if you'd like. Have you checked them out yet?"

"I have, but I'm heading that way again. Thank you."

He walked in the direction of the living quarters in the front and off to the side of the prison. The closer he got to the rooms he'd call home, the more excited he became.

As soon as he stepped outside the prison complex, he stopped. Caroline walked toward the door of the living quarters. *Could this day get any better?*

Before she put her hand on the door handle, she looked up at Matthew and smiled big.

He got control of his emotions and hurried toward her. "Caroline, what are you doing here?"

"I went by the jailhouse and one of the deputies told me you were here. I hoped I'd run into you."

He walked up to her and pulled her in his arms.

She looked around. "No one is here. You can kiss me, you know."

Matthew laughed. "You, young lady, have become quite brazen!" But he pulled her close and kissed her hard. His heart beat rapidly. When he stepped away, he looked into her eyes. "I'm so glad you're here. Do you want to see where I'll be calling home?"

Her face got serious, but then she smiled. "That's why I'm here."

He took her hand and led her through the door of the small brick building. "This front room is the living area. It's pretty small."

"But manageable."

He nodded. "Right. Manageable." It wasn't exactly what he wanted to hear, but at least she wasn't repulsed by the quarters. Looking at it now, he knew Caroline deserved more than this. The three storied house that Samuel was having built for her might be a little extravagant but these few rooms seemed totally inadequate.

Caroline looked around at the front area, then pulled away and walked into the room that would be used for a small bedroom. He waited in the living area.

She walked out with a smile on her face, but neither said a word. "Where's the kitchen?"

"Through that door in the back." He followed her into a decent size kitchen. A wood burning stove sat in the middle of the floor but had not been installed yet.

She ran her hand along the new stove. "I'm told this is where meals for the prisoners are cooked."

"You heard right."

"Are there workers to help with the meals?"

"Yes. In Jefferson City the wife of the jailer cooked the meals, but she had help with the cooking and with the housework. I'm assuming it will be like that here. Since I'm not such a great cook, I guess I'll have to hire someone to be the cook and do the housework."

"That would make sense since your duties running the prison would be much more important than cooking."

"Right."

"Or if you married you could have your wife run the kitchen."

Her words caught him off guard. What was she thinking? Was that just an off-the-cuff comment or should he read more into it than that?

He nodded. "I guess."

Caroline put her hands on her hips. "Do you ever think about getting married?"

He took a step backwards. "Of course, I do. I thought about it all the while I was taking care of my stepdad, and now that I'm here. . ."

The door opened and one of the men from the city council walked in.

Matthew took a deep breath. He wanted to spend time and talk with Caroline, but this man needed his attention. "Welcome, sir."

He walked up and shook his hand, then turned to Caroline. "And I'm sure you know Caroline Fletcher."

"Yes, I certainly do. I hear you've been working over at Douglas's vet office."

"I have been on and off. I love the animals on the ranch and it felt like the natural thing to get involved with."

"Makes sense to me."

"What can I do for you, sir?"

"I've been out of town. I missed the election. Didn't even get to vote for you, but I hear you pulled it off without my vote."

"Your vote would've kept my nerves a little calmer. It was too close for comfort."

"Yeah, I heard the Browns pulled their strings and got votes from all over the county." He looked at Caroline. "I'm sorry, Caroline. I forgot you're engaged to Samuel."

"It's okay. If you've been out of town, you probably haven't heard that we're no longer getting married."

He blinked. "No I had not heard, but I guess that's a good thing since the family might find themselves in deep water with the bank."

"I really hate it for them." She faced Matthew. "Johnny is in town and is heading back to the ranch so I'm going to ride along with him. I came here today to invite you to Christmas dinner. It will be in the afternoon. We'd all like you to join us. We exchange gifts after breakfast so I'd love for you to join us for the morning festivities as well."

"Thank you, Caroline. As long as nothing is going on at the jail, I'll be there."

She smiled at Matthew, then told the councilman goodbye.

"I hope I didn't interrupt anything."

"It's fine. Now what can I do for you?"

Matthew listened with half a heart. His mind was on Caroline and wanted to be with her, but he'd have to wait until Christmas. The man had news about the judge coming through town in three or four days and the council wanted to make sure Matthew had everything he needed to get started.

Matthew had everything he needed to start his job. The only thing he needed now was to figure out his life so he could offer himself to Caroline.

CHAPTER TWENTY-FOUR

Christmas morning brought freezing temperature and a light sprinkling of snow, but the black clouds in the north confirmed what everyone predicted. Much more snow would cover the land soon.

Matthew glanced up one last time at ominous sky over the rooftops as he walked to the stables to get his horse. He wanted to spend Christmas with the Fletchers, especially Caroline, but riding out to the ranch in this weather was not the greatest idea. He'd flung his saddle bags over his shoulders. In it he'd put two gifts for Caroline and a few pieces of candy he'd bought for the children, along with a few other small gifts.

He got to the stables and shoved open the big door. Stuart sat by a big iron kettle with a small fire burning. In his lap sat a big yellow cat with long hair.

"Hey, Stuart, you're here early on this Christmas morning. Merry Christmas to you."

"And Merry Christmas to you as well, Mr. Jennings."

"Would you please call me Matthew?"

"I guess I could, but next week, I'll be calling you Deputy Marshal."

Matthew chuckled. "I hear the judge is coming to town next week."

"We're all excited that you'll be running the new prison."

"Thank you, Stuart. I appreciate your saying that." He looked around. "Why are you here on the cold Christmas morning?"

"I woke up before sunup like I always do. When you're alone, it's better to be where you might be able to see other people. The stable is as good a place as any on a Christmas morning. At least the horses and this cat Shaggy here are good company."

Matthew walked over to the fire and petted the cat's head. "And I'm sure the animals are glad you're here to build this fire. It's freezing out."

"I don't imagine I'll have many needing horses this morning. You're not riding out, are you?"

"I was invited to spend Christmas with the Fletchers. I hate to miss that."

"Don't blame you." Stuart stood up. "I'll get Morgan for you. You should've told me yesterday you needed him early. I could've had him ready for you."

"It's fine. I wanted to make sure the jail was okay before I made definite plans for the morning."

"I would think it would be quiet on a Christmas morning, but who knows?"

"You're right. Who knows?"

He dug in his saddlebag. "Here. Merry Christmas." He pulled out a small package wrapped in a cloth and handed it to Stuart."

"You got me a present?"

"You're an important part of this town, Stuart, and you're always here to help. I appreciate you."

Stuart took the package and pulled out a bright red scarf. "Matthew, this is really nice." He put it around his neck and smiled. "Thank you. I haven't gotten a Christmas gift since my wife passed." His eyes glistened.

"Everyone needs a little something on Christmas."

Stuart nodded then headed toward Morgan's stall.

Matthew watched him wipe his face so his didn't say

any more about the gift. At the stall he rubbed Morgan's nose. "How you doing this morning, boy?"

Morgan stomped his feet and threw his head back.

"We'll be out on the road in no time."

"You be careful out there, Mr. Jennings. I think we're going to get a heavy snow."

"Hope it holds off until I get to the Fletchers."

He helped Stuart with the saddle, finished tightening the straps on Morgan, then led him out onto the street. Looking up to the north, he realized the black clouds moved faster now. He'd probably get caught in the middle of a snow storm.

"Not how I want to spend Christmas, but I really want to go the Fletchers, so let's go, Morgan."

The horse took off. Matthew let him run. The faster they got to the ranch the better off they'd be.

Matthew pulled his coat tight across his chest and his hat down over her forehead. The road had a light covering of snow on it, but not anything that would prevent a safe ride.

Looking up into the dark sky, he asked God to watch over him and Morgan.

~

Caroline took extra care with her hair, brushing it until it shone and letting it fall across her shoulders. The curls at the top were unruly so she attached a small red ribbon to pull it out of her face.

She got up from her dressing table and went to the window. Pulling the curtain back, she watched the snow come down hard. Disappointment swept over her. Matthew might not be able to join her family for their Christmas celebration. Selfishly she wanted him to ride out, but in her heart she knew the road could be dangerous, and the last thing she wanted for him was to have an accident.

If he didn't come today, she'd make a point to try to get in town as soon as the weather cleared to see him and to give him the present she'd sewn for him.

"Aunt Caroline, come see the presents," William yelled from the bottom of the staircase. "We all have presents, even you."

Caroline laughed. "I'm coming."

At the bottom of the staircase young William bounced up and down. "Quick, come see,"

She bounded down the steps, then at the bottom, swooped him into her arms. "Oh my, you're getting so big I can hardly pick you up anymore."

"I know. I'm six."

She put him down. "Lead the way, young man."

William took off running, but Lucas grabbed him as soon as he got into the living area. "Whoa, son, you can't run through the house like that. You could run over someone. You could hurt your grandmother if you knocked her over."

"I'm sorry, Father, but I'm showing Aunt Caroline all the presents."

"Let's take a quick look, but we'll open gifts after breakfast."

Lucas smiled and looked at Caroline. "We do have a lot under the tree, but then we have quite a few people living in this house."

"Don't keep reminding me," said Douglas as he came out of the kitchen. "I swear I'm making plans for Emma and me to start our house as soon as spring gets here."

Lucas put his arm around his younger brother. "I didn't mean anything by my comment. You and your family can stay here as long as you like. It's as much your house as mine."

"Now that you mention it, it is. Maybe you ought to move." Douglas laughed out loud. "Just joking, brother. You know I've always wanted a house down in the meadow near that stream. Emma loves that spot, too."

Caroline listened to her father and uncle joke about living arrangements. Remembering she almost married and moved into town sent a wave of sadness through her. Her life would've been totally different from what she was used to on Fletcher Ranch. She thought about Matthew. If he ever came around and realized how much she loved him, she wondered where he would choose to live. Being the County Deputy probably would require him to be near the prison. The small living quarters next to the prison was small, but she could picture herself making it into a home for the two of them.

Shaking her head, she followed the family into the dining room. Thinking about having a life with Matthew used to be so easy when they were younger. Now things were totally different.

Looking out the dining room window she saw nothing but white. Thick snow drifts formed along the fence line, and heavy snow still came down.

Lucas put his arm around her shoulders. "I'm sorry, Caroline. I know you wanted Matthew here with us today, but I don't think he'll be able to get here. Luckily Abigail's mother and Mason slept in our small bedroom last night so they could join us this morning."

"I guess I should've told him to come out last night. At least he would've been here, but," she looked at her father and smiled. "I'd rather have him safe in town."

Grandmother Fletcher came through the door looking as beautiful as ever, though she had started showing her age. Her hair had streaks of gray, her face was wrinkled and thin, and she walked slowly.

Caroline went over to her. "Merry Christmas, Grandmother. You look beautiful this morning as you always do." She gave her granddaughter a kiss, then headed for the table.

With one last look out the window, she turned and sat with her family at the full breakfast table. Her heart melted. So much love surrounded her in this home every day of the year, but on Christmas that love was extra special.

How she wished Matthew could have sat here with her.

CHAPTER TWENTY-FIVE

The arduous trek to Fletcher Ranch worried Matthew. Luckily he'd ridden this road enough to know how to keep Morgan on the right path. Several times he thought about turning around and going back to town, but the thought of not being with Caroline on Christmas Day kept him going.

Midway down the road, he heard something but wasn't sure what. "Did you hear that, Morgan? Was that a shout?"

Again, he heard a man's voice off to the south of the road. Matthew yelled back. "Where are you?"

"Here, by a downed tree. My horse threw me when it fell. I can't get up. Hurry."

The man's voice was strained and weak, but Matthew thought he pinpointed the direction.

Matthew turned Morgan. "You can do this boy. That man needs help." He guided Morgan off the road and into the thick brush. "Keep talking," he yelled. "I need to hear you to find you."

"Here. Here." The voice was weaker this time.

"Keep going, Morgan. Keep moving. He won't make it much longer in this snow."

Together he and his horse pushed aside brush and limbs and hoped he headed toward the man. Under the trees the snow wasn't as thick, but the brush blocked the path. He jumped off Morgan. "You can't go any farther through this." He tied him to a bush.

Heading away from Morgan, he yelled once more, but this time there wasn't an answer.

Matthew hurried toward what he hoped was the direction of the injured man. "If you can, make some noise. Anything. I need to know where you are."

"Here."

Matthew strained to hear, then headed forward. A huge tree lay fallen in front of him. Hoping this was the tree that the man was by, he jumped over limbs and shrubs, then saw the man almost buried by the tree's branches.

Matthew struggled to get through the tangled mess, but finally reached the man. His body lay under twisted limbs. He went to him. The man's face was streaked with blood.

"I'm here. Let's see what has you trapped."

The man opened his eyes. "Matthew Jennings." His words were but a whisper.

Matthew looked closer. "George Burge, I can't believe you're in this mess. What happened, and why in heaven's name are you out in this storm and off the main road?"

"Going to get a doctor. My wife is having a baby. One tree fell, scared my horse, and he headed into here, then this tree got caught up in the other and fell on me."

Matthew tried to lift a limb on the man's body. He pulled and pushed and finally was able to lift some of the weight off the man.

"Aaaah," George screamed.

"I'm sorry, but we have one of the limbs off. The other tree is still trapping you." He looked around for something to use as a lever to lift bigger limb. "You need to cover your face and try to protect your arm. I'm not sure where these limbs will come down." Again he used his entire strength on the limb being used as a lever, pushed and lifted. The limb rolled slightly. With the next push, it teetered slightly then rolled off George, but one of the branches toppled toward Matthew. He fell back when the huge limb gave way and hit him. He hit the ground with the limb on top of him. A sharp stick stabbed him near the neck.

For a second he thought the limb had simply scrapped his neck and shoulder, but then realized part of it was stuck in him. He grabbed it, held his breath, then pulled. The pain sent him to the ground. Warm blood gushed down his body. With one hand he pulled his neck scarf and shoved it into the hole to stop the bleeding. Losing too much blood would be the death of both him and George.

"You okay?" George whispered.

"I think so, but we need to get you out of here before you freeze." *And I bleed to death.* "Do you have any broken bones?"

"My arm. I think it's broken."

Matthew eased up off the ground, trying to keep the wound from shooting blood.

George squinted. "You're hurt bad."

"Lots of blood, but I think I'll be okay. Don't know if I can lift you though. I'm scared I'd lose too much blood."

"You're right." George pulled his bad arm to his body with a groan.

Matthew found a thick broken limb. "Here, see if you can raise yourself up with this. I'll try to help."

Together, the two men pulled and stood, then leaned against a nearby tree. Blood gushed from Matthew's neck area. He shoved the scarf back into the hole. "Can I have your scarf to hold this one on."

George, weak and pale, untied his scarf. Matthew took it and tied it around his neck, then waited a few minutes to see if he had helped the flow of blood.

"I think that helped. I don't see as much blood." George said.

Matthew nodded."My horse is not far from here. Is your house or Fletcher Ranch closer?"

"Fletcher. That's where I was heading to get Doctor Emma. My wife needs her bad, and now both of us do, too. I hope my Madeline is still hanging on."

Matthew felt his energy flowing out with the blood. "Come on. We need to get to my horse before we both pass out."

Holding each other up, they trudged through the thickness. At one point, George stumbled and fell pulling Matthew down with him. They both let out a scream, then lay still while the pain and the flow of blood lessoned.

"Ready?" Matthew asked, his words barely audible.

"No, but let's try it."

Matthew used a tree to pull himself up, but let George get up alone. He knew his limits.

"My horse shouldn't be far." In front of him, he thought he made out the horse's body. "There. There he is. Thank you, God. Thank you."

~

Caroline hardly touched her food, but when William jumped up and said it was time to open presents, she took a bite, and stood up with everyone else. Before leaving the dining room, she peeked out the window once more.

"I think the snow isn't as thick now." She leaned closer to the window. "Father, I think I see someone coming through the gates." She smiled big and turned. "Maybe it's Matthew."

Lucas looked out the window. "I think you're right, but our visitor is moving awfully slow. I'll put on my coat and go see."

Caroline followed Lucas to the front door and grabbed a coat and hat, then reached for her boots.

"You probably don't need to get out in this," Lucas said as he slipped on his coat.

"I'll be fine." No way was she staying inside if that was Matthew coming in the yard.

She followed Lucas across the porch and down the front steps.

He stopped. "I think that's two men. You stay here."

This time Caroline didn't argue. She stepped back up on

the porch, but as she did she recognized Matthew and another man on a huge horse. She held onto the railing then carefully stepped down the stairs. When her boot hit the grass below, she followed Lucas across the front yard toward the horse.

Lucas ran ahead of her. When he got to the horse, he took the reins and led the horse toward the house.

Caroline's breath caught in her throat. She was close enough to see that Matthew slumped over the horse.

She turned. Abigail was on the porch.

"Abigail, go get Emma and Douglas. Something is wrong."

Caroline headed toward the horse. "Matthew." She called out his name but he didn't look up. His head lay against the horse's neck.

"Matthew is bleeding bad," George shouted, "and I have a broken arm."

Emma and Douglas ran out. Douglas ran across the lawn, then helped Lucas pull Matthew off his horse. Carefully they laid him on the ground. Blood covered the front of his jacket and arm.

Caroline squeezed her eyes. Her lips quivered. Seeing Matthew in this condition tore at her heart. She knelt down by him and squeezed his hand, but he never opened his eyes.

"We need to get him inside," Emma stood up.

"I'll be right there." Lucas helped George down. "What happened out there?"

George gave a quick story. "Doctor Emma, my wife needs you. That's why I was trying to get here before the tree fell and trapped me."

Emma looked from George to Matthew. "Let's get Matthew inside so I can have a look at his wound. We need to make sure the bleeding quits before I leave him."

"I know, but. . ."

"I know you're worried about your wife. I'll go as soon as I can. I promise."

Caroline stepped back. Lucas and Douglas lifted Matthew as gently as possible and carried him in. She wanted to be near to Matthew but she knew she'd be in the way so she followed alongside.

Inside the house was a whirlwind of activity. Mason ran over to them and helped carry Matthew into a guest room on the first floor.

"Here're some towels." Abigail quickly laid them on the bed, then stepped back and put her arm around Caroline while the men laid Matthew on the bed. Emma and Douglas wasted no time in pulling off his coat and shirt, then easing the scarf off the wound. Blood flowed freely when they did.

"Get some more towels and someone get snow from outside. Make sure it's clean." Emma gave orders but expertly put pressure on the open wound and also on the vein nearby.

When Abigail came back in with a bowl of snow, Douglas wrapped some in a clean towel and laid in on the wound. "Sometimes the cold will help clot the blood." He looked at his wife. "If you want to look at George's arm, I'll keep the pressure on his neck."

Emma nodded and eased away from him while Douglas took his turn with his hand on the towel.

Emma checked George's arm and confirmed it was broken, but he wouldn't let her do anything. "Not yet. Please, let's go help my wife. After the baby and she are ok, then you can tend to the arm."

Douglas looked at Emma. "If you want to ride out to his ranch, it's not far. I'll keep the pressure on the wound. Mason, would you take her in the carriage? That way she and George can both go."

"Sure."

"I'll help here, Emma." Caroline stepped near the bed. "I've done this with some of the animals."

"Thanks. You and Douglas stay with Matthew. I'll see about a new baby."

When everyone had gone their separate ways to get ready to leave, Caroline pulled a chair up to the bed next to Douglas. "I can take turns with you. Your arm will be numb after a while."

"Thanks. We'll get this blood to stop together." He looked at his niece. "Some Christmas, huh?"

~

Several hours later Emma came back into the house and ran straight to the bedroom. Caroline had her head on the mattress. She looked up and smiled.

Douglas still had his hand on Matthew's neck. "I've never been so happy to see anyone."

"Has it stopped?"

Douglas nodded. "Pretty much, but we were afraid to take the pressure off."

"That's a good thing." She stooped down over Matthew and eased the towel off. Blood barely seeped through the wound.

Caroline stood up. "I've been praying that he hasn't lost too much."

"Me too." Emma smiled. "Me too." Carefully she cleaned the wound and finally wrapped a bandage around his neck. "I think he'll be okay."

Abigail came into the room. "We've set the table for lunch. Do you think any of you can join us?"

"I'll stay here with Matthew," Caroline said.

"We'll bring you a plate." Emma kissed her on the head. "Don't hesitate to call if you think we need to come back or if you see more blood."

"Emma? Is George's baby okay?"

"Yes, it's a healthy little girl. The mother might need to be in bed for a day or two, but she'll be okay as well."

For the rest of the day Caroline sat by Matthew. Even as the sun set and the room dimmed, she didn't bother to light a candle. Sitting by Michael and holding his hand was enough to make her happy.

She laid her head on the mattress and closed her eyes, but immediately opened them when Matthew squeezed her hand.

"Matthew? Are you awake?" She raised his hand to her lips and kissed it.

He opened his eyes and nodded. "Barely."

She heard his whisper so she leaned down near his face. "We've been so worried about you." She turned and grabbed a tin cup. "Please try to drink this." She lifted his head slightly.

He took a few sips. "Thank you. How's George?"

"He is at his house. Emma delivered his little girl and set his arm while Douglas and I stayed with you here. She had a busy day."

"Not the Christmas I wanted for you."

"I'm with you, Matthew. That makes my Christmas complete." She leaned over and kissed him on the forehead.

"Am I interrupting something?" Lucas walked through the door. "I wanted to check on you, but I see you're in good hands."

Matthew smiled. "The best hands ever."

CHAPTER TWENTY-SIX

The next morning Matthew asked Douglas to help him out of bed and down the stairs.

"You know my wife is going to have fits when she sees you up." Douglas held him tight as they took each step slowly.

"Blame it on me. I want to sit at breakfast with the family. I missed that yesterday."

Douglas opened the dining room door. The entire family sat quietly eating, but when the door opened Lucas and Caroline jumped up and ran to Matthew.

"Oh my goodness," she said as she took his arm. "Should you be down here?"

Emma walked over slowly. "I'll answer that with a definite 'no.' but since you're here you might as well eat. It will do you good."

"Yes, you didn't get to eat Christmas breakfast with us yesterday." Caroline put her hand through his arm and led him to a chair by her seat.

"Breakfast at Fletcher Ranch is always like Christmas." He took his seat carefully.

Bonita came into the room carrying a tray of meats. "Mr. Jennings, I'm so glad you're with us this morning."

"Me, too, Bonita. You have no idea how happy I am to be able to sit here and eat with the Fletchers."

Lucas sat back down in his seat. "We've already blessed

this meal, but let's bow our heads once more. Lord, we thank you again for this food, but we especially thank you for having Matthew feel strong enough to join us this morning. Amen."

Everyone joined in with amen, and after the prayer the mood at the table changed. The hushed tones became louder and happier and the meal continued.

Caroline took his hand once more. "I'm so happy you're here with us."

"I am, too, Caroline. I messed up your Christmas yesterday."

"It wasn't your fault. You were helping Mr. Burge. I hope he appreciated what you did for him."

"It doesn't matter if he does or does not. I'm simply glad he's alive and has that new little baby at the house."

She smiled. "A new baby is exciting."

"Yes, it is."

After everyone had cleaned their plates, Lucas stood up. "Matthew, we saved some of our Christmas to share with you."

Matthew sat up straight, not knowing where this was going.

"If everyone is finished, we'll go back into the parlor by the tree and finish opening gifts."

"Thank you, sir. I would like to get my saddlebag, or at least something that's in it, but I'm not sure I can walk all the way out there."

Douglas stood up. "I'll go get your saddlebag."

As everyone got up from the table, Matthew turned to Lucas. "Would you mind if Caroline and I stepped out on the porch for just a few minutes?"

Lucas nodded. "Sure. We'll be in the parlor."

"We won't be long."

He took Caroline's hand, led her to the door, then grabbed a coat from the coat rack and placed it around her shoulder. As soon as they stepped outside, he turned to her and kissed her. "Merry Christmas, Caroline."

"Merry Christmas to you, Mr. Jennings."

He stepped back and took her hands into his. "This isn't the way I wanted to do this, but I can't wait or I'll chicken out."

Caroline laughed. "You've never chickened out of anything in your life, Matthew."

"I might if I don't do this now." He swallowed. "I know you've just gotten out of an engagement and if you need time to think about it, I can wait for an answer. I don't want to wait, mind you, but I will." He cleared his throat. "I can't live without you. I was going to make myself exist without you when you were going to marry Samuel, but now that you are a free lady again, I want to know if you'd be my wife."

Caroline blinked. "Are you asking me to marry you?"

Matthew swallowed, then nodded.

She took both of his hands in hers. "Of course I'll marry you. I've been trying to figure out what you'd say if I asked you to marry me." She laughed. "I want to be with you for the rest of my life, Matthew Jennings." She reached up on her tip toes and kissed him.

He pulled her close and kissed her hard. "I can't believe you said 'yes.' You do understand that I can't give you the things that Samuel would have."

"Fiddlesticks. Do you think those things are important to me? I've told you before that I want to be happy, not rich. I want to have a family, your family, and to raise those children myself, not by some nanny. I want you, Matthew. Only you."

"And you can live at the prison for a while until I can afford to buy something else?"

"Definitely. I think it will be cozy. Our little love nest."

He pulled her close to him again. "I love you, Caroline. I always have. Merry Christmas."

"Merry Christmas to you, my future husband."

He kissed her again, then held her close to his chest.

"I've never been so happy. This is the best Christmas present I've ever received."

"I agree. Best Christmas ever. I'm as happy as any lady can be right now."

"We'd better go in. The family is waiting."

They walked hand in hand into the parlor. Caroline looked at her family with a huge smile on her face.

"Fletchers, I want to introduce you to my future husband."

For a second, no one said a word, then as if it took a second to understand what she was saying, they all whooped and hollered, then ran up to them and gave them hugs and kisses.

"It's about time," Lucas said as he shook Matthew's hand. "I thought I was going to have to hit you over the head with a shovel when you stood back to let her marry Samuel. What a mistake that would've been."

"Father! If that's the way you felt, why didn't you say something to me earlier?"

"Because you're always telling me you're not a child anymore. You had to figure out what you wanted on your own. I can only say I'm glad you finally did."

"Let's open more presents." Little Emma said as she ran to the tree.

"Let's do." Caroline took his hand. "I hope you're feeling well enough to do this."

"Nothing would drag me away from this."

Douglas came in with Matthew's saddlebag as they all gathered around the tree. Only a few gifts remained, and they were all for Matthew. Everyone had a little something for him, even Grandmother Fletcher.

Bonita came in with something wrapped in a cloth napkin. "Carmella and I baked you a loaf cake to take to the boarding house."

Matthew took it, then kissed Bonita on her forehead. "Thank you." He looked around. "I'm totally overwhelmed.

I can tell you I haven't had a Christmas like this since I left the ranch."

Caroline handed him a small package. "This is from me. I made it myself."

Matthew opened the package and found a blue shirt with silver buttons. He looked up. "I'm so impressed. This is wonderful."

"I'm glad you like it. You know I don't like to sew, but for you I did."

"It's wonderful. Thank you."

He opened the saddlebag and first pulled out candy for the children. They all shrieked and yelled. He'd bought lace handkerchiefs for each lady. Caroline loved hers, then he gave her a small present wrapped in a brown cotton cloth. "This was my mother's. I'd like for you to have it now and wear it when Preacher Smith marries us."

Caroline carefully removed the cloth and found a ruby ring. "Oh, Matthew, this is wonderful. I'll treasure this always."

He took the ring and placed it on her finger.

She held her hand up for her family to see. Everyone clapped, then came to her and kissed and hugged her.

Finally, she kissed Matthew on the cheeks and whispered, "This is the best Christmas ever."

He wrapped his arms around her shoulders.

"Are you still feeling okay?"

He nodded, even though he could feel his energy seeping.

Lucas stood up. "One more gift, Matthew. I've wanted to do this for some times now, but I needed the right time and since you asked my Caroline to be your wife, I think this is the appropriate time."

Matthew looked at Caroline, who shrugged.

"Douglas, Mother, and I want you to be part of this family, as we have always wanted. Douglas has acreage along the meadow east of this house. On the other side of that piece is about fifty acres. The stream running through Douglas's property continues onto the back of his fifty acres. Caroline loves that stream. We want you and Caroline to have it and to build on it, this is if you want to."

Caroline shrieked, threw her arms around Matthew and kissed him.

Matthew was stunned. He looked at Lucas. "Of course, I'd love to have a home on that property. I don't know what to say."

Lucas walked up to him and shook his hand. "You know we've always thought of you as a Fletcher. Now you are." He pulled Matthew to him with a big hug, then patted him on the back. "With your new position at the prison, you'll need to be in town a lot. This piece of land is closest to town and won't take long for you to come and go. What do you say? You think you could find a place to build a house on that piece?"

Emotions clogged Matthew's chest. He nodded. "Of course. Thank you, sir. No one has ever done anything like this for me."

"We Fletchers take care of our own."

~

With the door to the guest bedroom open, Matthew lay stretched out on his mattress with Caroline asleep in his arms. Emotions still clogged his throat. his full heart bursting with happiness. Never in his life did he imagine he'd own fifty acres of beautiful land. It would be quite a while before he could build a house for Caroline, but he knew when it was built it would be filled with love.

He closed his eyes and said a silent prayer of thanks. He had not gotten a chance to attend church since his talk with Preacher Smith, but the next Sunday he would walk through those doors with Caroline on his arm.

God had been good to him, saved him from disaster many times, and let him live through his massive loss of blood from the branch.

"What are you thinking about?" Caroline turned to face him. Her sleepy blue eyes shone with happiness.

"I was thinking about how I've been blessed beyond belief."

"So have I, Matthew. Do you realize how unhappy I would've been had I married Samuel?" She propped herself up on one elbow. "Would you have let me go through with that marriage?"

"I'm not sure. I wanted the best for you, but I can't say if I could've let you marry him. I don't know how I could've lived without you."

"I don't know if I could've gone through with it either. I had my doubts."

"But you loved him?"

"In a way, I did, but," she put her hand on his face, "nothing like I love you. I've always loved you even when you rode away from me years ago. I loved you from deep inside. Here." She moved her hand from his face and placed it on her heart.

He smiled. "Yeah, that day I rode away from you, I could hardly breathe. It was all I could do to keep from turning my horse around. I really thought I was doing what was best."

She snuggled up against him. "But we now know what is best for us. Thank you, Matthew, for coming home to Fletcher Ranch."

"The ranch has always been my home. Now it's official. One day we'll have a home here and fill it with children."

"Yes, children and horses."

He chuckled. "Of course, horses. Since we'll be living in town for a while, do you think you'll still want to help Douglas out at the vet office?"

"You wouldn't mind me doing that?"

He chuckled. "Why would I mind? If your dream is to work with animals, then that's what you should do."

"Yes, I would love to do that until we have children,

then they will be my life." She sat up. "I'm not sure I'll be able to do that, though if I need to cook for the prisoners."

"We can hire someone to do that." He kissed her. "We'll figure it out."

"Yes, we will." She lay back down. "I think I'll lie here and dream about our new piece of property. When you're up to it, can we ride out and see it?"

"Of course, we can. In fact maybe we can borrow one of the carriages and ride out today. I think I could sit in a carriage and do okay."

"Let's do."

Matthew lay back and smiled.

"Why are you smiling again?"

"Because my life has taken a turn for the best. I can't believe we'll actually have a home of our own on Fletcher Ranch."

"We will, won't we?" She snuggled closer to him.

He pulled her close and kissed her. "I love you, Caroline Fletcher. You and the Fletchers have made me one happy guy."

THE END

Fran McNabb, author of traditional, clean romances, recently moved to Louisiana with her husband of over 50 years. Even though she lived most of her life along the Mississippi Gulf Coast near the islands and the water, she feels she has come full circle since her father was born in south Louisiana. Visit her at www.FranMcNabb.com or Facebook at Fran L. McNabb or Fran McNabb, Author.

Follow me on Amazon

Other books by Fran McNabb
The Way Home
Paradise Lane
Return to Paradise
Paradise Found
Gulf Coast Romances